UNFINISHED BUSINESS

Also by Shankari Chandran

Song of the Sun God
The Barrier
Chai Time at Cinnamon Gardens
Safe Haven

SHANKARI CHANDRAN
UNFINISHED BUSINESS

ultimo press

ultimo press

Published in 2025 by Ultimo Press,
an imprint of Hardie Grant Publishing

Ultimo Press
Gadigal Country
7, 45 Jones Street
Ultimo, NSW 2007
ultimopress.com.au

◎ X ⨍ ultimopress

All rights reserved. No part of this publication may be reproduced, stored in a retrieval system or transmitted in any form by any means, electronic, mechanical, photocopying, recording or otherwise, without the prior written permission of the publishers and copyright holders.

The moral rights of the author have been asserted.

Copyright © Shankari Chandran 2025

A catalogue record for this book is available from the National Library of Australia

Unfinished Business
ISBN 978 1 76115 129 3 (paperback)

Cover design Courtesy of Audible
Additional cover design Andy Warren Design
Cover image by Madrugada Verde / Shutterstock
Text design Simon Paterson, Bookhouse
Typesetting Bookhouse, Sydney | 13/17 pt Adobe Garamond Pro
Proofreader Rebecca Hamilton

10 9 8 7 6 5 4 3 2 1

Printed in Australia by Opus Group Pty Ltd, an Accredited ISO AS/NZS 14001 Environmental Management System printer.

MIX
Paper | Supporting responsible forestry
FSC® C018684

The paper this book is printed on is certified against the Forest Stewardship Council® Standards. Griffin Press – a member of the Opus Group – holds chain of custody certification SCS-COC-001185. FSC® promotes environmentally responsible, socially beneficial and economically viable management of the world's forests.

Ultimo Press acknowledges the Traditional Owners of the Country on which we work, the Gadigal People of the Eora Nation and the Wurundjeri People of the Kulin Nation, and recognises their continuing connection to the land, waters and culture. We pay our respects to their Elders past and present.

This project is supported by the NSW Government through Create NSW.

For Rajan Uncle and Aunty Nalaini

'We must be the great arsenal of democracy.
For us this is an emergency as serious as war itself.'

PRESIDENT FRANKLIN D ROOSEVELT, 29 DECEMBER 1940

PROLOGUE

NOW (2009)

Ameena adjusted the laptop and read the editorial for tomorrow's paper one last time. Her ex-husband had been right about her. She loved the thrill of finding stories in dark places and forcing them into the light. She loved the feeling of the early morning's first copy, still warm in her hands, its ink permeating her skin.

He had also been right to leave her and take the children with him. She had put herself, and therefore all of them, in front of a loaded gun. Five years after their separation, she would have told him that—if he still spoke to her.

She saved the document again and closed the laptop. Tomorrow's piece was about the children being slaughtered in the north or forced to flee from one makeshift camp to another, walking for months through the jungle, their bare feet cut by the shards of splintered palm trees. Bombs falling from the sky, sent by President Rajapaksa, paid for by the Chinese, and ignored by everyone else.

The Sri Lanka Army had orders to find and kill the Tamil Tigers wherever they were. How were they to know which person was a refugee and which person was a Tiger? They didn't care. Things happen in the chaos. Things are hidden in the jungle. Things are forgotten in time.

The President of Sri Lanka and his cousin, Dilshan Perera, relished their power. They abused it with impunity.

'See, we told you. These Tigers are monsters. What kind of freedom fighters hide among their own people for safety?' President Rajapaksa declared.

'What kind of President bombs his own people?' Ameena wrote in return. 'You know they are innocent. You know they have no choice. And still you bomb them.'

Every day she had to write about this.

Had she chosen her job over her children, as her ex-husband had accused her? It wasn't a choice. Her job might kill her, but if she could write about other people's children, then she would have life beyond her own.

She shuffled the laptop and last documents into her leather satchel. One of the buckles had broken weeks ago, but she never had time to fix it. Her fingers still reached for the heavy brass, trying to thread the strap through its missing bridle.

From her study window, she could see the crows perched on the high brick wall around their home. The birds weren't afraid of the broken glass cemented to its rim. It rose like peaks of discoloured ice that defied the heat. A barrier of glass and a guard—these were her only concessions to the death threats. She didn't want a security system in her home. They were already being watched enough.

Sathyan stood at the door of her study. 'Are you happy with the editorial?' he teased. They had been together for a couple of years, so he knew she was never truly happy.

He kissed her lightly. Everything about him was light these days. It was good to see him like this, finally.

'Can I get a lift with you to Jeya Books? They're having a genre sale this weekend,' he said.

'Which genre?'

'Dystopian fiction.' He laughed at her expression.

She tried not to roll her eyes. 'I don't know why you love that stuff so much. We are *living* in a dystopia. *The Road* is hopeful compared to Sri Lanka.'

He nodded. 'The lift?' he asked again, checking the money in his wallet.

'I'm sorry, Sath. I'm not going that way. I need to drop documents over at Shirani's house first,' she said, putting her car keys in her pocket.

She rarely lied to Sathyan, but she was going to meet her source, not Shirani Dennis, her deputy editor.

She greeted the guard in Sinhalese, inched the car out of her driveway and surveyed the street. It was empty, save for the white van parked thirty metres down the road. Closer than usual today.

She cleared the gate, watched the rear-view mirror and made sure the guard bolted it shut before she began her journey.

There were many potential routes to the city. Sathyan had asked her to vary her journey. Her ex-husband had begged her to vary it. She ignored them both. She paid her taxes; these roads were hers too.

She slowed down at the corner of Saunders Avenue and Beira Road, approaching Kutty and his little stall. The old man sold cashews, toasting them with salt, honey or chilli. Usually he had a bag of chilli cashews ready for her.

Ameena ran a tab with Kutty and gave him reams of old copy paper. He preferred it to the newspapers other street vendors used to package their food, which bled ink into his cashews. Even *The Lanka Herald* wasn't good enough for his fare.

He wasn't there today.

She held out a 100 rupee note to the young man she didn't recognise. 'Is Kutty okay?' she asked.

'Kutty's fine,' he replied, revealing well-cared-for teeth. He gave her too much change and the right packet of cashews. She hadn't asked for anything yet.

She accepted the warm packet and returned a few coins, squaring her debts as she had been taught to do. The safest route was to continue down Saunders Avenue. Instead, she turned the corner into the side street which would take her past a small mosque and a Buddhist temple. She urged herself not to overthink as she checked the vendor in the mirror one last time.

At the next intersection, she noticed a new billboard. Dilshan Perera, the Under Secretary for Defence, smiling smugly down on them all, presiding over an image of the new port in the south that the Chinese government was constructing. Sri Lanka didn't have the wealth or military power to rival the countries next door, but it did have the geographical position of the nosy neighbour who sits in his living room and watches all the comings and goings of everyone else on the street.

Thinking about the new port, Ameena didn't notice that the white van had closed the distance between them. She didn't notice the two motorcyclists who met at the cashew vendor's stall immediately after she'd left, or the municipal garbage truck that blocked the traffic behind her, or the final two motorcyclists who cordoned off the street one hundred metres ahead with construction signs. All four of them on expensive bikes, with proper leathers and darkened visors, now converging on her.

She spotted the garbage truck first. The white van pulled away. Then she saw the motorcyclists behind her and the ones in front.

She cursed herself for not noticing them sooner and braked hard, skidding her silver Mazda to a stop. She heard the thud of a bullet against her windscreen, spidery lines reaching out across the glass from its epicentre, like the fault lines of an earthquake.

Her hands clenched pale against the steering wheel's black vinyl. Flecks of broken glass salted her hair and face.

Three motorcyclists hung back while the leader dismounted and walked towards her. She couldn't see his face, but she didn't need to. He possessed the unhurried gait of a man who had thought of everything. Who knew the roads were blocked. Who had done this before and would most likely do it again.

Another bullet shattered the driver's side window, spraying hot needles of glass into her. She ducked towards the passenger seat and the bullet cut past her ear, lodging in the torso of the passenger seat.

The window was wide open now. The sounds of angry horns and chaotic traffic drowned out the heave and splutter of her own breath. Her chest was wet. She looked down and saw the bloom from her right pocket like a fountain pen leaking red ink. She reached for it but couldn't make her hand connect with her body. Pain bolted from her chest, propelled by the last defiant beats of her heart. She tasted blood on her lips, every laboured breath delivering a little more.

She met her own eyes reflected in the polished visor of the stranger's helmet. She saw her tears. Angry tears. She wasn't ready. She wanted more time.

She didn't know who this man was, but she knew who sent him.

One bullet: Dilshan.

A second bullet: Perera.

A final bullet, then no words.

1

NOW (2009)

'You're sending me back to Sri Lanka?' Ellie asked, her heart pounding but her voice casual. The homeland of her grandparents held memories for her that she worked hard every day to forget. 'Am I being punished, Redmond?'

'You deserve to be,' Redmond replied. 'I benched you from fieldwork at your request. I agreed to transfer you to USAID until you were ready to come back to the Agency. You sold that to me as a short-term "secondment". You've been in the land of global aid, unicorns and rainbows for four years now. I've paid for your ongoing psychiatric treatment—'

'The US Government pays for that, as it should,' she interrupted, slapping the file back on her boss' desk. The desk was sparsely populated with personal touches. A photo of his three children on holiday in Paris. A snow globe of the Grand Canyon from his ex-wife. Apparently, it had come with a note: *Wish you were at the bottom of this, xoxo Louisa.*

'You have a varied skill set, Ellie,' Redmond continued as if she hadn't spoken. 'You're wasted in USAID drafting aid packages. And this self-imposed martyrdom isn't helping you.'

'Self-imposed martyrdom?' she repeated. She could feel the heat rise beneath her skin. 'Martyrdom implies the subject is dead. I am very much alive.' She was, but the others weren't. She reached for the snow globe and shook it.

'Alive but still malfunctioning.'

'I'm not going back to Sri Lanka, Redmond. My psychiatrist won't allow it.'

'Your psychiatrist works for me. He's signed off on it.'

'That's unethical and unprofessional.'

Redmond shook his head. 'You were recruited by the CIA straight out of college because your psychometric testing revealed, among other things, that you are comfortable with dishonesty. Until this gardening leave of yours, you worked for the CIA and entered countries using USAID as a *cover*. You went to post-conflict nations and pretended to be negotiating aid while gathering intelligence.'

'Back then, I believed in the higher purpose it served.'

'Higher purposes are for televangelists. You are a soldier, gifted with greater potential than most. I want you to use it again, and I want you to use it in Sri Lanka.'

In truth, Ellie had been recruited for more than her 'gifts'. Her Sri Lankan ancestry gave her entry into a whole region that Redmond wanted to infiltrate.

He pushed the file towards her. 'Look at Solomon's intelligence briefing at the back.'

She picked the papers up again and flicked to the briefing from the station chief in Sri Lanka. Her heart pounded as she scanned the report. Ameena Fernando, respected journalist and editor of *The Lanka Herald*, shot on her way to work. No other casualties. Four motorcycles witnessed leaving the scene.

The ice in Ellie's blood receded.

No other casualties.

Sathyan was safe.

She concentrated on her breathing again. She needed to see her psych. If she agreed to go back, cognitive behavioural therapy, martial arts and meditation weren't going to be enough. Three years ago, she had tapered off the benzodiazepines and 'graduated' to fluoxetine for her anxiety. Her psych might need to up the dose; she could feel the panic rising already.

'We've been instructed to investigate the killing,' Redmond said. He never told her who issued the instructions and she never asked. 'I want you on the ground because you're connected to . . . her.' He paused. 'But I *am* worried about you, Ellie. Will your mental state enhance or compromise your ability to do your job? I know you got burned last time.'

'*I* didn't get burned,' she corrected him.

'But you did get hurt, and honestly, I think going back will help you.'

'Are you ordering me back to Sri Lanka?'

'I'm trying to help you. Stop being so paranoid.'

'*Paranoid?* Remember what happened last time I wasn't paranoid enough?'

Ellie didn't need to remind him. Redmond had been there four years ago at Dover Air Force Base when she'd returned with the coffins. She had struggled to release them into the waiting arms of the Color Guard. She couldn't speak. She had focused on the flag at half-mast behind him, battered by the cold winter wind. He had made her look at him; made her let go. There was no judgement in his face, just the understanding of someone who'd made his own mistakes and learned to live with them.

She was still learning.

Redmond skated over the reference. 'It's been long enough, Ellie. You know Sri Lanka—its politics, its ways. This will be hard for you, but it could also be good for you.'

'If you use the word "healing", Redmond, I'm going to beat you with your snow globe.'

He looked at her seriously, his voice quiet. 'Nothing else has worked, Ellie.'

Her chest and throat tightened. She looked at the victim's photograph and swallowed hard. Ameena Fernando was striking—large, kohl-rimmed eyes, black hair in an elfin crop, a wide and unguarded smile.

Passionate, fearless and stupid.

It only ever ended one way for these people—a posthumous award from Amnesty International. Small comfort for the husband. Or partner.

'We don't usually get involved in local government hit jobs.'

Redmond nodded. 'The ex-husband is driving this with support from those fuckwits at Amnesty. He lives in San Francisco with their three children. Left Colombo in 2004, couldn't handle the death threats.'

'Smart man.' Ellie searched him on her phone. Anil Fernando was a journalist too. According to the news report, he was having Ameena's body flown to the US for burial near his children's home. That took some connections and money.

'Go to Sri Lanka and ask around. The State Department has to look like it's doing something—something but not too much. We don't want to antagonise the Sri Lankans.'

'Of course not.'

'But we need to listen to our citizens, hear the anger of our multicultural communities and show concern over this blow to freedom of expression.'

'Nice.' She was impressed. Redmond had incredible recall for government standard responses. 'And what about all the other dead journalists in Sri Lanka? Taken away in white vans in the middle of the night, on government orders?' Something crept up her throat from her gut, burning and bilious. Some lives were always more valuable than others.

'We're still looking into it.' He stood up. The meeting was over.

'The war's been going on for twenty-six years. From your briefing, it's about to end—badly,' she pushed.

Her three brothers had been sending her news clips and human rights reports, too. In all their messages, there was an unspoken question: could USAID do something?

'Like I said, we're still looking into it.'

2

NOW (2009)

A few hours after her death, Ameena Fernando's newspaper published an editorial that was essentially an obituary written by the dead journalist herself. It accused the Sri Lankan government of being responsible for her death and foretold that platitudes would be made, international outrage expressed and investigations ordered, but that those who had killed her would be protected, not punished.

The haunting letter was addressed to Dilshan Perera, the Under Secretary for Defence.

The day after the editorial, citing the safety of staff as the primary reason, the Minister for Communications shut down *The Lanka Herald*.

•

For a long time, Ellie had thought her work with the Agency was both noble and necessary. For the last four years, however, she had benched herself, opting for a policy role at USAID, utilising the experience of her former cover and making it her new day job.

Redmond had reluctantly agreed to the transfer, as long as she maintained her field training requirements and checked in with him to provide any intel she'd picked up through USAID. She accepted his accusations that she'd reduced herself. She had been too afraid to leave the familiarity of the Agency, but too repulsed by its failures—by *her* failures—to be more than an over-qualified contract negotiator. His request to return Ellie to Sri Lanka terrified and excited her.

She checked her inbox at the small kitchen table and found the email again.

From S. Navaratnam. She hadn't seen his name in four years, but she had read it several times since the email had arrived two hours ago. Memorised every word.

S. Navaratnam. Sathyan Navaratnam.

Sathyan. It meant truth.

She opened the email again.

> Sunday 11 January 2009
>
> Dear Ellie,
>
> This morning Ameena Fernando was assassinated. It's all over CNN, but no doubt you already know.
>
> She and I were together. Two travellers on this lonely planet.
> If you are in the region, I would greatly appreciate it if you could meet me in Colombo. I would like your assistance. Please don't feel obligated to come.
>
> With warm wishes,
> Sathyan

She swallowed hard.

Please don't feel obligated to come. Is that what was left between them? An obligation? Obligation was a long but not-quite-accurate word. 'Debt' was a smaller word with a far deeper meaning. She had a debt she owed him and others. A long-overdue debt.

She called Redmond.

'I can't just show up in Colombo,' she began. Her name would set off red flags everywhere from the Sri Lankan High Commission in DC to Sri Lanka's Criminal Investigation Department.

Redmond had been expecting her. 'You'll be helping our aid delegation. Keith Tenby was promoted to First Secretary last year, so he's leading this work, but he's getting bullied. Every Sri Lankan minister is angling for foreign aid and kickbacks. You have the contacts and the clout to help him. It's a solid cover.'

'Tenby's very good at his job but it's hard to negotiate against Sri Lankan entitlement and absolutism,' she said. Keith Tenby had started his career as a CIA analyst but after a mission had gone wrong years ago, he'd lost his nerve. She was in no position to judge him for it. Tenby had moved into high-level diplomacy, where he'd excelled.

'That's why he'll welcome your support over there. Read the whole briefing. You've got access, same codes as last time. The Embassy will issue you with a weapon when you arrive. Your logbook is up-to-date, so I know you remember how to use a gun.'

'I do, but I was never very good with it in the first place.'

'Your logbook says you're good enough,' he replied.

'There's a big difference between shooting at targets and putting a bullet in a person's head.' She pushed away an image. Blood seeping into the dark earth, swallowed by the jungle floor.

Breathe, she reminded herself.

'Ellie,' Redmond called her back, his voice soft but insistent on the other end of the phone. 'The latter is easier if that person wants to put a bullet in your head first. The draft aid agreement is on the system. Help Tenby fix it. Make sure it gives us what we need.'

'And what do we need this time?'

'A new world order is being created around us, not always by us,' he replied. 'If we don't stake a claim, we'll be left out. We need a seat at the table so we can help Sri Lanka with the post-war transition.'

'Post-war? The war is still going on.'

'It'll be over soon. All foreign journalists and NGOs have been removed from the war zone. The last UN truck was escorted out on Monday.'

'No more witnesses. BBC World says the Sri Lanka Army has pushed almost 300,000 refugees into a safe zone.' Reportedly four miles long and three miles wide. She brought up a map of Sri Lanka.

'It's called the No Fire Zone,' he said. 'There are a few of them. It's being fired on.'

'By whom?' It was never clear in this war.

'Our intel says both sides. The Sri Lankan government is firing on the Tigers. The Tigers are firing back, protected by their own people.'

'They're not protected if the government is firing on the civilians in a designated safe zone,' she said. Her eyes were drawn to Mankulam, the last place she'd been stationed before she was evacuated back to the US.

There had been no time to explain. Or to say sorry.

What could she have said to Sathyan? What words would have justified what happened?

Redmond interrupted her memories. 'The government says it doesn't need to comply with the Conventions because the Tigers are using their people as shields.'

'Two wrongs make an act of genocide.'

'We're not using the G-word yet,' he replied.

'Really? I'd like to talk to Rajapaksa and use the C-word and the F-word and then the—'

'This will be over soon. And when it's done, we want to help them establish a healthy, friendly democracy. Tenby will introduce you to Dilshan Perera. He's the Under Secretary for Defence. He'll work with you both on the aid agreement.'

'Dilshan Perera? He's the key suspect *and* my liaison for the aid negotiation? Am I liaising with him or am I investigating him?'

'Liaising and nothing more,' Redmond replied. 'He's too important—he's the President's cousin. Look elsewhere, find nothing, write a report and let everyone—including you—move on with their grief. The past is the past.'

Ellie closed the laptop. 'The past is never past,' she said, trying to remember the words and name of a dead white writer.

'Ellie—'

'I'll go, Redmond.'

'I know.' He had always known.

She had unfinished business in Sri Lanka.

3

THEN (2005)

Ellie needed this R&R in Colombo. The city was a welcome change from the tropical jungle Redmond had sent her into. She had three teams in the east of the island digging up bodies while she attended the human rights conference in the city. The project had taken six months of research as well as 1.5 million US dollars in funding from the Consortium of Islamic Development Organisations. USAID had provided the forensic pathologists. The Middle East had the funding to make it happen as long as USAID pursued their objective—the exhumation and proper burial of Muslims killed during the conflict.

The project gave the Agency a reason to be there, but Ellie's team were looking for more than bodies. Forensic investigators studying the bombing of the USS *Cole* in Yemen had matched its Semtex fingerprint with that of a bomb in Lyon. It also had the same fingerprint as the Semtex used to blow up a bus in Colombo. Bombs went off in Sri Lanka all the time, but Agency Forensics was all over this one because two American tourists had died.

The human rights conference in Colombo had hit its Day Three slump. The optimism was over, the rhetoric had reached its hyperbolic zenith, and now exhaustion was setting in. It was a well-worn trajectory.

Ellie looked at Keith Tenby, the US Embassy's foreign aid delegate and former mission controller. He was seated next to her, diligently taking notes. Last year, when he was in charge of an operation, he had completely choked and it had cost the lives of two agents, and Tenby had finally retired early from the Agency to enter the diplomatic corps. Still well connected and respected in Asia, he was much better suited to diplomacy.

The last speaker took the podium. Sathyan Navaratnam from the Anti-Landmine Lobby, a small but earnest Canadian NGO. Ellie was expecting practical insights into landmine treaty application.

After brief thank yous, the speaker launched into an angry but articulate polemic on why US trade subsidies for weapons companies were responsible for the radicalisation of Muslims all over the world, not just in the Middle East. His voice had the clipped vowels of a local educated in the West, like her father's. She watched the speaker at the front of the room and felt her heart rate quicken.

Sathyan Navaratnam was a young man, younger than his voice and experience indicated. He wore a white short-sleeved shirt, a pencil in his front pocket. His skin was the colour of palm sugar, his thick black hair cut short and neat. His eyes flashed with barely restrained emotion.

Ellie raised her hand. Tenby shook his head but she ignored him.

'Yes,' Sathyan motioned to her, thrown by the interruption. He hadn't yet called for questions, but she had another meeting in thirty minutes.

'Thank you.' She stood up and saw Tenby close his eyes pre-emptively. 'Landmines, used largely by non-state actors, kill thousands of US soldiers, militants and civilians in the Middle East every year. Reducing US supply still won't address Middle Eastern demand. I completely agree that there are too many sellers and not enough standards. But I don't think more non-proliferation legislation will stem the rise of all these Islamic off-shoots.' She had redirected blame for the underlying cause of the market's existence and deflected attention away from the use of landmines by state actors—their friends—in the Middle East. Tenby had to be happy with that.

'Islamic off-shoots? Seriously—that's what you're calling them?' Sathyan asked.

'Excuse me if that's not politically correct enough for you,' she replied. 'They are off-shoots of Al-Qaeda and they share an Islamic fundamentalist doctrine of raining down an Armageddon on America and its allies.'

He addressed the room. 'See—this is why they hate us.' The audience murmured its agreement. Everyone was paying attention now.

'Yes, that must be it. They hate us because I use culturally insensitive references to the New Testament when describing their military strategy.' Perhaps she should have called it Asymmetric Warfare instead. 'Raining down an Armageddon' *was* a bit dramatic.

'No.' He shook his head. 'The fundamentalists hate you because they hate everyone who isn't like them. You gave them a big peg to hang that hate on when you set foot in their holy land and started killing their children. The rest of the Islamic world hates you because you don't acknowledge that. And to add insult to a pretty big injury, you then lump all of them in with the crazies by calling them Islamic off-shoots. The Klan, which is alive and well, is a Christian off-shoot, just so you know.'

Fuck him. She wasn't going to take that, no matter how irresistible his dimples were. Could dimples exist in a frown?

'I know that,' she replied evenly, despite the flush she could feel rising. 'If it weren't for the Constitution, I'd carpet-bomb their meetings, too.'

Tenby's mouth twitched nervously, knowing she was serious. He moved his knee towards her, in an attempt to nudge her into silence. She stepped casually to her left, just out of reach.

Sathyan didn't laugh. He looked her straight in the face and said, 'The key rights in the US Constitution that protect those motherfuckers are also in the *Universal* Declaration of Human Rights.'

And that was it. Something about the way he said *motherfuckers* made her want to kiss him.

The crowd laughed and she could see the man to Sathyan's right shake his head with a 'Don't bite the hand that funds you' expression on his face. Must have been his boss, used to his outbursts but hopeful he could reign them in.

She loved that he couldn't reign them in. She understood that.

•

At the end of the seminar, Ellie hurried after Sathyan, touching him lightly on the arm so he turned around.

'I didn't catch your name,' she lied.

'You didn't listen to most of the presentations.'

'Yes, I did.'

'No, you didn't. You appeared to be catching up on work.'

'You noticed,' she smiled.

'I'm indiscriminately observant.' He shrugged and turned back towards the door.

'You still haven't given me your name.'

The man sighed. 'Sathyan—Sathyan Navaratnam. "Raining down an Armageddon?"' he quoted. 'A bit dramatic, but better than "Asymmetric Warfare", I suppose.' He didn't wait for a reply.

'I'm Ellie Harper.' She followed him out.

'Ellie Harper.' He turned the segments of her anglicised name over, looking for the real name it masked.

Ellora Rachel Harischandran.

In a migrant's attempt to assimilate, her father had changed his name from Surya Harischandran to Sam Harper when he moved to Australia years before she had been born.

When she escaped Australia on a university scholarship to the States, she'd in turn changed her name from Ellora to Ellie.

And Rachel. She loved the middle name that honoured her American mother.

'Are you stalking me, Ms Harper?' Sathyan asked.

'Have lunch with me,' she blurted, thoughts of her next meeting forgotten. They were blocking the path, and people around them were muttering. She was knocked too close to him. She could see where he had cut his neck shaving. He moved back, politely shaking his head, a smile tugging at the corner of his mouth.

She waited for the dimple to reappear.

'Is your social strategy much like your military one?' he asked. 'You know we don't want you, but you come anyway?'

Before Ellie could reply, Sathyan headed off, out the sliding doors and into the midday heat. He was untroubled, his eyes focused on the traffic, his right-hand twitching when a tuk-tuk approached. He looked back at her, then seemed to change his mind, heading briskly down the street.

'Lunch, please. Don't make me beg,' she said, a step behind him. 'You could berate me some more about the failures of US foreign policy.'

'Appealing but pointless.' He kept walking. 'You've heard it all before.'

'Dinner, then.'

Later, she would reflect on that first meeting and wonder why she had chased him. Sure, she initiated relationships, but she never chased.

'Definitely not,' he replied.

He darted quickly through the crowd for three more blocks, before finally slowing to take a left into an alley. He stopped at a small diner.

It was a Hare Krishna cafe.

'Is this where you bring all the . . . friends you want to hide?' she asked. There was a large mural on the wall of the blue god holding a flute, a young girl in a sari standing beside him. There were quotes from the Bhagavad Gita all around the cafe. 'It's a nice place,' she said, taking a seat opposite Sathyan.

'It is. Cheap and cheerful. And I didn't bring you here, you followed me.'

'Cheap and cheerful? That's a very British thing to say. Did you study there?'

He shrugged. 'All Sri Lankans have weird British-isms. We talk like an Enid Blyton book.' He put the menu down and called the waiter over.

Ellie nodded. Her father's vocabulary was the same. 'I'm pretty sure Enid Blyton never said *motherfucker*, though.'

Sathyan grinned reluctantly and she caught her breath. She wanted to make him laugh again, to see the spontaneous eruption of dimples in his cheeks and the furrowing of his eyebrows. He tilted his head a little, his body rocking back into the chair.

'And you?' he asked. 'You look Tamil, maybe mixed, with a name like Ellie Harper. Your accent . . . a lot of time on the west coast, perhaps?'

'You're a linguist?' she asked, suddenly afraid he might work for an agency instead of the Canadian non-profit. That would be complicated.

'No, I watch a lot of American television. Where are you from?' he probed.

'My father was originally from Jaffna, but this is my first trip to Sri Lanka,' she said, truthfully. 'I used to live in the Bay Area,' she added, vaguely. Her American accent was solid, the Australian tones of her childhood locked away when she was on the job. 'Now working for USAID in DC,' she said, seamlessly setting out her cover legend.

'That's a surprisingly unadventurous job, although you *are* here. In search of adventure in Sri Lanka? And am *I* a little local adventure?'

The waiter came over and Sathyan ordered for both of them, then turned back to her, waiting for an answer.

'This is not where I'm supposed to be right now,' she said instead. 'The Emir of Qatar is a key funder, and his eighth son is hosting a lunch. I should be doing a meet-and-greet with them.'

Sathyan showed no sign of being impressed. Instead, he asked, 'Are you meeting the Key Performance Indicators of your grant?'

'Mostly. My KPIs are about bodies exhumed. Yours?'

'Limbs saved. I work for the Anti-Landmine Lobby.'

'I know, I was listening. I like your voice.' She smiled. He had a beautiful voice.

Sathyan laughed and looked down at the redundant menu.

'No, really,' she assured him. 'When you speak, I want to listen to you.'

A slow blush was creeping under his dark skin. 'How long are you here for?' he asked. 'I mean—'

'I know what you mean. I'm here for as long as it takes, or as long as we can get funding.'

'Gulf funding is good, and they're pretty serious about returning their brethren to Allah the right way.'

'They are. I've been here for four months. Before that, I was setting up a USAID team in Pakistan.'

'Same thing? Looking for bodies?' he asked.

'No. My work varies from country to country. Looking for different things.'

'And do you like Sri Lanka? Is it everything you thought it would be?' His eyes were cast down as he blew onto the surface of his tea.

Ellie hadn't even noticed the waiter arrive with it. She needed to concentrate.

'Do I like Sri Lanka?' she repeated with a smile. 'It's hard to answer that quickly.'

'Try. This is the only time we'll eat together.'

'Harsh! Sri Lanka is a difficult place to understand. My mother was white, so we didn't grow up connected to a Tamil diaspora the way some people did. My skin is brown but I might as well be white, too. So, I experience this country—*your* country, not mine—from the outside,' she replied.

'That's not an answer. That's a methodological approach and an excuse. Try again, Ellie,' he said.

She gave it another go. 'People do things to each other here, terrible things, as they do all over the world. But there is a silence around it. It's almost as if it's not too impolite to take thousands of lives, but it *is* too impolite to talk about it. Grief, loss, truth—these things are buried as deeply in the ground as the bodies. That's no way to live, and no way to die.'

'You've understood us well, Ellie. So, answer the question—do you like Sri Lanka?' he asked again, his tone gentle this time.

'I don't know,' she replied. 'I like you—does that count?'

'A little.' He smiled slowly, his dimples reappearing.

When Sathyan had gone to the cafe bathroom, Ellie took his diary from his backpack and scanned through his upcoming engagements. He would be attending a dinner for the UN World Food Program hosted by the Norwegian Embassy tonight. Two phone calls later, so was she.

•

Ellie checked the table in the Embassy lobby for Sathyan's name tag but couldn't find it. He must already be somewhere inside. She lingered, noting the names from the Australian High Commission, and steeled herself for passive aggressive comments about patriotism, wrapped in boring job offers that would take her back home to Sydney. She was about to enter the ballroom when she saw Sathyan heading for the exit.

She called his name, and he turned and smiled, before remembering his earlier irritation with her.

She quickly closed the gap between them, caught his hand and held it tightly, drawing him towards her. She kissed him on the cheek, her lips grazing his earlobe and then pulled back. 'Leaving so soon?'

He waved his name tag at her. 'My boss has seen me. I've done my networking, and now you're cramping my quick getaway.'

'I'm only here to see you. If you leave, you'll cramp *my* plans.'

'How did you know I would be here?'

'All the conference delegates were invited to this one. The Norwegians are religiously un-elitist. And the pickled herring canapés can really pull a crowd. Stay a bit,' she cajoled. 'You can introduce me to tedious people as punishment—and as a reward, I'll get you fifteen minutes with the Under Secretary to the US Ambassador so you can talk to him about the landmine treaty.'

To her delight, he laughed. 'You're on.'

They walked through the lobby and up the sweeping staircase to the main ballroom. Ellie was wearing a sleeveless black satin shift dress with black sequins around the neckline. It was her standard gala outfit because it was uncrushable at the bottom of her suitcase. Unlike most of the men, Sathyan wore casual trousers and a tailored shirt, not a tuxedo.

He motioned for her to follow him, weaving through the crowd until he stopped at the person he was looking for. She recognised his boss from the conference and smiled when she saw the elderly gentleman he was talking to—her friend, Dougie Vanderstraaten.

'Kulen, this is the lady I was telling you about—my stalker, Ellie Harper, from USAID. Ellie, Kulen Thirarasa.'

Ellie shook Kulen's hand. 'Lovely to meet you, Kulen. Sathyan has described you to me far more generously.'

'Lovely to meet you, too,' Kulen replied, smiling warmly.

Sathyan tried to retreat, but Dougie herded him back into the circle with his cane.

'Delighted to meet you . . .?' Dougie extended a hand.

'Sathyan,' he replied.

'Dougie Vanderstraaten.' Dougie placed his cane down. 'From the Tea Council.' He was actually an agent under non-official cover. Espionage was a lifelong hobby befitting a man of his station, and he had no real ties to the British government he served, beyond his Etonian accent and Merchant-Ivory dress sense. He reached for Ellie's hand and brought it to his lips. 'My sweet. You look unusually clean.'

'Thank you, Dougie. You look typically ravishing. What brings you here?'

'The pickled herring. You?'

'The same.'

Sathyan looked between them, bewildered and annoyed. 'Kulen, Ellie would like to know about the new German landmine detection technology, which no country that actually has landmines can afford to buy. She has a technical mind and wants to know *everything*.' He turned to leave, but again, Dougie blocked his path.

'Stay,' he said, lightly rapping the younger man's shins with his walking stick. 'I'd rather drown in a vat of pickled herrings than listen to this, but she's more than a match for you, young man.' He turned to Ellie and dropped a quick kiss on both her cheeks. 'I'll see you at the next ball.' He bowed quickly and left them.

'Wonderful.' Kulen said, clearing his throat. But before he could speak, Ellie turned to Sathyan and said, 'The challenge with wartime technology is to develop something that helps the victims of war, not its perpetrators. Even with German sweepers, it would take four hundred and fifty years to clear the world's landmines. Maybe the new technology could improve the speed.' She shook her head. 'So, reduce that to two hundred years. That's still a lot of dead children.'

She had exhumed ninety-six bodies in the last four months and they had barely scratched the surface of the jungle's fermented earth. Sathyan had asked her if she liked Sri Lanka. She was repulsed by it and drawn to it, in equal measure.

Ellie wanted him to know that. She wanted to say she was more than another foreign aid worker with a danger pay uplift and hostage insurance. She wanted to tell him that the broken bodies and broken Conventions were starting to get to her. He seemed like he would understand.

'The landmines used by the Tigers are mostly recycled Russian-era models. They admit that,' Sathyan said. 'But the government secretly scatters the RN340s from the sky. Both are prohibited by the Mine Ban Treaty.'

'So how do you address the use of a weapon that the government doesn't acknowledge exists?' Ellie asked no one in particular. There was no answer.

'Do you work in the landmine sector?' Kulen asked.

'No, she's probably an arms dealer,' Sathyan said. He seemed upset with her, or perhaps himself.

Kulen took his words as a joke, Ellie did not. She *could* have been an arms dealer. In her experience, they never looked the way you expected. 'I develop post-conflict human rights frameworks. To implement justice after a conflict, you need to understand the conflict in the first place. What needs to be fixed is usually based on what went wrong.'

Sathyan's eyes were serious. 'What went wrong? As you've already observed, in Sri Lanka, we don't talk about that.'

'Maybe you and I could talk about it anyway?' she asked softly.

4

NOW (2009)

Ellie loved the flight from DC to Sydney. Business class, three movies and the sense of going home. She had left Australia in 1995, aged eighteen, courtesy of a Franklin Scholarship to Berkeley and her mother's US citizenship. She'd been seduced by US patriotism from childhood, and when the CIA had approached her in pre-law, she had been naive enough to be flattered.

She was older now and understood what home and homeland truly meant, and had learned the difference between expected and acceptable sacrifice. After that mission to Sri Lanka, she spent more time at home in Australia but maintained her brownstone in Georgetown as her US base. She accepted short-term USAID jobs in interesting, less volatile places than Sri Lanka, but always longed to return to Sydney and the comfort of her father and brothers. Ellie went straight from the airport to the Cinnamon Gardens Nursing Home.

•

She took a deep breath and entered the room her father shared with three other men.

'Ellora,' her father greeted her with her full name, as he always did. He had been named after a sacred place, and despite relinquishing it for the ease of Anglicised syllables, he had insisted on traditional first names for his four children.

He wrapped his hands around the armrests of the chair and braced himself. 'You're back,' he said, leaning forward.

'Don't get up, Dad.' She bent down and hugged him. She could feel the angles of the old man's shoulder blades beneath his flannel pyjamas.

'Happy birthday, girl,' he said. Despite his illness, he hadn't forgotten one yet.

'Thank you,' she said, holding on to him for longer. He was fragile but still an anchor for her and her three brothers. 'You warm enough?' she asked.

'Warmer than The Spitter,' he said, referring to one of his roommates. 'I could have sworn he died overnight.' He chuckled at her reaction. 'Kidding. You look beautiful, ende chelle cunju. Just like your mother.'

She looked at The Spitter, The Pray-er and The Crier, as her dad had titled them. He called himself The Wrongly Incarcerated. She and her brothers had offered to get him a private room, but he had refused. She thought he secretly enjoyed the company of his so-called 'cellmates'.

She opened his top drawer and rummaged through the underwear to the back. Her father kept his contraband there. She pulled out a small, greasy bottle.

'What's this?' She sniffed, and winced. The aroma was sickly sweet and familiar from years of mandatory church attendance.

'A gift from The Pray-er. Apparently baby Jesus used it and so should we.' He put it back in the drawer and pulled out the KitKat she was looking for. 'Bloody food fascists.' He offered her some between rebellious bites. 'I've earned this, darling.'

'Too right, Dad.'

He kept one hand firmly on the armrest of the chair, the tremor controlled but not hidden. His shoulders quivered if he lost concentration. The Parkinson's was progressing faster than the early onset dementia.

'I've got another trip coming up,' she said, not wanting to look at his face.

'So soon?' Her father locked his hands together in his lap. 'Where to this time?'

'Sri Lanka, actually.' She waited to see if he remembered what she was like when she had returned last time.

'Sri Lanka? Does the homeland need a new constitution?'

'Something like that.'

'The current one's not worth the paper it's written on.' He looked at her closely. 'My parents would weep if they knew what happened to our country. You'll be okay over there?'

'I'll be fine, Dad. Will you be okay without me? The boys'll visit.'

'Manankati,' he swore. 'Those boys don't come around as often as you.' His hands shook in his lap. Ellie held them.

'I'll be back soon, promise.'

Sometimes the good days were the worst.

•

Ellie entered her Sydney apartment and locked the front door behind her. She took her sidearm from the freezer and defrosted a portion of chicken biriyani.

She didn't feel anger anymore. Just sadness. Deep, aching sadness. The weight of it was exhausting and helped her go to sleep, but not to stay asleep—nightmares woke her often.

The last time she had drawn her gun was four years ago, in the jungles of northern Sri Lanka, protected by soldiers wearing thirty-five pounds of body armour. Their instructions had been to save a bullet for herself in case she was taken.

She had earned her right to the cosier postings of the last few years. Her father had snorted when she described Kathmandu as cosy, but it was, compared to Kabul or Islamabad. And tomorrow, Colombo.

•

The flight to Colombo passed slowly in a haze of fitful sleep and frightening dreams. At the mouth of the plane, Ellie peeled her shirt away from her body and flinched against the glare of the early afternoon sun. The humidity reached into her throat and constricted her airway.

At the bottom of the tinny stairs, she was greeted by a familiar face. Keith Tenby had grown a little chubbier in the two years since they'd last seen each other at a conference in Dhaka. At the time, he'd been presenting on US investment in Asian microfinance programs. She'd already transferred over from the CIA to USAID, despite Redmond's protests about wasting her talents. She was still trying to serve her country, but it often felt like she was just marking time.

When Ellie had emailed Tenby two days ago to say she was coming, he replied: 'Colombo: still the best Yum Cha. EVER. Can't wait to see you. xoxo'.

Now, on the tarmac of Colombo Airport, he was dressed for the climate in a white linen shirt and beige pants, the Western diplomat's standard Asian uniform.

'Tenner.' She reached out a hand but Tenby ignored it and pulled her into a damp embrace. She inhaled, coughed and laughed. 'Is that a new cologne, my friend? Very frankincense and myrrh.'

'That's me, a Wise Man. No one calls me Tenner anymore, by the way,' Tenby replied. He took Ellie's carry-on luggage from her.

In 2004, when they'd last worked together in Colombo, Tenby had negotiated a local sex worker down from thirty dollars to ten for a good time. She'd said that he had the most beautiful eyes and accepted the lower fee.

'Got it, First Secretary,' Ellie said affectionately. 'But you do have the most beautiful eyes.' She winked at him.

'Fuck off. Let's get out of this heat.'

'You're looking a little red there.' She motioned to the top of Tenby's chest where the skin peeped through his shirt, flushed and inflamed. 'Have you been sunbathing? Not enough work to do in Colombo?'

'There's plenty. I can't get the Sri Lankans to agree to anything—you'd think they don't want our aid. And yes, too much sun. You know I'm delicate.' He adjusted his collar and buttoned the shirt up to his throat as he headed inside the airport.

'You're tough enough to survive this political jungle. I'm proud of you, Tenby,' she said.

'Thank you, Ellie, that means a lot to me. We've got your other suitcase already, come this way.' He led her past the queues and armed soldiers, straight to the diplomatic booth.

An immigration official sat behind plate glass, doing a crossword. Tenby tapped his credentials on the window. The man looked up, irritated. He wiped the sweat from his wiry moustache.

Ellie slid her passport under the glass, expecting a wave and nod. Her credentials and passport were usually barely noted.

'*More* people from America?' the man remarked.

'We like the weather,' Tenby said affably.

'You like to talk, you Americans. Talk too much.'

A young soldier joined them at the booth. He had a T-56 assault rifle strapped across his green and brown uniform, one hand with fingers threaded around the trigger, the other supporting the weight of its body against his.

The immigration official muttered something in Sinhalese and shoved the passport back at her. An expression of relief flitted over the soldier's face before he jerked his head, indicating they were allowed to leave.

In the Arrivals lounge, Ellie clocked the agents, identifiable by their studiously casual attire over unusually athletic physiques. Indian, Chinese, British and others. The American agents were a mix of local assets and CIA guys. They far outnumbered the rest. The Sri Lankan agents were harder to spot but she counted three.

'Is it always this busy—and tense?' she asked when they had cleared the airport and headed towards the cars.

Tenby shrugged. 'The end of the war is nigh.'

A tall man approached them from the left and her heart raced as she recognised his silhouette and gait. Arjuna Diwela stepped forward, reaching out towards her, and his face turned away from her almost simultaneously.

She looked down at the hand. There was a small silver amulet tied around his wrist and his hand was covered in the keloid scar tissue of imperfect healing after deep burns. The scar crawled from his right hand, up his arm and under his shirt. She knew it carved a path across the lean muscles of his chest and back before it emerged from under his collar, spreading and twisting like a creeping ox-eye vine, before coming to rest across the left side of his face.

She smiled at Arjuna, tears in her eyes. It was her turn to ignore an outstretched hand. She put her arms around him and kissed first his right cheek, then his left, feeling him stiffen under the contact, then relax. He held her briefly.

'Welcome back,' he said.

'Thank you, Arjuna. You're driving for us?'

'The pay is good.' He smiled that ironic smile she remembered, now tilted on the left by the tightness of the scar.

'How's the family? Namalie still working at Hambantota District General?' The last time Ellie had seen Arjuna's sister was in the intensive care unit of a different hospital.

'She is, thank you for asking. She's a senior administrator at the hospital. The boys are studying hard.'

'They must be young men now.' She turned to Tenby. 'I thought people were nicer in the tropics,' she said, referring to the immigration officer.

'They *are* nicer.' Tenby opened the rear passenger door and cool air rushed out to greet her. Diplomats always had the best cars. Air conditioned and bulletproof.

'They just don't like *us* anymore?' she probed.

'I'm not sure they liked us before. You heard the man, we talk too much.' He took his seat at the front.

She was mostly silent on the journey from the airport to Colombo. Arjuna stole several glances at her in the rear-view mirror. She allowed herself to lock eyes with him once. In the sliver of a mirror, he looked exactly the same.

It was an easy drive, first along the palm-lined beaches and then inland towards the capital.

'Good highway, eh?' Tenby echoed her thoughts.

'*Very* good for this part of the world.'

'Chinese contractors.'

'Is there anything they don't own?' She frowned. Energy, weapons, technology, land and labour. The Chinese were buying, building or selling everything.

'A few things,' Tenby shrugged. 'It's a new world order and everyone wants their place in it.'

'A new world order but the story is as old as time.' She looked up at the Taj Samudra as they pulled into the circular driveway, the hotel's three magnificent towers the prongs of a trident facing the cerulean blue of the Indian Ocean. 'I'm staying *here*? Are you serious? Isn't there a recession? Cuts to foreign aid, a crackdown on junkets etc?' She grabbed her bag from Arjuna in case Tenby took her seriously and suggested she bunk with him.

'I thought you deserved a treat,' Tenby replied. 'The cocktails here are excellent. Run a tab under the Deputy Ambassador's name, not mine. You're expected at the Embassy for diplomatic drinks tonight, Ellie. Redmond's orders.'

'God, I hate those things,' she rolled her eyes.

'You're going anyway. Consider it your patriotic duty. I'm sending Arjuna, just in case you do a last-minute runner. Read the whole briefing before the party, please. No skimming.'

'I never skim.'

'You do, all the time, and you get away with it because you're smarter than the rest of us. Pick up is at 1900, drinks at 1930.'

Tenby shook her hand, then pulled her into an awkward embrace and murmured, 'I've put two weapons, eight rounds and a vest in your suitcase. Protection only.' He pushed her away, smiling. 'It's good to have you back, Ellie.'

5

NOW (2009)

Ellie put on linen pants and a t-shirt and pulled her hair back into a damp, messy bun. She hadn't lied to Tenby. She never skimmed or went into a meeting unprepared. She had many failings, but a lack of diligence wasn't one of them. She would read the briefing when she returned. Maybe after the party.

Arjuna would be back here in three hours. She wrote down an address and slung her bag over her shoulder, then hesitated. The guns were locked in the room safe and her Kevlar vest hung in the cupboard, next to the tuxedo she had brought for the evening function. Redmond had implored her not to be sartorially provocative; Sri Lanka was contradictory in its conservatisms.

Ellie had replied, 'Shelling children is okay, but androgynous evening wear is not?'

'We shell children too. Stop judging them.'

'I judge us all,' she had retorted as she hung up.

She touched the vest now. They didn't always work, and the extra bulk would be a hindrance for what she meant to do.

She left it next to the evening wear and pulled the cupboard door closed. Foolish perhaps, but sometimes she liked to tempt fate.

She strode out of the hotel lobby into the afternoon heat. A reluctant breeze sloped in from the ocean and shifted the still air. She pulled a light scarf from her bag and casually threw it around her hair and shoulders. The nearest doorman darted forward.

'Taxi, madam?' he asked.

'No, thank you. Just going for a walk on the Green.' She paused on the circular driveway, under the canopy that protected the Taj's guests from the sun. She scanned the parking bays for any familiar vehicles. She didn't recognise any, but her heart rate quickened. Years of active duty had given her a sense for when she was being watched.

Unable to identify where that sense was coming from, she walked out onto the road, hailed a tuk-tuk and thrust the piece of paper at the driver. The old man recognised the address and raised his erratic eyebrows. He opened his mouth, revealing betel-stained, gappy teeth. She pulled out a 1000 rupee note. The old man turned off the meter and took her in the direction she wanted to go.

•

Ameena Fernando's office was situated on the second floor of the Bishopsgate Building, precisely 1.4 km away from where she was shot dead a mere 280 metres from her home.

Three days after the journalist's death, the entrance to the building had become a shrine to her. Flowers and garlands, large photographs of Ameena, anointed with holy ash, sandalwood paste and blood-red kum-kum powder, the sacred adornments she might have worn on her wedding day. Cards, posters and messages of love and anger. Candles half melted in the sun, their waxy bodies finding each other and merging into a shining mass.

The main door of the building was locked. Ellie looked up at the second-floor windows. Surprisingly, they were not barred. *The Lanka Herald* had suffered repeated break-ins by paid government thugs or soldiers dressed in civilian clothing, with instructions to intimidate the staff, destroy property and hurt Ameena—a little, but not a lot. But Ameena had apparently refused to imprison her staff inside their office. She was quoted in her paper saying: 'Words, language and speech—they should be free and so should we.'

Ellie paid the tuk-tuk driver and sent him on his way, despite his protests.

'I will wait here, madam. No extra charge. It's not safe. Poor Ameena,' he had lamented, picking up the edge of his sarong to re-tie it around his waist. He pulled the dirty cloth off his shoulder and wiped the sweat from his neck.

She waited until the tuk-tuk had turned the corner and checked again to see if anyone was following her. A motorcycle, its rider in full leathers, drove past her, a flash of red on its exhaust pipe. It turned at the same corner as the tuk-tuk. She waited a few more minutes, then walked around to the side alley, and down the small stairwell that led to the basement.

She put latex gloves on and tried the basement door. Locked, but thankfully with something simple. There was no reason for her to be here, not without a local police chaperone and Ministry of Justice permission—which had been denied when Redmond made the request from DC. Arjuna and Tenby would never sanction her next move: she pulled out her pins and needles kit from her satchel and opened the door on the first try.

Ellie looked around the musty room. No internal CCTV so far. She waited and listened. Nothing. At the second floor, she took a small retractable knife from her P&N kit and slashed the police tape away. Three more needles and she was inside *The Lanka Herald*.

She pulled her scarf back and surveyed the room.

Look, but don't touch. Find something but not too much, had been Redmond's instructions. *Show the family in San Francisco we care.*

She was terrible with instructions.

Walking among the debris, knife in one hand, torch now in the other, Ellie found Ameena's office quickly. Everything was upturned, drawers smashed and pulled apart, secret compartments suspected and searched for. The whiteboard behind Ameena's desk was cracked but still whole. It had fallen off one of its brackets and now tilted precariously on the wall. The filing cabinet had been prised apart. Three locked drawers were now open and empty. The desk was the same; nothing but the stationery and a paperweight remained. She picked up the bronze obelisk paperweight. It was engraved:

The Lanka Herald, for fearless journalism
Thomson Reuters Justice Award
South Asian Sector, 2007

Ellie crouched to pick up a broken photo frame, and was relieved that Sathyan wasn't in it. Annoyed that she would have been jealous if he was. The photo instead showed Ameena, three children and a man. Her ex-husband. They were leaning against the rickety hull of a fishing boat, their arms around one another, palm trees towering behind them. One of the children, the older son, was tickling the younger one, their bare feet buried in the warm sand. They were happy together.

She pulled the photograph from its frame—nothing behind it. No hidden message from the dead woman. She put it in her bag and was about to get up when the lights came on. She ducked down, cursing. They had to know she was in here. Of course, they knew she was in here—she had cut their tape.

'Hello madam, Mrs American,' a man called out. 'Hello madam,' he repeated. His colleague laughed derisively. They muttered to each other in Sinhalese, but Ellie couldn't hear them clearly. 'Can we help you?' he tried again.

Ellie stayed on the floor, shoved her torch in her bag, and kept the knife poised. It wouldn't go deep, but when used properly it could go far enough. Stun and slow down. Don't kill. She hated killing. Other people had usually done it for her.

She looked under Ameena's desk, her cheek hot against the cool wooden floor, and saw two sets of heavy boots, the ankles covered in Army fatigues, the tip of a bayoneted service rifle resting against the black shiny surface of his shoes. The room was secure and she was outnumbered. She pushed herself into the corner of the desk and weighed her options.

She could put the knife away, take out her ID and come out with her hands up. Looking up at the wall and the whiteboard, she cursed the absence of windows.

She noticed then that the board was plugged in. It wasn't a whiteboard. It was a smartboard.

She followed the vein of the wire from the wall up to the dented body. Where the wire met the smartboard, there was a tiny black rectangular box, like a USB stick, still plugged into the port. It could only have served one purpose. She would not be allowed to leave with it. She might not be allowed to leave at all.

She took four deep breaths, in through the nose and out through the mouth, and placed the knife back in her bag. She relaxed her body from the centre of her forehead to her feet, located her inner energy in the base of her spine and visualised it coursing through her body.

She was ready when the first soldier came through Ameena's office door, his gun poised over her.

She stood up in a fluid motion, grabbing the device from the smartboard, shoving it in her trouser pocket and then raising her arms to show she was not armed. She walked around the desk, her arms above her head now dropped to her chest with her hands open, relaxed but ready, protecting her centre line.

The soldier opened his mouth to call the other man but she shook her head, smiled and uncurled her right hand to reveal the small device. Confused by the co-operative gesture, the soldier leaned forward and dropped the tip of his bayonet just a fraction.

Ellie pulled down on the lug of the weapon. The soldier tensed and tried to keep his balance. She relaxed even more and redirected the hilt of the gun in a fast, sharp punch to his gut. He doubled over and she grabbed the obelisk and smashed it into the middle of his back. Another deliberately shallow blow to the back of his head. Stunned, two broken ribs—but not dead. She caught him as he slumped and laid him gently on the ground. She put the device in her pocket and crawled towards the door.

She couldn't hear the other man, who should have been searching for his colleague by now. She stopped and listened again.

Nothing. Something was wrong. She stood up slowly, hands above her head, just in case, and edged around the door.

Arjuna stood on the other side of the room holding a rifle that didn't belong to him in one hand, his gun in the other. It had an eight-inch titanium hybrid silencer screwed in.

'It seems you've learned very little in your time away,' he observed, his tone even drier than she remembered.

'I'm better at unarmed combat than I used to be,' she replied, breathless.

'Unarmed won't help you in modern warfare. Unmanned, but not unarmed,' he said, referring to the US drones that were always above them. 'Let's go, the Ambassador is expecting you.'

'The other guy?' She looked around for a body.

Arjuna led her by the elbow to the office entrance. 'He should have been better at *armed* combat.'

'Oh God, did you . . .' The blood rushed to her head. 'Arjuna—'

'Don't be stupid.' He shook his head. 'Or *more* stupid. You took a huge risk coming here, but the last thing we need is dead soldiers. There's a Special Ops team on the way that wants to clean up your mess. Follow me.'

She opened her mouth but he cut her off.

'I've told them to stand down. But we should get out of here before your new friends wake up.' He led her down the stairwell, to the building exit. Outside, the sun was setting but the heat still felt oppressive. A movement caught Ellie's eye and she saw a rider sitting on a motorbike, diagonally across the road from them. His engine was running, like he was waiting for something. She couldn't be certain, but he looked very like the motorcyclist she had glimpsed earlier. Which would mean he was waiting for *her*. He could probably tell that she'd seen him.

He had no intention of hiding. That was unusual for agents, even local ones.

The initial briefing with Redmond returned to her. Four motorcyclists were seen leaving the site of Ameena's murder. Before she could mention this to Arjuna, he'd walked over to his car and unlocked the passenger door for her.

'We've got to go, Ellie. Now. Solomon will want your head and probably mine. Your cover's blown and you haven't even got over the jetlag.'

6

NOW (2009)

Arjuna drove through the high-walled security gate and let Ellie out of the car with a warning: 'I'll be back at 2300 hours. It's a party. Don't antagonise the locals. And don't run away. There are more CIA agents in Colombo right now than tourists. We will find you.'

She nodded, grateful he was coming back for her. Until she worked out exactly who was following her and why, she had to be more careful. Ellie crossed the external antechamber and walked through the steel doors into the US Embassy. Memory and the sound of music called her to the main ballroom. She searched the crowd for familiar faces. The Australians looked like they had been here for hours. They never could turn down free alcohol.

She pivoted and nearly collided with an old friend.

'Harper, you're back.' Bill Solomon extended his hand. His voice was as hoarse as she remembered, decades of cigarettes briefly interrupted by two surgeries for throat cancer. Solomon was the station chief for the CIA in Sri Lanka, and a lifer in Colombo. His breed of agent was essential for security in high-risk countries, although since Dar es Salaam and Nairobi, all American embassies considered themselves targets. 9/11 hadn't made the CIA paranoid, simply justified.

'Bill, you're still here,' Ellie smiled sweetly.

He was standing next to a broad Sri Lankan man in a tuxedo, whose thick moustache and corpulence she recognised, and not just because Sri Lankan men of a certain age and social class were all over-fed and redolent of Old Spice.

Solomon had a hard grip and he pulled Ellie towards him. 'Let me introduce you to Dilshan Perera, the—'

'Under Secretary for Defence,' she finished. 'You look just like your cousin, the President.'

'Thank you. The President is much better looking,' Dilshan replied.

'My boss, Mike Redmond, mentioned that you would be my liaison for the aid negotiations. I just got in this afternoon, but perhaps we could meet later this week?'

'Excellent. I'm honoured Mike sent you. You still have a reputation and friends in Sri Lanka.' Dilshan smiled, revealing perfect Western orthodontics. He had been briefed on her last mission here. 'I'll ask my office to call you. Bill will have your number, no?'

Solomon nodded. 'Yes, I know how to find her.'

'Excellent. I'll let you two catch up. Dr Harper, it was a pleasure.' The Under Secretary shook her hand, then joined a current in the crowd that took him to the next circle of diplomats.

'How's the Ambassador?' Ellie asked Solomon, bracing herself.

'Furious. He got a call from Perera.' Solomon stood head and shoulders above most of the room and kept monitoring the crowd, but here he stooped and pitched his voice for her ears only. 'He heard about your little side trip this afternoon. What are you playing at? You could have been killed.'

'If I didn't know you better, I'd say you were concerned about me,' Ellie said.

'I'm concerned about damage control. If you eat a bullet, I'm the one who has to clean up. You jeopardised our operation here and your role, and now I have to explain to Langley why you didn't follow protocol. I told Redmond this was a mistake, but he's getting soft.' He eyed her as he straightened once more to his full height. 'Actually, he was always soft on you.'

Her face heated. 'I wanted to have a look around without a state chaperone. You know how they operate. I'd have been shown the outside of the building and some carefully edited crime scene photos and advised to file a report.'

'That's exactly what you should do—file a report. You're here to help Tenby lock in an aid agreement. The other stuff is just optics. That journalist was living on borrowed time. Tell the family you investigated and found nothing solid, and you're sorry for their loss.' He acknowledged someone across the room.

'Say that a lot, do you?' Her voice wavered a little. She hated these people.

'I do, and sometimes I mean it. In this case, Fernando had it coming to her. This is Sri Lanka, not Sweden.' He dusted pastry flakes from his lapel.

'Speaking of Scandinavia . . .' She needed to get out of this room. Where was Tenby? 'The Norwegians are worried about what's happening up north.'

'Fucking bleeding hearts want us to intervene. Like that would do anything. Sometimes I just want to beat them with my nine-iron.'

'Maybe that's why you play alone,' she said.

'I *prefer* to play golf alone. I'm always listening to chatter. When I'm on the green, I want silence.'

She could understand that. Solomon had seen the bomb blasts in the capital. He had identified the bodies of Americans and bagged them for freight as methodically as he sent souvenirs home for his grandchildren. Everyone needed a little silence.

'The city still on high alert?' she asked.

'The city's been on high alert since 9/11.'

'And Rajapaksa's pledge to join our war on terror. Who would have thought he'd become such an enthusiastic and fluent speaker of Bush's anti-terrorism language?'

'That's *President* Bush. Watch your language, Harper. You're a guest here. This is my house.' Solomon was serious. He protected country above countrymen. Terrorism, he had once told her, was simply the same acts of war he had been fighting since Vietnam, just with more deadly tools.

'Ellie, you made it.' Tenby joined their circle and pretended not to notice the relief on her face.

'Yes, she did, by the skin of her teeth.' Solomon leaned into Tenby. 'Keep your agent in check and remind her who she works for.' He raised his glass in mock salute and left them.

'Christ, that was fast. It usually takes you twenty-four hours to piss off the establishment. You look beautiful, by the way.' Tenby pulled his collar away from his neck, adjusting the bow tie. 'Damn suit,' he muttered.

'Age is accelerating my superpowers, Tenby.' She reached up and straightened his tie, her fingertips touching the creeping redness at his neck. His heat rash looked more like a stress rash. Poor old Tenby.

He thanked her and pulled away. 'Did it ever occur to you that if you played ball with Solomon, he could help you?'

'He'll only help me if my interests are aligned with the United States.'

'Your interests *are* those of the United States. You should *always* be aligned with the home country, Ellie. You're not a free agent, even if all you do now is attend constitutional reform meetings in developing countries. You're always there as an agent of the United States and your refusal to accept that—well, frankly it's getting tedious.'

'"Frankly it's getting tedious"? That's the best you can do?' She ribbed. Diplomats swore like pansies, especially the newly promoted ones whose circles of influence were more politically powerful *and* more politically correct.

He smirked. 'Okay, fine, Ellie—it's fucking annoying. You make it seem like you're on the side of truth and justice and we're on the side of the American Way, and somehow those things are opposed to each other.'

'Tenby, that's the most honest thing you've ever said to me. Now, can you get me into the Frontal Lobe? I don't think I've got clearance for that anymore. Perhaps without Solomon watching?'

'You definitely don't have clearance for that. You're several steps up from a visiting academic, but several steps down from the inner circle of intelligence. What do you want there?' he asked apprehensively.

She took the USB device out. 'It's encrypted. I've tried six programs already. I took it from the smartboard in Ameena Fernando's office.'

Tenby choked on his drink. 'You stole evidence from a crime scene?'

'Correct.'

'Then yes, I can get you into the Frontal Lobe. We should connect it to one of Scottie's super-brain computers and see what it can do,' he suggested.

'Perfect. Maybe now? This party is painful.'

'Agreed,' he said, ditching his drink and leading her across the ballroom, through the kaleidoscope of well-dressed dignitaries. They had almost reached a side door when a woman in gold shimmered into their path.

Her jet-black hair fell like a sheet, straight and shining over one shoulder, plunging with her teasingly low neckline down towards her belly. The perfect dress for Embassy drinks, distracting but diplomatic. She whispered something in Tenby's ear, and he nodded, allowing himself to be directed towards an elderly gentleman. The man was fringed by heavy-set bodyguards who had surrendered their guns at Security Portal 1 but could still kill with their bare hands.

Tenby coughed and wiped the sweat from his palms on his suit pants. He always was a nervous sweater. 'Ellie, I'd like to introduce you to the Chinese cultural attaché, Mr Eric Kwan. Mr Kwan, this is—'

'We've met before, Tenner—Tenby.' Ellie smiled apologetically and warmly at her friend and then spoke to the Chinese diplomat. 'Mr Kwan, it's a pleasure to see you again. You've been promoted to the diplomatic corps? Or was it a demotion?'

The older man ignored the jibe. 'What brings you to Sri Lanka, Dr Harper?' he asked without smiling in return. 'Not secession agreements this time, it must be hoped.'

'Mr Kwan and I met at a forum about Tibet, hosted in New Delhi,' Ellie explained to Tenby. 'I was presenting on devolution agreements. You know, what does partial autonomy in trade, tourism, law and order et cetera look like?'

'It looked far too much like secession,' Kwan replied.

'Well, as you say, there won't be any secession agreements here.' Ellie shrugged, feigning indifference.

'Then why are you here?' Kwan asked again.

'I thought I could write the Sri Lankan government a new constitution. You know, one that sets out the rights of citizens and the responsibilities of the state. Maybe with pictures and diagrams, in case they still don't get it.'

Arrows, she thought. *Arrows might help.*

'Americans, always joking.' Kwan shook his head. 'Never listening. Never learning.'

Tenby answered for her. 'I'm finalising an aid agreement and Ellie has kindly offered to help. Post-conflict nation-building is her expertise for USAID. We're looking at the whole package that will be needed after the war ends.'

'Ah yes, thank you, Mr Tenby. Dr Harper called you Tenner?' he asked, raising an eyebrow. 'An unusual nickname.'

'An old and defunct nickname,' Ellie redirected quickly as Tenby flushed. 'Now we just call him "First Secretary".'

'Of course.' Kwan nodded. 'Mr Tenby, you've reminded me about the three R's of post-conflict: reconciliation, resettlement and reconstruction. Dr Harper presented a paper on it in New Delhi.' He looked at Ellie.

'You flatter me, sir,' she said.

'Not intentionally. The People's Republic takes its responsibility to Sri Lanka seriously. Perhaps between diplomatic parties, you will visit some of the hospitals and schools we are rebuilding. You might learn something.' Kwan held out his arm and the woman in the gold dress moved forward to take it.

'I'd like that. Perhaps your assistant will show me around?' Ellie looked at her.

'Daughter, actually,' the woman replied. 'Su Lin Kwan. I would be delighted to show you our work with rural communities here. As my father says, we could teach the Great White Saviour something about empowering partnerships.'

Ellie smiled. People did like to consider her white when convenient. 'There's a fourth R in my paper, Ms Kwan. But the State Department edits my lectures, and in the case of the People's Republic, you edit all incoming information, too.'

'With good reason,' Kwan said. 'Wrong information can be corruptive.'

'What's your fourth R?' Su Lin asked.

'The rule of law. Post-conflict reconstruction has to be underpinned by the rule of law.' Ellie actually believed that. She had just never seen it done effectively. 'Sri Lanka doesn't score well on the Rule of Law Index.'

'If Guantanamo Bay was a country, it wouldn't score well, either,' Su Lin replied. 'You're so convinced that you know best; that you—and only you—know what countries need to succeed. And yet you lack the self-awareness to acknowledge that all you're really doing is building puppet democracies, defined by a Western-normative model that protects your imperial interests.'

'Is what you're doing any different?' Ellie asked. It wasn't a challenge. She wanted to hear this woman's perspective.

'No. But *we* are honest about it,' Kwan replied for his daughter. 'Enjoy your trip here, Dr Harper. Sri Lanka is a busy country. How is it you Americans say? Take a number.' He nodded to indicate that they were excused.

Tenby grabbed Ellie's hand, muttering under his breath as he took her out the side door, through two corridors and the industrial kitchen. 'I don't even want to talk about that.'

'Oh, come on,' Ellie protested. 'That was at least a bit of fun in an otherwise dismal party. I *am* sorry about the Tenner thing, though. Old habits.'

He waved off her apology as they descended two flights to another corridor. Tenby led her past the rec room where the Special Ops guys were hanging out, waiting for a call.

'Where's the armoury?' she asked. It used to be somewhere around here.

'Other side, next to the gym. Different security system. Why?' He took her to a door with a dimly lit panel beside it. 'I can get you whatever you need.'

'No, thank you for the gear.' Two guns and a vest were more than enough.

Tenby inserted a key below the panel, then placed his palm on it and entered a code with his other hand. Finally, he spoke into the monitor: 'My voice identifies me as Keith Simon Tenby.'

The panel lit up green. A voice crackled through the monitor. 'I see you've brought an old friend, Tenby.'

'I have, Scottie—an oldie but a goodie.'

'I'll be the judge of that. Verify yourself,' the voice instructed.

Ellie stepped forward and placed her palm on the panel. Her left hand was about to punch in her former security code, an unconscious muscle memory.

'That won't be necessary. I'll bypass the code,' the voice interrupted her. 'I just need your voice signature.'

'My voice identifies me as Ellie Rachel Harper. Date of Birth: 12 January 1977.'

'Happy Birthday, Ellie,' the voice said.

'Thank you, Scottie.'

The panel lit up green again and the reinforced metal door opened.

They entered the intelligence room known as the Frontal Lobe—walls of screens, satellite images, maps, movements of US military personnel, banks of computers. There was a small team of analysts, some on headsets, all working data. Each US embassy had an intelligence room. In some countries, the US had several in different secure locations, all networked to their station office and each other. The Frontal Lobe in Colombo was small but networked to its counterparts in India.

Scott Barnett stood up from his cluttered desk to greet her with a bear hug. He looked older than before, more lines on his face, less ash-blond hair on his head, but the same intelligent eyes and quick smile, and still strong and lean for a man who only left this fortified room to have a smoke.

He sat down again in front of a computer with three screens. Two showed reams of data. The third was *Dance India Dance*.

'Complex encrypted data embedded in that one?' She motioned to the screen.

'Highly complex. I've been taking classes on YouTube.'

She laughed. 'What else do they have you doing here in Colombo? I thought you'd have asked for a transfer by now,' she said, taking a seat next to him. 'Somewhere less prone to malaria and genocide. You deserve it.'

'And miss all the action in the Thoroughfare?' Scott replied, pulling up a map on one of his screens.

He took a stylus and drew a line on the screen from the Middle East to Pakistan, around India and Sri Lanka. He threaded the line through the Strait of Malacca and parts of Asia, around to China. Then he drew an X on Sri Lanka.

'From here, you can watch the movement of a fleet above the water or below it. You can refuel and restock your own fleet to fight it. You can deploy planes and short-range drones. Every colonial and superpower has wanted Sri Lanka, so they can watch all of this.' He drew a ring around the region. 'From right here.' He rested his stylus on the X. *That's* why I'm still here,' he said. 'And good thing for you that I am, I'm guessing. What can I do for you, Ellie?'

'Do you think you could decrypt this for me, please, Scottie? Then we can talk Bollywood moves or Sri Lanka's strategic advantages, your choice.' She gave him the device.

'Where did you get a Tardis from? Do I want to know?'

She shook her head. 'Tardis?'

He inserted it into one of his hard drives. 'This is high-level data mining technology, with capacity to transport massive amounts of information through space—hence the name.' He played around with various screens and prompts, each one bringing up a file lock. 'It's not a passive storage unit like a USB stick. The Tardis is an active leech with five levels of security and encryption.'

'Don't tell me you can't crack a journalist's security system.'

'A journalist?' He looked dubious. 'This tech is expensive, and you can't just buy it at Walmart. You program it, then plug it in, and it automatically, intuitively draws out all the data it finds. And it finds everything, even data that's heavily protected.'

'Impressive.'

'It's a sophisticated toy. Once it finds what it wants, it transmits the data to an off-site location.'

'Anywhere off-site?'

'Anywhere in the world,' he confirmed. 'It packages the data, bounces it to a satellite which bounces it to whoever put the

Tardis there in the first place. Not many countries have this technology.' Scott took the Tardis from one hard drive and inserted it into another.

'*Could* this belong to a journalist, rather than an agency?' Tenby asked.

Scott shook his head. 'Like I said, not many people have the tech. Unless your journalist was aligned to . . . a state party?'

'Unlikely,' Ellie replied. Ameena Fernando attacked all players equally. 'But I'll look into it. Next request: can you access local CCTV footage?'

'I can, although not directly. I tap into the Station and they're hacked into the local system. I'm just a spectator. What do you want to see?' He opened up another program.

She pulled out a folded square of paper. 'I need to know what happened between 0900 and 1200 hours on 9 January 2009. These are the coordinates of the kill zone. I also want footage of the two weeks prior, to see who scoped the kill zone, plus the forty-eight hours after, to see who's returned to dispose of evidence.'

'You're here to investigate that?' Scott asked. 'You know who they suspect, right?'

'I know.' It was more than a suspicion. It was an accusation from the dead woman's grave.

'And Redmond still sent you to investigate it?'

'She's here to help me on the aid agreement,' Tenby interjected. 'Redmond asked her to make inquiries about the other incident, but as usual, she's been doing more than that.'

Ellie shrugged. 'I also need all of Ameena Fernando's phone records. Let's look at the last six months for now. And track her location too, please, if you can.'

'Sure. Anything else?' Scott asked, bemused.

'Cross-reference the phone numbers with bank records. I also want you to look at this list of persons of interest.' She turned the paper over and showed Scott the list.

'You have POIs already?' Tenby peered over Scott's shoulder.

'Just based on the key exposés the paper ran over the last two years. I need vital stats, phone records, criminal records and known associates of staff, same timeframe.'

'You suspect her staff?' Tenby asked. 'As I understand it, the paper was run by a loyal team of radicals.'

'I suspect everybody.'

'Eighty per cent of homicides are committed by someone intimately known to the victim,' Tenby pointed out. 'Like a husband or a lover. Are they on your list?'

'Naturally,' she replied, not entirely truthfully. Anil Fernando and Sathyan Navaratnam were on the list, but far below others. She would need motive and means to move them up.

'It's been a while since you used your investigative skills, Ellie,' Tenby said. 'I'm impressed that it's coming back to you so fast.'

'I've been watching a lot of *NCIS*.'

'I've often wondered who watches that show,' Scott mused.

'Old men in nursing homes and their dutiful daughters. Send everything straight to my inbox, if you can.'

'Ellie.' Tenby weighed his words carefully. 'No offence, but you're basically a lawyer now, not an intelligence analyst and certainly not a detective . . .'

'So?'

'He's saying that you attend conferences and make human rights recommendations that no one reads—'

'I'm not offended by that at all, thank you, Scottie. Please continue to minimise my career.'

'I'm *saying*, what does Redmond actually expect you to achieve?' Tenby tried to appease her before an argument broke out, scratching the rash on his neck.

'With your help, Tenby, he wants me to make reasonable efforts to find out what happened to the journalist.' Her voice came out harsher than she had intended with her old friend. 'Her ex-husband is a high-profile US citizen, he's asked for help and we've got to show we're taking this kind of thing seriously.' She wasn't exactly sure what she meant when she said *this kind of thing*—the assassination of a journalist, the threat to freedom of the press, or the decline of the rule of law in the region.

'Okay, okay,' Tenby placated, his hands raised in the air. 'I'm allowed to ask, Ellie, so I know how to help you.'

She took a deep breath and turned to Scott. 'Can you get me the footage or not?'

'I can—here.' Scott pulled a flash drive from his computer. 'I can insult you and illegally download CCTV footage at the same time. It's yours. Go crazy, detective.'

•

That night in her hotel, Ellie tidied the draft agreements into a pile on the bedside table. She opened up the encrypted laptop Scott had given her, punching in the three codes and placing her hand on the screen to read her biometric data.

She opened up the file of the CCTV footage and located the timeframe of the murder, giving herself a margin of thirty minutes on either side.

Her CIA briefing had showed twelve cameras between Ameena's house and where she was assassinated. Twelve across only four blocks. Colombo was on high alert for terrorism, but the government watched terrorists and citizens alike.

The second camera at the main junction after Ameena's house showed her in her silver Mazda, stopping at a cashew vendor's stall, buying food and then turning left. The third camera showed no trace of the journalist at all.

Ellie checked the footage on all the cameras, flicking back and forth. She had her, and then she lost her. A grainy image of a hand reaching through the window to give cash and receive food. Ellie froze the image and expanded it as far as it could go. She looked at Ameena's hand, noting something there that had caught the light. A ring perhaps. She tried to zoom in and enlarge, but couldn't. Scott would have to help her with that. She let the footage continue.

One second, Ameena was there, and then in the next, she wasn't. Nothing. Ellie checked the time stamp. It was accurate. She checked the footage again and again. Perhaps she had made a mistake.

The footage showed people, but not the person she was looking for.

No silver Mazda, no assassins on motorcycles, no shooting and no dead woman.

7

NOW (2009)

After her frustrating review of the CCTV footage, Ellie read Redmond's briefing, and after that litany of horrors, her dreams were even worse than usual, filled with images of dead bodies, old *and* new. She slept through her alarm and three phone calls from Tenby.

She arrived at the Under Secretary's office an hour late. His personal assistant looked like a flight attendant, ushering Ellie into the back of the small, crowded conference room.

Staff from various government departments were on one side of the table, with Dilshan Perera in the middle. The American aid delegates were seated on the other side: idealists and logistics experts who always looked like they'd just come in from the field, tempered by the accountants in freshly laundered suits.

Ellie recognised many faces on both sides of the table. Some of them bristled when they saw her; some of them smiled.

Dilshan looked up when she took her seat next to Tenby. 'Good to see you again, Dr Harper. I'm so glad you could join us. Have you found our country much changed since you were last here?'

Everyone in the room turned to her. She answered diplomatically for Tenby's sake. 'It's as beautiful and full of potential as ever.'

Tenby exhaled quietly and turned back to continue the discussion. From his brief, Ellie knew that the Sri Lankans wanted a long list of projects funded in the south of the country: irrigation schemes, investment in industries and hotels. She let the negotiation meander for as long as she could bear.

'What about the north?' she interrupted finally, images from the country briefing still vivid in her mind. Men who looked like her uncles and cousins. Children who looked like the ones she had encountered on her first mission here.

'Excuse me, Dr Harper?' Dilshan asked.

'The north,' she repeated. 'This is a critical time for Sri Lanka. Our satellite reports indicate you're making the final push in the north and the east.'

'Yes,' Dilshan replied. 'US satellites have been an important part of our successful military strategy. You are our primary eyes in the sky.'

'We are your *only* eyes in the sky. I'm keen to hear your plans for the north when the war ends and reconstruction begins,' she said. If the government didn't invest aid into the conflict zone, generations of Tamils displaced by war would be disempowered by poverty.

'You're here on behalf of your government, Dr Harper. Your country analysis is hardly objective.' Dilshan's tone suggested no further response was needed.

'We're in the middle of something here, Ellie. Let's cross that bridge when we get to it.' Tenby raised his eyebrows meaningfully at her.

'Let's *build* that bridge, while we're here,' she replied. Tenby was a good operator, but the Sri Lankan government was a completely different adversary. They felt entitled to hurt their own people—both Tamil and Sinhalese—and would not comprehend the assertion that their acts were criminal.

He dropped his voice. 'We're working through an agenda. You can't come out swinging, Ellie.' He smiled apologetically at Dilshan and his colleagues.

She had read the minutes of the previous negotiations. Tenby's approach of give-and-take diplomacy wasn't working here, with China making fast, bold offers they couldn't compete with. The deals were being done before Tenby even got in the room. The rising superpower had already secured the larger reconstruction contracts. Even the Australians had somehow negotiated a role for their navy, helpfully 'patrolling' local waters to catch people smugglers. The US was left to throw aid money at the Sri Lankans without asking for enough in return.

'I think swinging hard for the sucker punch is all we've got left, Tenby,' she whispered. She was about to say more to him but changed her mind. 'If you'd excuse us for a moment, Minister,' she said, standing up and tapping Tenby's shoulder for him to do the same.

'Please,' Dilshan replied. 'Take more of our time.'

She took Tenby down the empty corridor outside the conference room but kept her voice low, for his hearing only. 'If they want help from us in the south, then let's at least make them agree to basic principles before we give them aid or trade.'

'Like what?' he asked.

She sighed. 'Like: "We will invest in a desalination plant in the south, if your soldiers stop raping women in the north".'

'I can't say that.' Tenby looked around nervously.

'We're *supposed* to say that. That's why we're here. Read the list I sent you last night—ask for the human rights protections they'll never agree to, then concede to a softer option you're still comfortable with.'

He shook his head and made his way back to the meeting. Ellie had no choice but to follow him in and take her seat. Everyone was staring at them.

'Dr Harper, would you like to share something?' Dilshan's voice cut across the room.

'Yes, of course, sorry. I was just telling Tenby here that aid experts usually have more degrees than balls. But Tenby's got balls, sir. *He* was just about to say that we'll fund a desalination plant in the south, if your soldiers stop raping women in the north. What do you think?'

'I think our soldiers don't rape women.'

'Then you should have no trouble putting that condition in the agreement,' she said.

'Perhaps we can leave the delegates to talk, and you and I can have that briefing?'

'Of course.'

Dilshan led her out of the conference room. They were greeted by his PA, who accompanied them to his office. It was resplendent with enlarged photographs of him and the President, as well as other world leaders.

'You can't manipulate me with your fancy lawyering, Dr Harper,' Dilshan said as he took his seat, gesturing her to another. 'We are entitled to protect ourselves.'

'I don't question that, sir. I'm here to ensure that Sri Lanka is given the aid it needs, and that it complies with the Conventions that govern it.' She turned at the sound of the door opening.

'Remarkable, isn't she?' Tenby entered the room. 'Ellie is a true believer, one of our last. It's one of the reasons we love her so much.' He sat next to her and nudged her foot. Hard. She moved it away. She hated it when he did that.

'I even believe in the doctrine of universal jurisdiction,' she said. 'For the International Criminal Court.' There were many who thought the Sri Lankan president should be tried at the ICC, including her family.

'Open your eyes, Dr Harper,' Dilshan retorted. 'These are not the universal laws of international human rights in operation. These are the eternal laws of survival and commerce. For example, you need oil and you need someone to do business with to get it. As soon as Saddam stopped being that person, you ignored the laws of territorial integrity, invaded Iraq, and replaced him with someone else.'

'I think it was more complicated than that,' she replied.

'Yes, fabricating the existence of weapons of mass destruction and coercing sovereign countries to invade another sovereign country for no reason is very complicated indeed.'

Tenby paled but Ellie burst out laughing. 'I'm sorry, sir. That's the kind of thing I get in trouble for saying.'

'I hope you *won't* get into trouble while you're here, Dr Harper. Help us finalise the aid agreement, and then go to one of our many beach resorts with the rest of the diplomatic corps. My treat.'

'Thank you, sir. But that's not necessary.'

'Of course, it is. We're keen to build long-term partnerships with our allies, including the United States.'

'I know, we are too, sir,' she replied, on message again. Hopefully Tenby would report back selectively to Solomon. 'Which is why I wanted to apologise for my intrusion into *The Lanka Herald* office and my behaviour with your men. My curiosity and reflexes got the better of the respect I have for your country.'

Redmond always said offence was the best defence, including a pre-emptive and fulsome—and completely disingenuous—apology. Dilshan knew she had been to the journalist's office. He knew she wasn't here for just the aid negotiations. She had given him that. Solomon was right, she had fucked up.

'Ah yes, Ameena Fernando's death,' Dilshan responded. 'That was such a tragedy. She was an accomplished journalist. Misguided at times, but accomplished. If you believe everything you read about her, she was a veritable saint. A paragon of integrity and ... fidelity.'

Ellie waited for him to continue.

'Her husband will tell you there was much more to her than her public persona. What kind of woman leaves her family for her job? Have you asked yourself that?'

'I haven't had enough time to look into it, sir,' she deflected.

'The President and I knew Ameena well. She was a far more complex person than she seemed.'

In Ellie's experience, this was true of everyone.

'We'd like you to discontinue your investigation into her death,' Dilshan said.

'There is no investigation,' Tenby replied. A pointless lie. Half-truths were always better.

'There *is* an investigation,' Ellie contradicted him. She felt Tenby tense. 'Her family demands it. But I can make my investigation into Ameena's death disappear.' Half a truth, half a lie.

She hated these people. She hated herself. She hated how strong her old instincts were, despite four years of pretending they did not exist.

'Solomon will talk terms with you,' she continued. 'There are contracts I'm sure he'll want you to reconsider.'

Dilshan nodded, suspicious but intrigued.

She felt last night's canapes rise from her gut. She *could* make the investigation disappear, like the missing CCTV footage. Disappear, like the children in the jungle. Disappear, like Ameena Fernando. She could, but she wouldn't.

•

Dilshan Perera's office overlooked Viharamahadevi Park. Ellie scanned the parked cars and, most importantly, the motorcycles. She didn't recognise any of them, but she wasn't sure what she was looking for yet.

She waited for a gap in the traffic, linked arms with Tenby and crossed the road. They took a seat on a wrought iron bench under the largest frangipani tree she had ever seen. It was the lone and rebellious native in a sea of Norfolk pines.

Tenby wiped the sweat from his face and neck with a handkerchief. 'That could have been worse, I suppose,' he said. 'I thought I was going to have a heart attack when you told him about the investigation.'

She put her arm around him. His benign plumpness was reassuring. 'Oh Tenby, you need to relax. Try Wing-Chun, my psychiatrist got me on to it. It's relaxing and aggressive at the same time.'

'Wing-Chun?' he repeated. 'I need Valium and a whisky chaser.'

'I don't think you're allowed to safeguard US diplomatic interests or operate heavy machinery after consuming psychoactive drugs. And benzos don't play well with others, so skip the whisky.'

'Shut up.' Tenby laughed reluctantly.

'I think that went really well,' she said, picking up a flower. A sunset of colours radiated from the centre to its creamy white, curled edges. She breathed in its perfume, imagining its sweetness cleansing her body.

Tenby shook his head. 'Ellie, people disregard advice from Dilshan Perera at their own peril.'

'Advice? First, he wanted me to look into Ameena's personal life, then he instructed me to end the investigation. It's classic misdirection, followed by a warning.'

'Then listen to the warning at least. You've created an opportunity for Solomon out of yesterday's colossal cock-up,' he said.

'Lemons, lemonade, something like that,' she quipped. Lime juice actually. She needed lime juice to stem the nausea.

Tenby sighed. 'I worry about you, Ellie.' He shoved the handkerchief back into his pocket.

'As long as you don't pray for me, Tenby.'

'I'm serious. We almost lost you last time.' He reached out and squeezed her hand. Four years ago, when she returned to DC after her last mission, Tenby had called her every week for months, checking on her under the pretext of needing her expertise on Colombo politics.

She smiled at him. 'I want you to help me instead of trying to protect me. I know where you're coming from and I adore you for it.' She put her arm around his shoulders again and presented him with the flower. 'Meet me later for the finest whisky the Taj Samudra has to offer. But no Valium.' She kissed him on the cheek and left for her next appointment.

•

Arjuna took her to the crime scene. It had been four days since the assassination and Beira Road was still closed and guarded. Small crowds of people gathered at the barricades, some leaving flowers and memorials, many weeping.

As soon as news of her death hit the wires, the Coalition to Protect Journalists had sent a large delegation from their offices in Bangkok and Beirut to set up camp at the crime scene. They televised reports and would continue to do so until the Sri Lankan government worked out how to quietly deport them.

Behind the crime scene, parked to the side, was a white van. Its front passenger window was halfway down, and from time to time, Ellie caught the twinkle of the sun glinting off a camera lens—or a sniper lens—trained on them.

'We have company,' she remarked to Arjuna.

'You've only just noticed? This investigation doesn't stand a chance.'

'Okay, when did *you* notice them?' She had also observed a green sedan following them from the hotel to the crime scene.

'At the hotel. Five cars behind the green sedan. The sedan, by the way, has been with us from the airport. How do you think the soldiers knew you were at the office?' He shook his head and looked disappointed.

'I'm more concerned about the motorcycle,' she said.

'I've seen him too,' Arjuna responded. 'He's much better at his job than the others.'

Ellie continued to inspect Ameena's shattered car, her eyes resolutely not straying from it, but her mind was pulled in the direction of their stalkers. 'It's a white van,' she observed.

'It is. We'll make a detective out of you yet.' Arjuna smiled. He too didn't look back at the vehicle.

'Death squads?' she asked. People who were abducted by those vans never survived.

'I don't think they call themselves that. You know what to do if you see one coming towards you.'

'I drop to the ground and let you draw your weapon?'

He laughed. 'You run. And yes, I'll draw my weapon.'

Ellie retraced the road Ameena Fernando had taken from the cashew vendor to this point. She walked the route repeatedly, spotting the twelve cameras that must have seen the journalist's final drive, yet conveniently not recorded it.

She stood on the driver's side of the silver car, its body riddled with bullets. The glass crunched underneath her feet. Eventually this street would be reopened. Cars, tuk-tuks, buses and trucks would trample over the shards of glass, grinding them into the pores of the road. But for now, the Coalition to Protect Journalists had preserved the crime scene without even intending to. It was impossible for the police to evict the foreign protestors and remove evidence without sparking an international incident.

The windscreen had splintered onto the dash, but the seat had been protected from the spray of glass by a body. Ellie peered through the driver's window to the passenger seat. It was also clean. Glass was wedged between the backrest and the base. More on the floor, like diamonds. Something had been on the passenger seat. Something large, like a briefcase or a file. She checked the inventory of the crime scene that Tenby had given her; there was nothing appropriate on the list.

She looked at the place where Ameena had died. Bloodstains all over the seat, its back and base, the mist of arterial spray and then the deluge from chest wounds. There were bloodied handprints sliding down the dashboard. Ameena had reached over and placed her hand on a small image of the Buddha, Blu-Tacked there for protection.

Ellie re-positioned herself as though she were the killer, holding her hand out, fingers curled into the shape of a gun. The final bullet would have been delivered through the shattered window. It had penetrated Ameena's body and burrowed into the seat. She could extract it with her P&N set.

'Don't even think about it,' Arjuna warned her as she leaned in. 'That's called tampering with evidence.'

'We have no evidence.' There was another bloodstain on the side of the car, a clear right-hand print, but partial only. Rust-coloured and dried against the silver surface like an autumn leaf, its fingers pointed down to the earth. She hovered her right over the blood, her living hand casting a shadow over the dead one.

She pulled back and took photos.

'The assassin's?' Arjuna suggested.

'I've never been that lucky.'

He circled the car, aiming his laser pointer at the holes and following the path of the bullets where they tore through metal and flesh. 'What does the crime scene report say?'

'Nothing. This was efficient and economical. Bullets were obviously extracted from the body but not from the car yet. It will be towed this week according to a CID email.'

'You're reading CID emails now?' he asked. The Criminal Investigation Department was Sri Lanka's FBI with the modus operandi of a CIA off-the-books unit.

'The CID doesn't believe in inter-agency cooperation.'

'No agency believes in inter-agency cooperation. That's just something they put on the marketing literature. What else do the emails say?'

'That the investigation is ongoing.'

'Ongoing or not going?' He bent down with the laser and his torch, checking under the vehicle from each side. 'Nothing—no casings.'

'According to the crime scene report, the preliminary ballistics on the body and car indicate Beretta M9s with silencers. That's an expensive weapon, not one for petty criminals. No casings and no CCTV footage.'

'No footage at all?'

'Well, there's footage, but it doesn't show anything. Either it's been replaced with dummy footage, or Ameena Fernando had an invisible car that was attacked by invisible hit men.'

Arjuna looked around and asked the question that had plagued her all night. 'Who has access to erase and replace CCTV footage from that many cameras? The Sri Lankan government?' he suggested, his eyes lingering on the white van.

'And others,' she replied. 'I've asked Scottie and Tenby to look into it. Let's get back to the hotel. I need a drink.'

•

Ellie and Arjuna entered the hotel bar, its marbled walls and mirrored ceiling rising like an incongruous cathedral around them. Tenby was waiting for them, an empty glass in his hand. 'Shirani Dennis,' he said by way of a greeting.

'What?' Ellie signalled to the waiter.

'You asked me about the newspaper staff, if any of them might have a motive. Shirani Dennis has been with Ameena from the beginning. She was her best friend, deputy editor and second-in-command. She also had marital problems a few years ago.

The rumour at the Ceylon Cricket Club was that Ameena was involved.' Tenby raised his eyebrows knowingly.

'Are we treating the CCC as a legitimate source of intel these days?' Arjuna asked, ordering a mineral water.

'As soon as news of the shooting came out, Shirani went to the office, not the hospital, Arjuna,' Tenby said. 'She put the obituary online *immediately*—and if that's not suspicious, she's also booked a long family holiday. I think it's worth exploring. Widen the search before you narrow it, isn't that what they say?' Tenby checked his watch.

'Thank you, Tenby,' Ellie replied. 'Do you have time for another?'

'No, I'm going to catch a late mass.'

'Christ, you *do* still pray excessively.' She pinched his cheek.

He swatted her hand away. 'It helps me be a better person. You should try it some time. After that, I've got to get back and review the draft agreement. The Sri Lankans conceded to some of your inclusions, by the way. Make sure you come to these meetings, Ellie. You're good at your job when you choose to be—and I need you.'

'I'll be there,' she replied.

She didn't ask if Dilshan had called Solomon yet. She had offered the Under Secretary something—an end to her investigation—in exchange for *what?* That would be up to Solomon and Dilshan to negotiate.

He gave her a quick buss on the cheek and left.

Arjuna cleared his throat. 'You've been here twenty-four hours, and you haven't visited him yet.'

Ellie swerved. 'Romantic advice, Arjuna? You've been spending too much time with your sister.' Tomorrow. Tomorrow she would see Sathyan.

'I *live* with my sister. It was inevitable I'd start to sound like an auntie. I'll try to marry you off soon. I know a lovely thirty-six-year-old dental surgeon, by the way.'

She laughed.

Arjuna shook his head, speaking into his iced water. 'Check out the guys who just walked in. Chinos and chambray shirts. They need to learn to dress differently.' He leaned back in his seat. 'Indian secret service.'

'Are they still involved in Sri Lankan politics?' she asked. 'After Rajiv Gandhi?'

'No. Once assassinated, twice shy. They try to keep an eye on things, though, given China's soft colonialism. India's a dark and edgy horse.'

'A dark and edgy horse with nuclear weapons.'

'You still think you should be the only ones allowed to have nuclear weapons, Ellie? The Nuclear Non-Proliferation Treaty was racist,' Arjuna said matter-of-factly. '"America and our Allies can have something lethal but you brown countries can't." The treaty wasn't just about protecting the world from nuclear weapons, it was about entrenching existing hierarchies.'

She nodded. 'Sorry. Old patriotisms die hard.' She scanned the room casually, taking in everyone, including the two Indians in chinos. She spotted the Australians in the corner, who she had missed on her first assessment of the bar. They were more likely to help than hurt her, but she still needed to pay attention.

'Old patriotisms, old racisms.' He shrugged. 'India is a rising economic power, with not-so-secret aspirations to be a regional superpower. They should be taken more seriously.'

'I'd take those guys seriously. Especially the one on the left with the strong jawline.'

'You should, Ellie. They're armed and not afraid to show it.'

'Like you, then,' she teased. 'Do you miss your old life?'

'Do you?' he countered, wiping the droplets of condensation from his glass. They puddled in a perfect ring at the base, drifting onto the marble benchtop.

She noticed the sacred pendant he was wearing around his wrist again. The silver amulet was tied in place with a black string. She touched the aged silver gently, remembering another pendant from four years ago, then reached for his hand, still a comforting hand to hold. 'I don't know how I feel. I thought four years would be enough to work it out. I thought staying away might help. Then I thought coming back might help.'

'Has it?' He stared at her hand.

'No.' She blinked back sudden tears. 'What am I going to say to him? I'm *sorry*?'

'It's the best and hardest place to start.' He squeezed her hand once and then pulled away. 'I think I'm ready for a whisky now, please. Top shelf.'

She called the bartender over and ordered a twenty-year-old Yamazaki. He nodded appreciatively and placed it in front of her with a bowl of caramels. She pushed the whisky towards Arjuna.

Something had been troubling her since she had seen the map of the No Fire Zone. 'Human rights lawyers are saying the Sri Lanka Army is bombing the NFZ, and they're hitting more than the Tigers. They're saying the Army *intends* to bomb the Tamil civilians. It isn't just collateral damage.'

'You're a human rights lawyer. What do you say?'

'I'd say the government's present strategy solves the post-colonial and post-conflict land-sharing problem that started all of this in the first place.'

'Too wordy for a t-shirt,' Arjuna replied.

'How about: We're all collateral damage.'

'Better. You worked for the Agency. You understand the moral compromises of war. Rights versus security.'

'It was always someone else's rights sacrificed for our security. That's why I left.' She wanted a sip of his whisky.

'That's not *exactly* why you left. And you haven't properly answered the question.'

She swallowed hard against the tightening around her throat. 'I think it doesn't matter. Those civilians are dead anyway. Just like Ameena Fernando. Hers is the cleanest kill I've ever seen, right down to the cashew vendor who's disappeared. Four bullets from a distance, to stop the car. Two bullets in the body, to stop her. And then one more, up very close and personal, to kill her. They gave her a moment to think about her life.'

'How do you know that?' he asked.

She reached over and took a caramel from the bowl. It was soft between her fingers, its amber colour and sticky texture familiar. 'I've seen enough executions.' They both had. She took a sip of his whisky and slid off the bar stool. She kissed him gently on his right cheek and then on the scarred left. Once again, she felt him tense then relax.

8

THEN (2005)

Before Sathyan led Ellie through the heavy doors, he took a caramel from his pocket and gave it to her.

'It helps with the smell,' he said.

When he called to suggest a holiday north together, she hadn't hesitated or asked questions. Now she wished she had. She moved the caramel around her mouth, soft remnants sticking to her teeth, as astringent chemical vapours hit the back of her throat.

'This is my favourite place in the whole world,' Sathyan told her.

'Your *favourite* place in the whole world?' she clarified.

'Yes.'

'You need to get out more. We're in a prosthetics factory,' she said. 'Let me guess, you love the smell of bleach, resin and polyethylene in the morning?'

'I love the smell of egg hoppers in the morning, but this will do. I'll show you why.'

She followed him out of the warehouse, passing people working on different parts of the process. Women in protective jumpsuits at a production line, guiding overhead vats across a series of moulds. Men sorting arms, legs, hands and feet. Old women sitting on the floor, checking legs against diagrams pinned to clipboards. One anointed a prosthetic leg with holy ash. She prayed to it, reached for her scalpel and began to carve. Her callused hands worked quickly and confidently, creating smooth brown grooves, planes and tendons, the angles of bone and the softness of human tissue. Something sinewy and real. Something that could be strapped to a mutilated body for support, but also for beauty.

Ellie had not expected that.

'She's our head sculptor. She used to make clay statues of the gods for the village temples that are now being bombed.' Sathyan turned to face her. 'I wanted you to see there is beauty and hope, even in the debris.'

•

Inside the school hut, Sathyan and Ellie sat down with a boy, Sathyan speaking rapidly in Tamil. Ellie recognised a lot of the words. The boy was nine years old and he liked cricket. But she also missed a lot of words. The Tamil spoken in the north was a purer, faster version than what she had studied at the Agency and picked up through work, and she struggled to keep up.

The boy looked from Sathyan to Ellie to his leg, then nodded. He placed his feet on a chair, rolling up the edges of his shorts to show her the socket of the prosthetic where the flesh of his actual leg sat in the plastic.

'The mine took off most of the leg to here, exposing the femoral artery,' Sathyan explained, motioning to what remained of the child's thigh. 'He nearly bled to death, but he was lucky.'

'And strong.'

'Mostly lucky,' he replied. 'Not all children are lucky.' His eyes shone with pain. The boy reached up and patted him on the arm.

'He's doing really well,' she said. She had seen the impact of the mines in other conflict zones, where she'd been tracking Semtex sellers. But in this prosthetics factory and refuge for survivors, the damage was more real. The failures of her work were more painful, the successes more urgent.

She repeated herself to the child, haltingly pulling the Tamil words for 'well' and 'strong' from the recesses of her mind.

The boy hooted at her colloquial vocabulary and then nodded shyly.

'My Hindi is better,' she said to Sathyan, embarrassed.

'That's very useful if the subtitles for a Bollywood film fail,' he deadpanned. He helped the boy down from the desk. 'For many amputees, when the arm or leg is taken from them, they still feel like it's there for years afterwards. The older they are, the harder it is to understand that the limb is actually gone. They reach for things with hands that are not there, take steps with legs that are missing. The mind doesn't believe what the eyes are seeing.' They watched the boy hobble away. 'The mind looks down and feels pain in a limb that has gone. It functions as if what was taken from it, what was stolen from it, is still there.'

'The phantom limb,' she replied. She wanted to ask Sathyan what was stolen from him, but she had learned to wait.

•

She had forgotten that the male form could be so beautiful.

Sathyan sat up in the bed and pulled the sheet back across the lower half of his lean and muscular body. Sweat lingered on the contours of his dark skin and caught in his hair. 'I read your op-ed for *The Washington Post*.'

Damn the internet. 'And?' She braced herself. Her article was about how the Iraq war had been the brave choice for the US, a necessary intervention.

'You know that more people died last year from gun violence in the US than in 9/11? You don't see emergency sessions of Congress being called for that, do you?'

'9/11 was different.' She probably needed to put some clothes on for this ambush.

'9/11 happens all around the world, all the time. It's just that it finally happened to you, and in your own minds, you are very important.'

'Thank you for minimising the pain of thousands of American families, Sathyan.' She sat up and dragged the sheet back to her.

'That pain will once again make you respond with disproportionate violence, setting more heathen feet on Muslim land and creating the threat of eternal occupation.'

'Seriously, this again? You seduced me in order to give me the rest of your presentation?'

'*I* seduced *you*?'

She smiled, relieved to have distracted him. 'We seduced each other. I own my choices.'

'More people should,' he replied. 'But that doesn't change the point of my presentation. You give the fundamentalists exactly what they want—a reason to hate you and a way to radicalise hundreds of thousands of Muslims who would otherwise have wanted to live peaceful lives.'

'You think it's as simple as that? That we're playing into their hands?' she asked.

'Yes, I do. Because while the jihadists have no playbook, you do. American foreign policy has been ticking boxes on the same playbook since 1945, and the jihadists have read it. Even though you don't give them credit for historical literacy.'

'Well, the history of those conflicts is hindsight, and you know what they say about hindsight.' Ellie dropped the sheet and pulled herself onto his lap, holding the headboard on either side of his head. They had one hour before his next meeting at the factory.

•

They lay on the bed, staring at the ceiling fan.

'This is unexpected,' Sathyan said.

'What, this?' She motioned between the two of them.

'No, *this* was entirely expected. Planned actually. I moved my afternoon meeting.'

'Are you saying I'm easy?' Ellie quipped.

'I'm saying you were right.' He rolled over and ran his hand down her side.

'Then what's unexpected? That you want to do it again, immediately?' She hoped his hand would keep going.

His hand stopped at hers, locking fingers with her, surprising her. 'It's unexpected how . . . comfortable you are here, in Sri Lanka, in the north. You were born and raised in the West. You look like us but you're not us. And yet, here you are, surrounded by the muck of war. Refugees, widows, orphans. People whose bodies and families and souls have been maimed beyond repair.'

She turned to face him and waited. She could see the story in him, wanting to be told, waiting for the right person to tell it to.

He began, slowly at first, and then the words tumbled out. 'My father was a teacher at St John's College, the boys' high school in Jaffna town. He taught history and geography. He loved the past and he loved the world. He said the two should always be taught together. He said you could understand the way the world was divided in the present if you understood the past. Understanding how it was divided helped you understand how to put it back together.'

She drew their entwined hands to her heart, kissed them, and waited again.

'We have family in London and Toronto. They begged us to join them, but he wouldn't leave. He loved this place. He said, "This is our viidu, our home." He refused to join the movement, but he also refused to relinquish his home.'

He paused, letting the final memory surface. 'The police had raided the school before, accusing the staff of teaching the children propaganda. Accusing the school of recruiting children for the Tigers. The principal tried to tell them. They would never allow the boys to fight. They wanted them to study and to leave the country, to leave the violence. One night, police came to the principal's home and took him away.'

'And then?' she whispered, even though she already knew.

'And then, a month later, they came and took Appa away. My younger sister, too.'

She pulled him into her arms and held him until he slept.

9

NOW (2009)

Arjuna drove her to Ameena's house, checking the rear-view mirror often. In her side mirror, Ellie could see a motorcyclist weaving through the traffic behind them. He was too fast for her to tell if it was the same one as before.

They pulled into Ameena's street and stopped at the front gate in view of the security camera. The guard house was empty. Ellie sat motionless in the car.

'Are you going to tell him why you're here?' Arjuna asked. 'Actually, remind me, why *are* you here? Official story, that is.'

'To help secure US interests in the post-conflict reconstruction of Sri Lanka through the strategic provision of aid.'

'That's right, I forgot that you're Redmond's best student of subtext. Are you going to get out of the car?'

'Sure, in a moment,' she replied.

'What's that expression you Americans like? Chicken shit,' he mocked gently. He turned off the engine and left her alone. He walked to the gates and called out. 'Hello? Sathyan, it's us. Anyone home?'

Ellie saw his silhouette first, tall and slim, standing on the verandah. He stepped into the sun, his hand shielding his eyes, and she saw that he was dressed in jeans and a Springsteen t-shirt. His face was drawn, shadowed with neglect, his hair longer, more casual.

He smiled and she wanted to cry. She swallowed back the tears and exhaled deeply, finally getting out and coming to stand at the gate. Sathyan waved and walked towards them.

'Use the side entry, it's easier,' he said, approaching the door near the guard house that was padlocked too. He concentrated on the lock as he reinserted the key at a different angle, and then another. Ellie recognised the furrowing of his forehead and noticed the grey hairs now at his sideburns, speckling up towards his temples. The padlock clicked open at last and slid to the ground.

'Come in, come in,' he said. 'Leave the car there. I'm not very good at all these locks. I had to let the guardsman go. Got a new security system and padlocks instead. Thank you for coming.' He was nervous too.

Arjuna nudged her as he passed. Sathyan embraced him with ease, kissing him on both sides of his face.

And then he stopped to look at Ellie properly for the first time. Before she lost her nerve and before he could put distance between them—more distance—she stepped forward and put her arms around him. She had to stand on her toes, over-balancing a little. He held her, closely and securely. An exhalation of muscle memory. He smelled of sandalwood soap. The tendrils of the musky fragrance had never really left her. She could recall it, recall him, at will.

They fit together and then separated. Another exhalation of muscle memory.

•

The three of them sat in the living room. It was littered with piles of books, newspapers and magazines. A tower of *Readers Digest* magazines held a window open.

Weathered teak armchairs with frayed rattan seats were arranged around a calamander coffee table, its surface tattooed with the circles of past cups of hot tea, carelessly left while the drinker sat lost in a book. The shelves were interspersed with dusty photo frames. Ellie recognised Ameena's family alongside photographs of Ameena and Sathyan.

Sathyan waited for the ayah to leave a tea tray on the table. He spoke to her kindly in Sinhala and she nodded.

'I tried to fire her too, but she won't leave,' he told them as they collected their teacups. 'She's the third generation to work for the Fernandos.' He cleared his throat. 'Thank you for coming.' His hands clenched around the hot cup.

'You don't need to thank me—us,' Ellie replied. 'I'm sorry—I'm sorry for your loss.' She cursed herself. It was such a pedestrian opening. 'Do you have any idea who would do this to Ameena?' she asked. A direct but necessary question. She had to focus on the investigation, skip the small talk, skip the personal talk. At least, that was what she told herself. *Focus.*

'Too many ideas. There was a queue of people wanting to kill her.'

'There was a longer queue of people who loved her,' she said softly.

He looked up, startled by her kindness. 'Yes.' He nodded and cleared his throat again. 'The media says it was the Tigers. She'd run several features on what they're doing in the north.

Forcing their people to fight, recruiting anyone who can lift a gun.'

'Nothing new there.' She pulled out her notebook.

'No, not new, but worse than usual.' He shrugged. 'It could have been the Tigers.'

She didn't think so. The assassination required planning and money. There was the missing CCTV footage, too. The Tigers couldn't pull that off. 'From the outside, the government is the prime suspect,' she said. 'Suspected, but not publicly accused or investigated.'

'Except by Ameena. That's who she thought would do it. She knew they would get her in the end, and yet she still . . . she still did her job. She was a lot like you in that way.'

It was her turn to look up, startled by the comparison. 'She was much braver than me.' Ellie was a coward. She had been one four years ago, and she was one now. A coward and a liar.

'She was braver than all of us. You would have liked her.' He put down his tea, walked over to the bookshelf and touched random spines, trailing a line in the dust that had settled on them. 'The government's death squads have taken eleven journalists in the last year. Our friends. So many . . .'

'The previous attacks on her life and the newsroom?' she prompted.

'The last attacks were claimed by the Eastern Freedom Organisation, a Tamil Tiger splinter group funded by the government. She wrote a piece about how the different Tamil groups were turning on each other, doing the Army's job for them. They didn't like that.'

'Did you hire the guard after that?'

'Before that, actually. Ameena had taken shots at various presidents over the years, but Rajapaksa's retaliations are particularly well-executed.'

They both paused at the choice of words.

'He isn't used to being publicly challenged,' Sathyan continued. 'They were trying to scare her but not kill her, not yet. You have to understand—Ameena was very high profile. She was, as you say, loved. She was also connected. She was Sinhalese, moneyed and educated. Her family has owned tea estates since the late 1800s. She had a family membership at the Cricket Club. She was established. It made her betrayal of the establishment all the greater, but it also protected her, for a while.' His voice faltered. He returned to his seat, reached for his cup of tea, and then changed his mind.

Ellie was rapidly forming a textured portrait of Ameena in her mind. Sathyan was right, she would have liked her. 'I read that she was being sued by the government?'

'Yes, by Dilshan Perera, the Under Secretary for Defence. The most recent lawsuit started three months ago. Ameena made allegations about an arms deal with a Chinese company. She had a trustworthy source, so she printed. They sued for defamation and demanded a retraction.'

'Ameena didn't seem like a retractor,' she observed.

'No. Before the injunction was delivered to the front door of *The Lanka Herald*, she printed another piece, this time linking to primary sources on her website, confidential emails between the Under Secretary, the new Chinese cultural attaché, Eric Kwan, and a Chinese agricultural manufacturer.'

Ellie made a note to investigate her old acquaintance from the diplomatic drinks the other night. Kwan was a senior diplomat now, but the first time she'd met him at the Tibetan forum, he was a general in the PRC Army. 'I know Kwan.'

'That makes sense,' he replied.

'I couldn't find the primary sources, just references to it,' she continued. 'Even Wikileaks didn't have it. Our own intel doesn't go further than that.'

'Unless your boss isn't telling you everything. He's very need-to-know, from memory,' Arjuna pointed out.

'I think this is something I would need to know.'

The corner of Arjuna's mouth twitched.

'*Why*, Ellie?' Sathyan asked. 'Why are you here? If you came because I emailed you, then I'm grateful. I can't do this on my own, I don't even know what I'm looking for.'

She looked away without answering him. She was here to make it *look* like she was negotiating an aid agreement and *look* like she was investigating Ameena's death. But now she wanted to know the truth. She wanted to do this for Sathyan. She owed him that, and she struggled to look him in the eyes and lie again.

'After the second piece, the government shut the paper's website down,' he went on when she didn't answer. 'All of Ameena's research was removed. A lot of papers and files about other things, too. They were looking for her source.'

'Do you know who the source was?' she asked.

'No, of course not.'

'So, the website's down, the files are gone. What was it about that deal that was worth killing her for? Why now?' she mused. Ameena had run features on government corruption and bribery scandals before. Sri Lanka had bought arms before. What was different about *this* deal with the Chinese?

Sathyan shook his head. 'She didn't tell me more than what she published. She was particularly careful about this story. Sometimes I helped with the proofreading, but she kept me far away from this one.' His voice stumbled and then recovered.

'Perhaps she was trying to protect her source? Or you?' she suggested.

'Perhaps.'

'And the Chinese company—what was its name?' Ellie flipped through her notebook.

'Ming-Na Wu Holdings—MNW. An internet search doesn't tell you much about them. They have a mixed portfolio of products; mostly chemicals for agriculture and weapons on the side, or vice versa.'

'Of course. That's a logical fit.'

'Absolutely. They probably produce vaccines, too,' Sathyan said.

She laughed. He smiled back, tentatively. She remembered that smile so well.

'I'll see what we can find on MNW. Scott back at the ranch is pretty good.'

'The guy that was here the last time? He's still at the embassy?' he asked.

'A lifelong patriot,' she replied.

'Like you.'

She didn't comment. 'Do you have anything left? Any research, printouts of the correspondence between Kwan and the government?'

'The evidence is all gone. After her death, the police came here again and took whatever was left. The house was searched. The office, too. They were thorough, as though they knew what they were looking for. Even the garbage and the shredder. Her notebooks—I used to love reading those . . .'

'How soon, Sathyan?' Arjuna asked softly.

Sathyan stared at him, confused.

'How soon after her death did the police come here with a warrant?' Arjuna clarified.

'That morning.' Sathyan closed his eyes briefly. 'She had barely reached the hospital.' He looked around the room. 'Only Ameena's books were left.' He walked over to the bookshelf again, crouching to a row of travel books. 'I've been meaning to return your *Lonely Planet* to you, Ellie. The one for the USA. I never made it out there in the end. But it's been here, waiting for you.' He pulled a book out. 'I like the maps. Washington seems like a beautiful city.' He handed it to her. 'But difficult to understand without the key.' He dropped his voice, and said for her ears only, 'When you work it out, please tell me what it says.'

She nodded, putting the *Lonely Planet* away in her bag quickly. She scanned the room for the surveillance devices he was worried about. 'Thank you,' she said. 'My brother was looking for this.'

She suddenly thought of something else. Rummaging around her bag, she took the photograph she had retrieved from Ameena's office and gave it to him.

Sathyan touched the glossy photograph lightly. 'This was taken at their beach house in Negombo. It's been in the family for decades. Happier times. Did you meet them in San Francisco?'

'No, but her husband, ex-husband, is launching a campaign. Do you know him?'

'Yes, I've met him. Is *that* why you're here? Because of his campaign?' he asked.

'You know why I'm here,' she replied. She couldn't look at him.

'Thank you.' He walked back to the books and placed the photograph on a shelf. 'Ameena's ex-husband is nice,' he said, reaching for less painful territory. 'A great journalist himself. I need a bit of time, but then I'll help him. Maybe we can make sense of this together, or put it to rest together. Make peace with it.'

'Who do *you* think it was? Who did this to her?' she asked. It was a slightly different question from her first.

Sathyan looked around as if expecting soldiers to storm through the doors. He lifted his gaze to hers. 'I told her to drop it so many times. So many times, we all warned her. Who do *I* think did this to her? She did,' he answered. 'She did it to herself.'

•

Sathyan closed the front door and bolted it shut. From the window, he watched Ellie and Arjuna lock the gate and test the padlock. His hand went reflexively to the keychain around his neck. He needed to get better at the new lock, needed to be able to open it faster under pressure. He had a ladder and rubber mats positioned at the wall behind the house. He could place the ladder against the wall, throw the rubber mats over the shards of glass and jump into their neighbour's garden. He had made Ameena practise.

He knew in truth that if anyone came for him, it would most likely happen outside the fortress their home had become. It would be the white van that trailed him everywhere since her murder.

If they really wanted to break into their home and kill him there, they could. Whenever he returned, he switched every light on and walked around each room, willing his steps to be quiet but confident. He checked each room for intruders the way his mother used to check each room for snakes.

Sometimes at night, he unlocked the padlocked gate, left the front door unbolted, turned off the alarm and the cameras, and slept without his shoes on. Sometimes he went to bed and, before he closed his eyes, he thought about Ameena, the choices she had made for all of them, and he said, *fuck you, too.*

10

THEN (2007)

Sathyan wiped the camera lens with the edge of his shirt. The Anti-Landmine Lobby wanted photographs of the victims to go with the testimonies he was collecting. He had a spare disk in his pocket as a decoy in case the Army showed up. Ellie had once taught him how to eject a disk and insert it into his thick watch strap, a sleight-of-hand that required practice. Two years after she had left Sri Lanka, it still hurt to remember all the dimensions of her sleight-of-hand.

The driver, Rick Woodham, stopped the jeep outside the refugee camp. He was ex-Australian military and now drove supply trucks for whoever paid the most—the Army, the Tigers, cashed up journalists and foreign NGOs. The other passengers, like Sathyan, would have offered a hefty fee to visit the camp. Rick had taken them off-road in the war zone using a network of paths through the trees and riverbeds. For hours, they had listened to the jungle brushing the windows of their jeep, interred by the shroud of a camouflage net. Each passenger had been lost in their own work and thoughts. Two journalists, two human rights lawyers from Amnesty, and Sathyan.

Now, Rick pulled the camouflage netting off the vehicle and hurried them out. He called his contacts on his satellite phone. Sathyan couldn't hear the words, but the tone was that of a negotiation.

'We've got an hour, no more,' Rick said, ignoring the muttered complaints from the group. 'The Army's coming. ETA three hours. The doctors are packing up. They're moving those that can move.'

'And the rest?' Sathyan asked. He saw doctors, nurses and others, their faces covered in grime and exhaustion. This camp had been set up in a school hall and Tamil families had collapsed around it, pitching small tents with plastic sheets. They were enclosed by rusted bikes, dilapidated cars crammed with entire households, and emaciated donkeys that were now being loaded with towers of items strapped together with rope. 'The rest?' he repeated when Rick didn't answer.

'Not your problem. Get your interviews and then we're out. I need two hours to clear this camp and put a safe distance between us and what's coming.' Rick set the timer on his watch.

Sathyan watched as Ameena Fernando did the same, and he copied her. She had sat with him on the drive up from Colombo and they had talked a little, but when the jeep left the demilitarised zone and entered the war zone, everyone had fallen silent.

He had recognised her immediately, and when she had gotten into the vehicle, he hadn't been able to hide his surprise. He'd seen her last week on the television, commenting on the rocketing rate of unemployment while the President employed his extended family in the government. *Jobs for the boys* had become *jobs for the cousins.* She was a regular on panels, discussing the erosion of the rule of law in Sri Lanka, criticising both the President and the Tigers. He wasn't sure if he had felt safer or more vulnerable with her in the jeep.

Ameena was more beautiful in person than on television. Her face was bare and tired, but he liked the determination in it, the efficiency of her hands as she did a quick inventory of her bag and equipment, and the economy of her answers to his questions. It was what he liked about her articles—they were brave. They said what he thought but was too afraid to say.

He tapped his pocket to make sure his decoy flash card and spare battery were there and began his work.

The wooden shutters of the hall had been removed and used for firewood a long time ago. The noise hit him first, a kind of low-level humming. As he got closer, he realised it was the sound of people, adults and children, crying and moaning. Then came the smell. He recognised the cold, metallic tang of blood. He could see the drip and drag marks, rusted and ground into the earth. The pathway looked like an abattoir floor, blood pooled in the divots and undulations of the earth.

He stopped for a moment at the hall entrance, its walls pockmarked with shrapnel. Ameena, who had walked ahead, now turned back towards him, her face shadowed in the dim light. She stood frozen. His eyes adjusted and he realised why when he saw the horror on her face.

Sathyan touched her arm. 'Let's go,' he said. 'We don't have much time.'

•

'How can you listen to these stories day in and day out?' Ameena asked. She lit a cigarette and passed it to Sathyan.

Everyone smoked to mask the smell. 'We've interviewed thirty-two people, most of them parents without their children.' She lit another cigarette for herself.

Their children. Left in fragments by the roadside. Was that better than no pieces? No body? He had wanted to hold his brother one last time.

When he said nothing, she prompted him. 'You handle it well.'

'I've been listening a long time.'

'You're not old enough.'

He shrugged. He had worked out that he was younger than her, but he felt old beyond his years. He'd been listening to the stories of the dead and the dying ever since his father and sister had disappeared in the middle of the night. 'It helps me—to listen. And I think it helps them to talk. I record each story, give each child their name, age, ancestral village, their family lineage and one comment. Then I write up each case study and send it back to the NGO. But I also keep a logbook for them.'

'Like a wedding register for the dead? That's a little perverse isn't it?'

'I suppose. I read the names from time to time and try to remember their stories. Srini Manmohan, aged twelve, played cricket, fast bowler. Rajani Kesavan, aged seven, was convinced she was a fairy.'

'Why?' Ameena drew from the cigarette again and held the smoke in her chest.

'Because all of my case studies are about where they died and how they died. What kind of device was it, mine, gunfire, mortar fire, Semtex explosion? Did the injury kill them, or the blood loss and secondary infection? What kind of treatment were they given and where? I record the demographics of the injury. Not the details of the injured.' He pulled out his clipboard and flicked through the sheets. 'I want to remember who they were before they became a statistic in a human rights report that no one will read.'

'Why do you keep doing this if you think no one will read it?'

'Why do you?'

Ameena smiled. 'I'm self-absorbed and attention-seeking, of course. I'm a terrible mother and a worse journalist. Haven't you heard?'

'Aside from that?'

'Because I keep thinking that someone *might* read what I write. Someone with real power and they might do something about it. Because if you put it down in words, you hold people accountable for their sins. You might not be able to punish them; you might not be able to prevent it from happening again. But we are all of us accountable to each other.' She exhaled a long stream of smoke. 'I want to give words to grief and loss and injustice. You?'

'Me?' The smoke spiralled away from him as he considered whether he would give her the truthful answer or the polite one. He chose truth. 'I seek out the dismembered because I feel dismembered, and recording the losses of others helps me make sense of my own. There will be no cemeteries for my people. No memorials or national days of remembrance, no records of family trees or family histories. No records at all, in many cases. Birth certificates, photographs, school reports, medical reports, driver's licences. Everything's destroyed. That's how amputation works. Complete removal of the limb that burdens the body. No record and no memory of the loss.'

'Their families will remember,' she said.

'Sometimes an entire family walks over a landmine together. Or cluster bombs fall on an entire village—generations, gone in seconds. Sometimes it's better that way.' He reached for another cigarette. 'I met a mother once who carried the torn foot of her dead child for twenty kilometres wrapped in a banana leaf, like some weird parody of lumprice,' he said, weakly attempting levity.

'What?'

'You know, lumprice—except inside the banana leaf was a foot instead of curries.'

'Thank you for that,' she said ruefully. 'I'll never be able to eat lumprice again.'

'Made you laugh, though.'

'What happened to the lady?'

All levity abruptly disappeared. 'She went mad with grief, attacked a soldier at a camp and begged him to kill her. He pushed her back with his rifle and pointed it at her. It was bayoneted. She threw herself onto it. That's what I heard. I wasn't there.'

'I'd probably do the same, although that wouldn't be my preferred method of suicide-by-soldier.'

'No? What would you do?' Sathyan asked.

'Probably try to contrive a firing squad. I'm squeamish. Not all rifles are bayoneted, so she must have thought about it beforehand. Funny how in this world of abundance and scarcity, there are so many ways to be killed but actually not that many ways to kill yourself.'

They were silent again. He watched the smoke curl in front of him and drift with the evening breeze. 'You have children?' he asked.

'I do—three. Chitran, Niru and Rohan. Maybe that's what makes this harder for me. When each of my children was born,

I held them and counted their fingers and toes. I ran my hands over their arms and legs and ears. I marvelled at how complete, how whole they were. It seemed like they would remain that way forever.'

He didn't have children but he once had siblings. He imagined that if he were a father now, he would look at his children and think: *If only your beautiful, dirty feet were not battered by the roads and the jungles and the walking. If only you could walk another path, another road. Where some bastard hasn't hidden a landmine.*

He inhaled the last of his cigarette and ground it into the dirt with his whole foot.

•

Patient number thirty-two, name Pradeepan, aged two. He photographed the scrap of paper pinned to the child's t-shirt. Status: Critical 7. The child lay on newspaper on the floor, his sweat, blood and urine seeping through it into the earth beneath. Sathyan wondered how many levels of critical there were before you were dead.

The boy's head was cradled in his mother's lap. She fanned him gently with the pallu of her sari, flicking away the flies that darted between his wounds and his face, exposing her blouse without care.

Sathyan touched her arm gently. Ameena looked at him, dazed and exhausted. Tear tracks stained her face and ran small rivers down her dusty skin.

She licked her cracked lips and asked, 'Enne, enne vehnem?' *What do you want?*

Sathyan wanted to know how a two-year-old boy ended up with a leg blown off. He looked at the mass of dirty bandages wrapped tightly around the stump, blood soaking a hungry red stain over the bandage and up the remains of his thigh.

Sathyan called for the nurse, Sister Punitha, who came over with fresh bandages and gave him instructions. He lifted up the stump. The child cried out in pain, jerking up from his mother's lap, his eyes suddenly wild and open.

'Vedengo, vedengo,' his mother said. *Leave him.*

Sister Punitha looked at her and then the child. She took the fresh bandages away and returned with a plastic bag that she tied around the stump. Infection containment for the others. Her face contorted and then she regained control. She was still young enough to weep for her patients.

'What happened?' Sathyan asked the mother in Tamil. 'Where are you from?'

Tears fell from her eyes onto the child's face. She rubbed them into his skin, cleaning the dust from his cheeks and arranging his hair neatly. It was plastered to his head with sweat. She tore her eyes away and looked at Sathyan.

'Who are you?' she asked.

'Sathyan Navaratnam. My people are from Teliveddy. This is my friend, Ameena. We want to write about what happened to your son.' He showed her his clipboard and digital recorder. 'We want people to know what's happening.'

'Why?'

'So that maybe we can stop it.'

'You can't stop it.' She shook her head. The rise and fall of the child's chest was becoming shallower and slower.

'Tell me, please. We can't help Pradeepan. I am sorry. I am so sorry. But we can try to help others. Please tell me what happened.'

The mother stared at her son's face, his eyes now open, looking unseeingly up at her. 'Padango mahan,' she soothed him.

Sleep, son. Sathyan's mother used to say the same thing to him. To his brother. She didn't take her eyes from her child as she spoke. 'We are from Manipay. Do you know it?'

Sathyan nodded and switched the recorder on.

She spoke slowly and clearly in Tamil. 'We have been moving for a long time now. Our village was shelled twice and we stayed, hiding in the fields. When it was over, we returned to bury our people. We didn't know where else to go. Eventually when we couldn't find enough food, we left. The fields and plantations were bombed. They wanted us to starve.'

'Who? Who was bombing you?' Sathyan asked.

'Helikaptar.' She took her hand from the child's body and with one finger made a swirling motion.

Only the Army had helicopters.

'Helicopters bombed you?' he asked, moving the recorder closer to her. The hum around him was getting louder, and he didn't want to miss anything.

The woman seemed to be listening to something inside, one hand returned to her son's chest, the other still stroking his hair. She smiled at Sathyan kindly. She shook her head with patience and relief. 'Helikaptar,' she repeated more emphatically. 'Ippe varar.'

Helicopter, coming now.

He reared back, dropped his recorder and toppled into Ameena.

'What is it, what did she say?' Ameena asked.

Sathyan stood just as three nurses rushed in. They were terrified but efficient, loading medicines and bandages from patients into soiled pillowcases and plastic bags. More people came in, families locating their injured. Some were carried out, some were left behind. People on the ground cried out for help;

others were too tired to cry. The hum swelled towards them. People outside screamed in terror.

Rick burst through the doors. 'We have to hustle now. Now!' Three children ran past him to the mother beside Sathyan. 'Come on. This place is gone. Now, now, now!' He ran down the aisle, stopping at Ameena.

'What about these people?' she shouted back. 'You said we had more time. *They* had more time.'

'Can't trust the fuckers,' he snapped. 'Time's up. Get your gear and get into the jeep. I'm starting the engine in three.'

Sathyan looked at the mother and her dying child. The other children were cowering around her, crying and shaking. Two young boys, maybe five and six, and a girl, slightly older. 'Come with us.' He tried to lift the dying child, who was slick with blood. The boy's head fell back over Sathyan's arm.

He was about to stand when the mother pulled at his arm. She shook her head.

'Vedengo, mahan.' *Leave him, son.*

He hesitated and then placed the boy gently back on the ground, back in his mother's lap. She nodded and pushed her remaining children towards him.

'Pohngo, pohngo,' she cried. *Go, go.*

Sathyan looked at Ameena, and without speaking, they pried the children's small hands away from their mother and ran out of the school as its walls began to vibrate like the chambers of a broken tin heart. They didn't look back.

Outside, people were running, grabbing meagre belongings, stuffing shopping bags with clothes, cooking utensils and bags of rice. The cars had already left. A man smacked a donkey on its rump and then its hind legs, urging it to walk.

Sathyan ran around the mess, checking that Ameena was still with him as they reached the jeep. The doors were flung open, the others already in, seatbelts on.

'What's this?' Rick pointed at the children. He cursed and jumped out of the jeep.

'We're taking them. We can take them. There's space,' Ameena shouted above the screams around them.

'Doesn't matter, we're not allowed. There's no fucking way I'm getting through the checkpoints with them.'

'I'll pay you more money when we get to Colombo,' she said desperately. 'My paper will pay. I can pay.' The children were holding each other, the smaller boys crying into the older girl's chest.

'Fuck the money, I can't get them through the checkpoint!' Rick shouted. 'You're not hearing me.' He tried to push her into the vehicle, but she pushed him back.

'Then take them as far as you can take them and drop them in the jungle,' she insisted. 'They've got a better chance that way. You said it yourself, this place is gone.' She shuddered as an Army helicopter flew ahead and the ground burst with machine gun fire. She pushed the children into the jeep and then turned back towards the camp.

'Ameena, get in,' Sathyan shouted.

She shook her head. She reached up to speak into his ear above the noise. 'I have to write this.' She ran back into the crowd as the first bomb fell.

'Take the children, instead of us,' Sathyan said to Rick, who swore again.

'Two of them for two of you,' Rick replied, pushing the boys deeper into the jeep, then pulling the girl out.

Sathyan didn't have time to argue. He grabbed the girl, turned and ran after Ameena, pushing through people to catch her hand. Ameena was about to say something when the helicopter passed over again, banked left and returned. This time he could see the machine guns mounted on each open door, the Sri Lanka Army soldiers at their helm.

The helicopter dropped towards them. The crowd surged at his back, pushing him forward. He stumbled and Ameena steadied him. She spotted the child clutched in his other hand and looked at him for an explanation, but he shook his head.

The child tripped and he lost his grip on her. Ameena bent down to pick her up as another volley of bullets hit the ground. People scattered. Sathyan covered Ameena's body and the child's with his own. He could hear screams and realised they were his own. The thrum of the helicopter blades receded. It would turn and come back.

'Come on!' He stood and pulled Ameena and the girl in her arms with him, checking them both for injury. Ameena was by his side, running, her breath heaving. He took the child from her and they kept pace with each other, passing families, being overtaken by others. 'Which way?' He stopped and looked at the crowd. Was there safety in numbers? The child's arms were tight around his neck, her breath fast against his cheek.

'The road. The road's that way. Follow the people.' Ameena pulled at his shirt.

'Rick brought us off-road for a reason,' he countered. 'We go back and find his path. We should have followed him out.'

'Please Sathyan, we follow them. They know where they're going!' she cried, dragging him with the mass of people.

'No one knows where they're going, Ameena.' He saw a second helicopter, its shadow like a winged metallic monster.

It swooped, then swerved left, a teasing gesture. It circled back and did the same thing again. People screamed and ran to the right. Towards the road.

He looked ahead and saw doctors and nurses also shepherding people that way. His heart was pounding, sweat pouring into his eyes, blurring his sight. Something was wrong, but he couldn't hold on to the thought. It swooped towards him and then suddenly banked left, like the helicopter.

'Okay,' he nodded and they followed the crowd. Running, walking to rest, shifting the child from one hip to another until they hit the road.

'Church, church,' a woman said as she stumbled against him. Her left arm was shredded by bullets. Ameena took the screaming child from Sathyan and he held the young woman up. It was the nurse from the school hall, Sister Punitha.

'Church?' he asked her in Tamil.

'St Paul of the Cross,' she whispered. Blood on her lips as another nurse came and took her away. Sathyan stopped. His side covered in Sister Punitha's blood, warm and sticky.

'Keep going.' Ameena pushed him forward. Around them people were running, families unable to carry their injured, leaving them to save their other children, to save themselves.

He couldn't move. 'I just need a minute,' he said, coughing. He raised his hand to cover his mouth but it was bloody. He wiped it on his trousers in confusion. His hand was intact. Shaking and red, but whole.

He looked up into the skies but couldn't see the helicopters. He looked around. Nuns, nurses, doctors. He couldn't identify the others. It didn't matter.

And then he heard it. A dull explosion, like thunder under water. People screamed. They all looked up. Nothing in the skies.

Then more explosions. Three ahead and one behind.

Bish, bish, bish, bish.

Like dark magic. People exploding from their feet up. Then the screaming. So much screaming.

So much blood. A crimson geyser reaching up to the indifferent heavens.

'Don't move.' Sathyan tightened his grip on the child and put an arm out to stop Ameena.

An explosion went off in front of them. Burning hot earth sprayed into his face, singeing his skin, stinging his eyes, choking him.

Don't move, he tried to scream again. He vomited dirt, his body heaving forward onto his knees.

Ameena caught him and held him upright. The child slipped from his arms.

Sister Punitha lay on the ground with her hands over her stomach. Nothing lay below it. Pieces of her spilled out.

'Landmines!' someone shouted.

'Don't move!' Ameena was still frozen at his side, holding his hand. Where her skin met his felt safe. Only then did he realise that the child had let go of his leg. The little girl had recognised someone behind the remains of Sister Punitha.

It was her mother.

Sathyan shouted in Tamil, but too late. The girl ran towards her mother who was shaking her head and crying. The woman's sari was soaked with the blood of her infant son. Her feet, bare and torn from running, stood on something metal, hidden under the dirt. So small and hard.

The little girl threw herself into her mother's arms. The movement made the woman rock a little. Just one step back. The child was in her arms.

Bish, bish.

Sathyan watched the woman crumple to the ground. Blood gushed in a pool around her. Red running mercury. She held her daughter as long as she could, then the child slipped towards the ground. Sathyan lunged a step forward. He was almost there. He could catch her. He could save her.

Bish.

11

NOW (2009)

Ellie fumbled with the padlock at the side gate. She could feel Sathyan's eyes on her from the window. She turned when she heard Arjuna swear. 'What is it?'

'The car.' All four tyres were slashed. Arjuna shook his head. 'I've only got one spare. This is coming out of your expense account.'

They looked down the street. It was quiet. She saw glass shards on the ground and looked up. The camera above the wall had been smashed.

'I'll call for a car,' she said.

'It'll take too long. We'll walk. The main avenue is three blocks to the south. We can catch a tuk-tuk from there. I'll let Sathyan know.' He set off down the street, his phone already to his ear.

Ellie heard and then saw the white van before he did. It crawled behind them, at a steady, confident pace. 'Company,' she said.

Arjuna looked back. He put his phone away and unholstered his sidearm, but didn't take it out.

'Who is it?' She forced her eyes ahead.

'Talk later. Walk faster. Don't run yet.' He picked up his pace.

She could feel her shirt sticking to her body. Her breath shortened, but she forced her shoulders back and down. A receptive position, not a combative one. Her left arm tightened over her handbag, pressing it and the coded message it contained closer to her body.

Arjuna led her off the empty road and towards the footpath. She didn't like footpaths. They could be pinned against the wall there. But she trusted him.

The van closed the gap between them.

They approached the first crossroad. She exhaled with relief when she saw cars passing. A bus slowed down at the stop as they began to cross. A motorcycle brushed past her and turned the corner. She caught the red flash of a sticker on its tailpipe that looked familiar. She wanted to get a better look at the rider, but Arjuna's pace was quickening, his body limber and poised to bolt soon.

There was a small park on the other side of the crossing. Mothers, grandmothers and children playing. A billboard of the President smiled benevolently over a stone statue that stood in the middle.

'Across the park, now!' Arjuna shouted as he broke into a run and darted diagonally through the gate. He hurdled a manicured hedge and simultaneously pulled out his weapon, keeping it dropped but ready at his side. He wasn't going to start a gunfight in a playground, but she knew he would finish one if necessary.

The van accelerated. She followed Arjuna through a sandpit and around a beached pirate ship, running towards the statue.

The van sped along the park's fenced boundary. They would converge at the top corner if Arjuna didn't change direction soon. They reached the statue.

'Stay down,' he ordered, pushing her behind the stone plinth.

'Give me your back-up.'

'No, stay down. They want you. Not me.'

'Which is why they'll kill *you*, not me. Give me your back-up!' He was such a fucking hero sometimes.

The window of the van slid down. The occupants weren't visible, but Ellie didn't miss the black barrel poised on the glass as the van skidded to a halt.

Arjuna pushed her back behind the stone.

'What are you doing?' she screamed.

'Testing a theory,' he answered, raising his weapon. He flipped it so he was gripping it by the trigger guard, not the handle. He raised his hands either side of his head in surrender.

People darted for cover, grabbing their children, ducking and tripping over each other as they ran.

Arjuna pointed up but didn't take his eyes off the van.

Ellie followed his finger. The statue they sheltered beneath was a life-sized one of Lord Buddha, standing protectively over them, his hand raised in blessing, his eyes closed in prayer.

'It's a full moon day today,' Arjuna murmured. 'Poya. Bad luck to shed blood on the Buddha's day of the month, at the Buddha's feet, no less.'

'*That's* your theory?' she hissed at him. Jesus Christ, they were dead. The government's death squads killed on any day of the month.

'Have faith, Ellie.'

The barrel of the gun retracted, the window rolled up, and the white van drove away.

•

The motorcyclist watched the targets rest underneath the statue. The burned man had gambled and won. The American woman was lucky. He watched her lean against the stone plinth and close her eyes for a moment, the relief palpable even from his vantage point across the park. She used her sleeve to wipe her face and neck.

The motorcyclist muttered a resentful rendition of his prayers and called his employer.

'They visited the boyfriend. What do you want me to do?' he asked, firing up the bike's engine again. Fumes charged out of its tailpipe, the Rolling Stones sticker vibrating as though Mick Jagger's lips were actually singing.

'Are you certain?' he asked. Confirming instructions was an important part of the process for his extensive and irrevocable services. He was excited by the answer. It wasn't creative but it required skill.

12

NOW (2009)

Back at the hotel, Ellie opened the mini-bar and took out a small bottle of whisky. She opened it with shaking hands and poured the contents into a glass. She set it down on the table, next to the *Lonely Planet* guide, and stared at the book through the oily filter of the amber liquid.

'Are you going to drink that?' Arjuna asked.

She shook her head. 'Do you know who they were?'

He reached over and drained the glass, wincing as the whisky hit the back of his throat. He coughed. 'Not personally. Generic hired thugs in a white van, same plates as the one at the crime scene. You should open that.' He motioned to the guidebook. 'The suspense is killing me.'

She found her medication in her toiletries bag and took a double dose of the beta-blockers. The effects of the adrenaline would take hours to subside without it. She opened the tattered cover of the *Lonely Planet* and flicked through its pages. The middle segment had been removed and replaced with a notebook, its pages a little smaller than the rest, its spine firmly glued to that of the guidebook. She prised it out and opened the first page. Handwritten notes cascaded across the lined paper and along the margins, words heavily underlined, numbers, question marks, arrows between parties and more question marks.

On the inside front cover, it read: *Ameena Fernando, December 2008—6 out of 6.*

Sathyan had given her a way into Ameena's mind. He had tried to understand it himself, but as he had cautioned her that afternoon, the notebook was hard to understand without the key.

'Six out of six?' Arjuna asked.

'Perhaps the sixth notebook out of six.' Had Ameena suspected this would be the last?

'The other five?'

'Gone—presumably confiscated with the rest of her work.' She leafed through the pages. 'There are multiple references here to Narada.'

'Who's that?' he asked. 'Aside from the character in Hindu mythology, it's not a common name.' He took another bottle of whisky from the mini-bar and poured it into his glass.

'Code name perhaps. There are dates, times of meetings. Notes from Narada about MNW.'

'The Chinese arms company?'

'Yes.' She pointed to handwritten lists of letters and numbers. 'What do you think these are?' There were pages of them. They looked like serial numbers. 'Account numbers maybe?'

'Not Sri Lankan accounts. Those always start with SLN.'

She opened up her encrypted laptop and punched in some of the numbers. Nothing came up. She searched the name Narada and read aloud from the description of the mythological character. 'Says here he's closely associated with Vishnu, the Hindu god of protection, and he's an all-round troublemaker. Spreads bad news and tells scandalous stories. Good code name for a source.' She reached for the whisky but Arjuna moved it away.

She called Scott on her satellite phone and put the phone on speaker. 'Scottie, I need you to run a couple of searches.'

'Sure, I'm not doing anything important in the defence of our great nation. What do you need?'

'The name Narada. Check our databases, see if we get any hits. Check Chinese and Indian businesses too, as well as foreign agents. Ameena Fernando's informant might have belonged to another agency.'

'First hit is an Indian energy storage company,' Scott replied. 'Then a Romulan mining vessel in the new Star Trek movie. There's an Indian exec who owns a beach house in Galle. I'm sensing they're not who you're looking for.'

'Thanks, Scottie. Maybe the exec. A full search on him and the energy company please, just in case. Now some serial numbers, see if these are more meaningful.' She read five of the numbers to Scott.

'Nothing, sorry, Ellie. Where are you getting these from?'

'Just a scrap of paper from Ameena's office bin. Someone forgot to take out the trash. They could be encoded numbers, too.'

'I'll try our encryption programs and get back to you. Hey, those photos of the handprint you sent me?' Scott asked. 'From the crime scene, the driver's side of the car . . .' he prompted.

'Yes.' There was something about that bloodstain that she couldn't insert into the timeline of the kill. Why would an assassin place his hand there, in that way?

'We got a hit on the print. It's Ameena Fernando's. Not your killer, I'm afraid.'

'Thanks, Scottie. I just wanted to make sure.' Something still didn't feel right. She turned the pages of the notebook quietly until she found what she was looking for. 'One last thing, Scottie.'

'Only one?'

'MNW—Ming-Na Wu Holdings. It's a Chinese weapons and agri-business.' She could hear Scott typing rapidly. 'Ameena investigated the company for an arms deal brokered with the Sri Lankan government. Can you get me anything on MNW? Who owns them, who's in charge, who are their representatives here? Cross-ref Eric Kwan, the new cultural attaché. He's ex-military but I don't know about his corporate affiliations. This could be one of them.'

'I'll get you what I can. I'm still working on everything else you asked for, Jethro Gibbs.'

'That's Special Agent Gibbs, to you. Mark Harmon is a hottie, Scottie, and one hell of an investigator. Plus, he married Mindy from *Mork and Mindy*, so what's not to love about that man?'

'Quite right. Your *NCIS*-inspired search query has yielded something I want to flag with you. I'm emailing you an address now. Ameena made frequent payments to an account registered to it. The payments were relatively small, one thousand US dollars each time, but that's worth a lot more here. They started eight months ago and they don't fit her spending profile.'

'Her spending profile?'

'We all have a spending profile based on an algorithm that— never mind. Just trust me when I tell you that this isn't a bookstore or stationery wholesaler. It seems to be a residential address in Colombo 7.'

Colombo 7 was an exclusive neighbourhood, populated by the moneyed classes, politicians and diplomats. 'Did you—'

Scott interrupted her. 'Yes, I also watch *NCIS*. I cross-referenced it against all of her known associates, including family—nothing. Then I checked it against her mobile phone tracking. She started visiting the location eight months ago—and made a payment each time afterwards.'

'Thank you, Scottie. That's great work.'

'She visited the address twice in the week before her death.'

'I'll check it out tomorrow.'

'Take a responsible adult with you, please. By that I mean you, Arjuna.'

'God damn, Scott, how'd you know I was here? Are you watching Ellie's room?' Arjuna asked.

Scott scoffed. 'Nothing so Orwellian. I track your phones so I know you're safe. I can see that either you're together or she stole your phone.'

'It's possible. She has some weird habits.'

'You were moving a little too quickly this afternoon. Do I need to upgrade your security classification, Ellie? Assign you a team?'

'Not yet, Scottie,' she said firmly. 'You know I don't like company. I've got Arjuna. Send me the mobile phone tracking for the week before Ameena's death, please. And call me back as soon as you can on MNW.'

'You know, Solomon wants me to log the time I spend on your investigation. He wants to see what searches I run for you.'

'He said that?' She chewed her lip. Solomon was a creature of protocol and process, but he wasn't a micromanager.

'Tenby told me. He's really worried about you, too. Please watch yourself, Ellie. No trouble this time, okay?'

'Promise.'

Scott sighed and ended the call.

'You didn't tell him,' Arjuna observed.

'What?'

'That you have one of Ameena's notebooks.' He tapped its cover.

'The notebook doesn't tell us much if we can't decode it. But someone wanted all of these. Only Sathyan could have given it to me, and I'd rather keep him out of this.'

'He's already in it. You can't protect him.'

She paged through the notebook again. 'I've never been able to do that.'

Ameena's script was elegant but scrawled quickly. Truncated words and symbols were used consistently in her own shorthand. One page was a diagram, a family tree of sorts, connecting MNW to the Sri Lankan government with a question mark above 'MNW—parentage uncertain'.

Her eyes fell on initials that pricked the edges of her memory. 'What's this about? Here—' She pushed the notebook towards Arjuna and showed him the words:

Narada 12/8/2008: $ for completion of HM port from PRC $ needed for resett. of local SN ppl, highway project to the deep north. How much palm sugar?

'HM—Hambantota,' Arjuna suggested. 'It's the President's personal electorate in the south. The development of a new port started in early 2008, but it's already over budget.'

Ellie pulled out her own notebook from her bag and flicked through the pages, stopping when she found what she was looking for. 'Ameena was being sued by Dilshan Perera. She accused the Under Secretary of taking bribes from the Chinese in relation to the port. It's in your neck of the woods, isn't it?'

'Yes. Namalie complains constantly about the trucks and the traffic. The port is called the Magampura Mahinda Rajapaksa Port.'

'The Supreme Overlord named it after himself?'

He nodded. 'Of course. It's cost Sri Lanka billions of US dollars in soft loans from China. The President wants to turn his home town into the commercial centre of the country. You know, golf courses, resorts, cricket stadiums. A sort of Dubai-meets-Shanghai.'

'Tasteful.' She looked again at Ameena's shorthand. 'And then this could be "resettlement of local Sinhalese people".'

'That makes sense. He couldn't just push the local residents aside the way he has in the north and the east. The south is a Sinhala stronghold and his voter base.'

'What if he moved them north?' she asked.

'What do you mean?'

'I mean, what if the People's Republic of China also built a highway for the Sri Lankan government? A highway going north after the war ended. It could be used for access, for the Army and trade and the "resettlement of local Sinhalese people".'

Resettlement and reconstruction, and the overlooked R of post-conflict nation building, reconciliation.

'What about the Tamil people who are there now?' Arjuna asked. She could see from his eyes that he already knew.

Ameena had known too. And maybe it was a plan worth her killing for.

•

Ellie shut the door behind Arjuna and checked her watch. It was lunchtime in DC.

'I was expecting you to call earlier,' Redmond said. He sounded like he was eating.

'We had a little trouble,' she replied.

'You okay?'

'Sure. Arjuna was with me.'

'Good man.' Redmond had worked with Arjuna in Mumbai.

'Solomon said he warned you not to send me back here,' Ellie began. She didn't know what she wanted to know from Redmond. He had been her recruiter, her handler and her mentor.

'He *did* warn me. He thinks you'll never recover. "Unhinged by trauma" was his expression.'

'Why did you send me back, Mike? Tenby will finalise the aid package eventually, with or without me. He's doing as well as can be expected. Solomon has made it clear there's no point investigating Ameena's death and angering the Sri Lankans. The Sri Lankans have made it clear that my presence is . . . not welcome.'

She waited for Redmond to respond.

'Hello? Are you there?' she prompted. 'Why did you send me back?'

'Why did you agree?'

'I asked you first.'

'I sent you back because there's no such thing as a great secret agent, Ellie. That's a myth created by James Bond and perpetuated by Jason Bourne. There are only two types of agents. Dead ones and living ones. You are neither. You are stuck in limbo, working for USAID and recovering from the CIA. I want you to choose a side.'

'Choose a side?' she repeated. She had chosen a side once, and then she had made a mistake and it had cost more than one life. That was the job. To subordinate all lives to protect the state. God bless these United States of America. God forgive her.

13

NOW (2009)

Ellie paused at the entrance to the hotel cafe and watched Dougie Vanderstraaten flirt with the waitress. The woman was used to wealthy old men. She smiled warmly at Dougie's jokes and politely moved away from him before his hands found their mark.

Ellie walked over and, before he could stand up, bent down and gave him a kiss. He was freshly powdered and immaculately groomed. She affectionately loosened his cravat. 'It's far too hot for one of those.'

'I can't very well wear my fedora without a cravat.' He motioned to the hat on the table. His hands had developed a tremor she was familiar with.

'You are your own stereotype, Dougie. They broke the mould when they made you.' Ellie picked up the glass on the table and inhaled the sweet aroma of Hendrick's.

'I am the mould; the rest of these neo-colonial Nancy boys are mere pretenders.' He took the glass from her and drained it, crunching ice between perfectly crowned teeth. 'It's good to have you back, Ellie. What brings you to this historic place at this historic time?' His hand rose in a florid punctuating twirl, then smoothed the thick silver lines of his hair into place.

Dougie was a Sri Lankan Burgher. Descended from Dutch traders, his family had inherited wealth for twelve generations, each one squandering a little more than the one before it. The old man was a British NOC, a Non-Official Cover operative, recruited shortly after the fall of the Raj. His views on Sri Lankan politics were non-partisan. 'Bring back the British,' he had once told her. 'They did a much better job than these donkeys.' With his mixed Dutch and Sri Lankan heritage, he was a little of each but not too much of either. The British found his colonial affectations flatteringly foolish and the Sri Lankans found them repulsively aspirational.

The waitress returned and stood safely next to Ellie. 'What would you like for breakfast, madam?'

'*Not* what he's having,' she replied. 'Espresso, no sugar. That's it, thank you.'

'Tut, tut. You weren't always so judgemental, were you? Oh, that's right, you were.' Dougie smiled and signalled the waitress to bring him another round. 'You should try it before you judge it. And the desserts here are splendid, much better than the Cinnamon Grand. Have one for breakfast, live dangerously.' He shivered with mock excitement. 'Now, you were going to tell me why you're here, in this fine land of Serendib. I hear you've been asking after Ameena Fernando, may God rest her overly inquisitive soul.'

'Dougie.' Ellie shook her head and bit back laughter. 'I am looking into her death, among other things.'

'"Among other things",' Dougie quoted. 'My, my, Ellie, you must be a secret agent with talk like that. Or a lawyer. Or perhaps a secret agent posing as a lawyer.'

'I prefer to think of myself as a lawyer posing as a secret agent. What can you tell me about Ameena, Dougie?'

'I can tell you that it doesn't matter who killed her. Ameena Fernando, the patron saint of free speech. She's dead and martyred, just the way we like our heroes. And our terrorists for that matter. Your priority should be keeping yourself alive.'

Ellie nodded, thinking of the man hunting her on the motorcycle, and the four who were most likely responsible for Ameena's death. Her stalker could have been one of them.

'Did the government order the hit?' she asked, hoping the second Hendrick's would take effect quickly.

'Almost certainly. It's called power with impunity, Ellie. I know you're familiar with it. Why are you pursuing this? For the family back in America? Or for that boyfriend that you let down?' His acquisition of local intel had always been impressive. His tone was light and his lips were shaped into a smile, but he watched her closely.

'Leave him out of it,' she replied calmly. She didn't have Dougie's decades of deception, but she was trained to confront tougher opponents than an ageing, alcoholic British spy. She tried another approach. 'I need to give the family something they can use to close this chapter of their lives. I'd like your help. No one knows Colombo the way you do. Ask around for me, will you?' She placed a hand on his arm. His suit was a deliciously soft but firm cotton. 'Nice. Savile Row?' she asked.

'Flattery will get you everywhere. I will ask around, as you say. But as an old spy—nay, as an old friend—let me tell you: you shouldn't have come back. You won't expunge the sin. You won't pay back the debt you think you owe him. Guilt doesn't work that way. I know—I've tried. All you will do is expose everyone to danger again.'

She nodded and squeezed his arm. Her phone vibrated. It was Tenby, waiting with a car. She signalled the waitress for a third Hendrick's before she left.

•

'I hope you don't mind me joining you, Ellie,' Tenby said as he opened the door to the Anti-Landmine Lobby. They were greeted by warm air churned up by the standalone fan. 'Solomon just wants us to look eager to help.'

Ellie shook her head. She *was* eager to help. 'Stop fretting, it's fine. As long as you're not here to escort me to the aid meeting afterwards.'

Tenby looked away, nervously.

'Seriously? Jesus, Tenby. I'm not a child.' She was about to say more when she noticed the logbook at the empty reception desk. She flicked through it to the days before Ameena's death. Nothing stood out.

'Ahem,' Sathyan interrupted her, his eyebrows raised. 'You don't have the unfettered power of the State. Don't you need a warrant for that?'

'Probably,' she smiled and kissed him on the cheek in greeting. He held her arm gently, an old instinct. Then he remembered and let go, turning to Tenby.

'Mr Tenby, thank you for coming today. And thank you for your card and beautiful words about Ameena.'

'Please call me Keith.' Tenby reached out and took Sathyan's hand in both of his. 'We were shocked and saddened by what happened. Ameena's courage emboldened all of us.

The Embassy offers its full support, so please reach out whenever you need something.' He was sincere.

'Thank you, Keith.' Sathyan led them down a corridor formed by cubicle dividers. 'Where's Arjuna?' he asked Ellie.

'He'll pick me up later. He said . . . he said you visited him a lot during his recovery.'

Sathyan shrugged. 'He was kind to my brother. I think being with him helped me more than it did him. Come this way, we have a meeting room at the back.'

'The place looks . . . emotive,' she said, looking at the posters of an old man missing a leg, the remains of a nurse lying in the dirt, a little girl crying out in pain and clutching wounds in the aftermath of a landmine.

'It is an emotional issue,' Sathyan stopped at an image of Lady Diana Spencer walking down a dusty road in protective gear. 'Do you think we could get Michelle Obama to do that here?' he asked. 'Or too derivative?'

'I think so. Homage only works when it's Daniel Craig emulating Ursula Andress.'

'That's what I said to our marketing girl. She's young and keen, wants us to get funkier or something.' He shrugged.

'A funky campaign about the illegal use of landmines. That's a challenging spec.'

Sathyan took them into a small room. He played with the remote control for the air conditioner and then gave up, opening a window and letting in the noise from the generator below. 'Sorry. We're better funded than we used to be, but you know how it is in this sector.'

'The Gates Foundation will fund new prosthetics factories but not your air conditioning?'

He smiled at that and then they sat in silence. Tenby shifted uncomfortably, sweat softening the collar of his shirt. Sathyan was calm, almost detached. She wondered if it was grief, fatigue or medication.

'I tried to call Shirani Dennis,' she told him.

'Oh yes?' He looked interested. 'And?'

Scott's searches had corroborated Tenby's research about Ameena's work colleague. Ameena and Shirani spoke several times a day, which was to be expected. But his searches also revealed that Shirani's husband, Sachin, called Ameena more times than one would expect. She didn't have the nerve to ask Sathyan about the best friend's husband. She answered flippantly but honestly. 'She hung up on me twice, abused me once, and won't take any more of my calls.'

Sathyan laughed outright at that, mouth wide, eyes closed, dimples darting. She wanted him to keep laughing. She wanted to make him laugh and laugh and never cry again.

'I've tried her house and her gym, but she's elusive,' she continued.

'It's the best way to stay alive in Sri Lanka,' he replied. He was serious now, though the laughter hadn't completely left his eyes.

They were silent again.

'I need to ask you some more questions.' She cleared her throat. 'I'm sorry to have to ask you.' She coughed again.

'Just ask me. You do that cough thing before you have something difficult to say. And before you lie.'

She looked at him sharply. 'I'm sorry,' she repeated. 'Did you get the financial records I sent you?'

'Yes, thank you for those. Ameena and I don't . . . didn't have any joint accounts. She just paid for the house expenses and I paid for as much as she would let me.'

She straightened the papers she had taken out of her bag. 'Have you had a chance to review them?'

'Yes, I followed up a few things I didn't understand.'

'Such as?' Tenby asked, leaning forward to look at the records.

Sathyan was startled by his voice. They had both forgotten he was there. 'Nothing troubling, Keith. Just some things bought online, mostly books for her children and rare ones. Ameena likes—liked—reading.'

'Yes, the outgoings seem largely predictable. There were only a few big spends. For example, a new laptop?' Ellie noted.

'That was for me. The police took that too.'

'Was there anything that seemed unusual to you? Any big payments you didn't understand? Anything regular or one-off that didn't quite add up?'

'Are you asking me if she took bribes?' Sathyan asked, his tone finally rising.

'I'm sure what Ellie means—' Tenby tried to explain but Ellie cut him off.

'That's one question but there are others.'

'Ameena was an honest person who died because of her stupid integrity and unwillingness to compromise,' Sathyan said fiercely. 'She didn't take bribes. She reported on those who did.'

'Okay. Does this address mean anything to you?' She showed him the address that Scott had given her, in the posh part of town. 'She made frequent and significant payments to this place over the last eight months, every time she visited it.'

'I see.'

She told him what Scott had discovered that morning after some cyber-reconnaissance. The place appeared to be a high-end brothel. She saw the confusion in Sathyan's eyes and gave him her theory quickly, not wanting to hurt him. 'I think she went there to meet a source. It's a safe and discreet place in a town that has eyes and ears everywhere. Three months ago, Ameena published her piece on MNW and the arms deal with the Sri Lankan government. It makes sense that, eight months ago, she started meeting her source there.'

Tenby had suggested other theories about why Ameena might have visited the establishment, including habits she might have been hiding. Ellie doubted it, but she hadn't ruled out blackmail.

'Have you spoken to the owner yet? Are any of the staff her source? Or the other clients?' Sathyan asked. Ellie noted that he'd said 'other'.

'I haven't gone in yet. I'd have to get a search warrant to look at records, *if* they keep records.'

Tenby smiled ruefully at her suggestion. 'No judge in the country would give you that search warrant. You'd find out about their colleagues or themselves. We have some contacts—do you want me to ask around?'

'That would be great, thank you, Tenby. The Supreme Court of Sri Lanka is more likely to take your calls than mine.'

She waited, unsure how to probe Sathyan more, but unwilling to leave. 'I'm at a dead end with Ameena's money. She inherited a considerable estate from her family but she seemed to put most of it back into the paper to keep it afloat. Aside from mixing personal finances with professional ones, the money trail looks clear.'

'That was how she felt about the paper and her life—a mixing of both.' He looked at her sadly. 'It was impossible to know where one stopped and the other started.'

Ellie recognised the conflict of priorities where one life was always competing with the other. Where one life was always destined to win.

'There is something I wanted to tell you,' Sathyan began. 'It seems innocent. I don't know. Ameena and I share an Amazon account. She uses it to order books for her children online, novels and a few biographies. They get delivered directly to San Francisco. But a few months ago, she ordered a really big shipment of textbooks and educational resources.'

'Educational resources?'

'Yes, like electronic Lego sets . . . the kind teenage boys like. The textbooks are in Sinhalese and Tamil, used by our schools, not American ones, which is why I noticed. I asked her about it, and she said it must have been a mistake, that she would look into it. But I didn't quite believe her; something wasn't right.'

'Perhaps she was helping someone training to become a teacher,' Ellie suggested. 'Or a student? Maybe she was helping a student.'

'Or a lover? You can say it. I've thought about it too. Was she having an affair with a teacher?'

Shirani Dennis' husband Sachin was a teacher. She waited again.

'It's out of the question. I would know,' Sathyan said. 'I would know.'

Ellie wasn't so sure. 'Do you have the books? Perhaps there was something else in the delivery. An encrypted message, another delivery within the delivery.'

'The books didn't come here,' he replied.

'Where did they go?'

'To the address you just showed me. To the brothel.'

14

THEN (2005)

Sathyan opened his suitcase and pulled out the gifts from Canada. The plastic canister of maple syrup had made it unbroken through the flight, a long road north and four Army checkpoints. This time, he had even managed to bring in a Lego Technic set for Gajan.

He had divided the paracetamol, Ventolin inhalers and batteries across his three bags. He couldn't bring much more into the north without raising suspicions at the checkpoints. He opened the lining of the suitcase into which he had sewn small packets of money for his mother to buy goods on the black market.

'I want you to speak to him, son,' Amma pleaded. 'Speak to him right way.'

'Amma, give me some time. I can't just come back and order him around. He's a young man.'

'He's a boy. He's fifteen years old.' She started to cry again.

'He's been a man since Appa was killed,' he replied. He felt the familiar tightness around his chest when he thought of his father.

'The Army is watching all the young people, checking every week to see if any are missing or have joined the Tigers.'

'And the Tigers?' Sathyan asked.

'They can't come into Jaffna right now, but we know they are asking each family for a fighter.'

'Do they ask, or do they demand?'

The Norwegian ceasefire, brokered in 2002, was failing. The Tigers were recruiting again and the Sri Lanka Army was restocking. The Norwegians were determined to resurrect the fragile peace, but the rest of the world had little tolerance for terrorists or freedom fighters after 9/11. Mahinda Rajapaksa, Sri Lankan Prime Minister, was campaigning for the presidency on a mandate of ending the Tigers' claim to a separate homeland, whatever the cost.

His mother wiped her face. 'I know he wants to join them. He wants to fight; he wants to defend our homeland. He's so angry, Sathyan.'

He nodded. He understood his brother's motivations and they terrified him.

•

Sathyan picked his way slowly through the scrub, carefully pushing aside the mesh of thorny karai bushes, his bare feet seeking the dirt path beneath. The heat radiated through the earth into his skin.

Gajan was sitting on the bank of the creek. A jute fishing line dangled from the branch of a tamarind tree, bobbing with the occasional current or curious tug of a catfish under the cloudy surface of the water.

'You're not going to catch anything like that,' Sathyan said, taking his place next to his brother.

'I know,' Gajan turned towards him and smiled. His eyes were large and framed by long lashes, like their father. 'I like to sit here and think sometimes.'

'What do you think about?'

'Did Amma send you to talk to me?' Gajan guessed.

'She did, but I'd like to know what you think about anyway. It's beautiful here.'

The creek wasn't much, but its underground tributaries fed into their village well. The water was salty and tasted like a paler shade of the Indian Ocean.

Gajan was a skilled fisherman and set traps all along the water, sharing the catch with their neighbours. He knew how to read the creek.

He picked up a stone and threw it in. 'Sometimes I think about the fighting. I think about Balu, Sarangan and Prana, and all the others who've gone to fight. I wonder if I should join them.'

'Have you thought about what it would be like to kill someone? You play cricket and build Lego robots. Look at your hands.' Sathyan reached over and caught Gajan's hands before his brother could throw another stone into the water. He held them tightly. 'You do all the things a boy should be doing. You still collect marbles.'

The boy pulled his hands away. 'There's no place for cricket and Lego anymore. And I *have* thought about killing someone. I want to kill the people who killed Appa and Manju Acca.'

'Those people are long gone and killing them won't bring Appa or Manju back. Thinking about killing is different from *actually* killing. It won't be the way you imagine it.' Sathyan knew he couldn't take a life. He had been around the dead and dismembered for too long.

'I want to fight.'

'And I want you to stay alive,' Sathyan replied. He cursed the Sri Lanka Army who made it so easy for children to be radicalised against them. He cursed the Tigers, too. They wouldn't win this war, but they wouldn't end it, either.

'We've lost so much. I owe it to Appa to fight. You should fight, too, Sathyan Anna,' Gajan addressed his older brother respectfully, without accusation.

'I am fighting, but not with guns or bombs. Appa wouldn't want you to fight like that either.' Sathyan thought of his father and younger sister. 'He taught all of us that nothing will come of this war but our destruction. If you owe him anything at all, it's to stay alive.'

Gajan said nothing in return, pushing at the dirt with his bare feet. Sathyan tried again. 'You know I've been working for an organisation in Canada.'

'The one-legged people?'

He laughed in spite of himself. 'You are surprisingly rude for such a sweet-looking boy. They are not "the one-legged people". It's called the Anti-Landmine Lobby, and I'm researching the ability of amputees to become economically viable members of society.'

'Do you even know what that means?' Gajan asked.

Sathyan slapped him on the back of the head. 'Yes, I know what it means. It means that if I can finish my study, this Canadian NGO will fund another prosthetics factory in Jaffna.'

'Sounds important. Appa would be proud of you.'

'It *is* important. It gives me papers to come back here every few months. If we're successful, it could help a lot of victims. Appa would be proud of both of us, Gajan. You look after Amma, you do all the things Appa would have done. You get the water, go to the market, fish and help her take her sewing to her clients. She said she's even been teaching you to sew.' He paused. 'I've been talking to my boss in Canada.'

'No,' Gajan said quietly.

'Please, listen to me. I have letters of recommendation from the NGO. I can get you out of the militarised zone and take you back to Colombo. From there, we can work out what to do.'

'No. I won't leave the north. Colombo isn't safe either. There are bombs everywhere, you know that.'

'Yes, but it's worse here. The ceasefire is ending, the way they all do, and soon the war will start again. The shelling and landmines and death squads and torture. There are still police coming in the middle of the night—'

'I don't want to run away from that.' Gajan pulled the fishing line hard, snapping it. He unspooled more jute from a ball next to him, concentrating on undoing the knots.

'Running doesn't make you a coward. Most of the north would leave if they could. They're getting on shitty boats and going to India or anywhere. No one expects you to stay.'

'The Tigers expect *all* of us to stay.' Gajan retied the line as he spoke. 'They're fighting for us, for our homeland. What's the point if we run away?'

'The point is that you'll live.'

The silence between them was heavy.

'Do you think about them?' Gajan whispered.

Sathyan nodded. He thought about them all the time. 'You?'

'A bit. I remember Amma crying, mostly. I can't remember Manju's voice. I try to hear her laughter in my head.'

'It sounded like a snort. Kind of a snort, kind of a burp.' She had only been thirteen.

'Sometimes I sit here,' Gajan said, 'and I wonder what would have happened if she'd been at school that day, or at a friend's house.'

'Then she'd have lived longer,' Sathyan answered without hesitation. 'Just as you will live longer if you come with me to Colombo.' He caught himself from saying *Canada* just in time. He had to work on getting his brother out of the north first.

'It's not right that some people get to live longer, and others just die. Who decides that?'

'In our country, the Sri Lanka Army and the Tigers. Gajan, I am begging you.' Sathyan tried to keep the rising panic from his voice. 'We're all Amma has left. Once the fighting starts, it will be harder to leave. We need to go now, before the Army suspects you or the Tigers recruit you. I will never forgive either of them.'

Gajan gave up on the fishing line and threw a handful of stones into the water. The ripples crashed into each other on the surface. He smiled and Sathyan's heart broke a little more. 'No one will take me, but I believe in the Tigers, Anna. Would you forgive *me* if I joined them?'

'I would forgive you anything,' Sathyan replied.

•

Sathyan placed the bags on the table. A small UN ship had unloaded food rations at Ponnalai. He had lined up at 3 am, taking shifts with Gajan, until eventually, nine hours later, he'd presented his papers and been given three plastic bags of rice, yam flour, lentils and milk powder.

Families depended on the UN rations. People tried to grow king yams, snake beans and bitter gourd on their land, but the earth was hard and water was scarce. They often hid their meagre harvests, because if the Sri Lanka Army was moving through, the soldiers stole from the hungry.

Sathyan rotated food out of the go bag, replacing the old food which they would eat tonight with the fresher dry goods.

The go bag was his father's idea: a backpack ready to be picked up and run with. It contained a rudimentary first-aid kit, food, matches, a torch, batteries and a large, tightly folded square of plastic for shelter. On each trip home, Sathyan added another item to the sack. It made him feel like he had some control over their survival.

In Canada, he had bought a small camping stove but hadn't worked out how to smuggle it in yet. Fuel canisters weren't allowed into the north.

'Will he go with you?' Amma swept grains of rice from the table into a container to be saved.

He shook his head.

She sat at the table, placed her head in her hands and sobbed, defeated. 'Please, son, please. Maybe he could get a scholarship to Toronto like you. Ravi Anna said he overheard Gajan and other boys talking about running away to find the Tigers. We're running out of time.'

Sathyan thought about Ellie. Perhaps she could help them. USAID had connections on the ground. She would know what to do.

'I'll try, Amma. I'll try.'

•

He woke to the sound of heavy wheels on dust. A voice crackled over a speaker, tinny and piercing. They were being attacked. He ran into the kitchen and rifled through the cupboard, grabbed the go bag and called out to his mother.

He stumbled out onto the front step of their small house. Amma was there already, standing in her batik kaftan. She had been up at dawn, sewing. Gajan too, on the lower step, in his shorts, his bare chest heaving. Sathyan frantically searched the sack and found the inhaler, shoving it at his brother. Gajan pushed his hand away and tried to slow his breathing down himself.

Their mother moved to crouch on the step above Gajan. She wrapped her arms around him, holding his scrawny body to her chest, as if that would make all the difference.

The Army jeeps drove in convoy, tearing circles around the streets of their small village, striped green, black and brown like a herd of mechanical jungle animals. The vehicle in front had a siren that bayed, making Sathyan wince every time it passed their home.

All the neighbours stood outside, watching. Eventually, the jeeps stopped on the main street, which housed the well, the Ayurvedic doctor and their one bus stop. In the middle of the dusty street, there was a small Ganesha temple.

Orders were barked over a speaker, calling the people out of their homes. They hurried back inside to change their clothes and hide what little wealth they had.

Sathyan hid the go bag under a pile of his mother's sewing and surveyed the house. There was nothing of value except the sack, the food and his brother.

'You stay here, son,' Amma said to Gajan.

'They already know I'm here,' he replied. 'It's better we go out to meet them.' He went to the small shrine, touched the picture of Appa then the picture of Lord Ganesha, and took his blessings.

Sathyan stood next to him and held him, swallowing back the fear. The Sri Lanka Army could arrest Gajan just for suspecting that he wanted to join the Tigers. They could arrest him just for being Tamil.

They heard the wail spiral from the main street. A woman screaming, a man crying, too. Sathyan and his family ran outside and down the road, clutching each other's hands, terrified of what they would find.

The soldiers had dismounted from the jeeps, leaving one at the helm of each vehicle with a machine gun trained on the villagers lining the street.

Some of the soldiers had gone into old Uncle Skanda's general store and were helping themselves to his scant supplies. Uncle Skanda stood silently outside, his feet frozen to the hot ground. He didn't make eye contact with them as they left, arms full of soda, Sunlight soap and tins of milk powder.

'Keep going,' Sathyan whispered to his mother. They followed the sound of the crying, which had become more muffled after the initial howl.

At the well, they found the rest of the soldiers, some drawing water and refilling large canisters. Most of the villagers were standing in loose lines, their hands folded together in a gesture of prayer and greeting, their heads bowed respectfully, fearfully.

Collapsed against the small temple were Sarada and Venkat. They were holding Balu, their sixteen-year-old son. Sathyan heard Gajan stifle a cry. Gajan and Balu had been in the same cricket team at school, before Balu had run away last year to join the Tigers.

Balu's grandfather stood to the side, holding back the other children, who were also crying.

Sathyan couldn't tell if Balu was alive until he saw his legs move.

'Thank God,' Amma said.

'Something's wrong,' Sathyan whispered. The Sri Lanka Army didn't bring wounded Tiger soldiers back to their families. They killed them and left the bodies where they lay.

Sarada looked up and motioned to the women at the well for water. One of them rushed over with a small cup, but just as she reached Balu's mother, a soldier knocked it out of her hand with the butt of his gun. The water splashed to the ground, beading in the red dust like blood. Sarada cowered over her child. Venkat wrapped his arms around them both, trying to push them into the wall of the temple. Lord Ganesha sat impassively over them, his bulbous stomach glowing in the morning sun.

A man stepped forward in the bright green beret of an Army leader. His skin was dark and shiny with sweat, the cuffs of his uniform rolled up to his elbows to reveal burns and scars along his arms. 'My name is Captain Devage. This boy has betrayed his country. He is a coward and a traitor,' he said in English. 'There is no Tamil nation. There is only Sri Lanka. This boy has chosen to fight for terrorists. We are in a war against terror.'

There was no sound except for Sarada's quiet whimpering. Balu did not speak or cry. He had left his home to fight for his homeland. In the short time he had been with the Tigers, he had seen a lot. He knew what was coming.

The captain motioned to two soldiers behind him. They stepped forward and tried to pull Balu from his mother's arms. Venkat threw his body over his family again, swatting the soldiers away until one of them flipped his gun around and drove it into the top of Venkat's neck.

Sathyan heard a sickening crunch as Sarada screamed, clutching Balu tighter.

'Forgive us,' she cried in Tamil. 'Forgive him, he's only a boy.'

He's only a boy.

The second soldier reached down and grabbed Balu's legs. Balu tried to kick them away. His clothes were torn as though he had been running through thorns and scrub. His feet were bloodied around the edges of his sandals. Sathyan was close enough to see masking tape holding the sandals together. The tape snapped and one of them flew into the air, slapping the soldier in the face.

Balu stopped moving and his mother stopped crying, shocked. The soldier froze in surprise. He touched his face. Registering the insult, he slammed his fist hard into Sarada's face. Thick blood gushed from her nose, spilling onto Balu's clothes. She drew her hands to her face, then, realising what she had done, reached for her son again, but it was too late. The soldier gripped the boy by the ankles and dragged him towards the well.

The first soldier stepped forward and blocked Sarada's path, leaving her collapsed over the body of her unconscious husband, calling out to God and beating her chest with bloodstained hands.

Sathyan stood beside Balu's grandfather and younger siblings. The old man stared at his family in horror, his arms around the two small boys in matching Spiderman shorts and dirty singlets.

'Kanne moodengo,' Sathyan whispered urgently to the grandfather. 'Kanne moodengo.' *Close their eyes.*

The old man looked at him blankly, then understood, drawing the children into the folds of his sarong and turning their faces away. He inched back and Sathyan stepped forward to block their view.

The soldiers hauled Balu to the well, his belly leaving a deep smudge in the dirt, his hands scrabbling and clawing, the dust choking him as he inhaled it into his lungs. The ochre earth of Jaffna in his blood and in his breath. They lifted him up so he was leaning against the crumbled brick wall of the well.

'This boy is our gift to you,' the captain announced. 'And our warning. Tell the Tigers, the next time we find one of their soldiers alive, we will come back to their villages and we will kill the rest of their families. Tell the Tigers, if they want to send children to fight us, then we will kill their children. *All* of them.' He looked at the little boys hiding behind their grandfather and Sathyan, then raised his gun and shot Balu between the eyes.

The hollow crack of the bullet ricocheted in the well, followed by the sound of Balu's lifeless body landing in the water below.

15

NOW (2009)

Ellie stood at the entrance of the Dali Butler store. From here, she could see the gate of the school across the road. She scanned the street for white vans, the previous surveillance vehicles and most importantly, the motorcycle.

Seven missed calls from Tenby and three messages. She hadn't listened to them but could guess what they were about. She was two hours late to the next round of aid talks. There was even a voicemail from Solomon. You knew you were in trouble when the station chief called you.

She rolled down the sleeves of her cotton blouse and checked that her hair was tucked into her headscarf. The faded olive-green silk and dark glasses were the best she could do to fit into the predominantly Muslim neighbourhood she was loitering in.

She brought up a photo of a car and number plate to cross-check against the growing line outside the school. At 13.27, the car she was waiting for glided past the queue and pulled into the last spot. Shirani Dennis was either running late or deliberately just on time. Ellie suspected the latter when she saw a white van drive past the school, also searching for a place to park. The packed queue forced the van much further down the street.

Nicely done, she thought.

The car door opened and Shirani emerged. Her headscarf slipped, revealing greying hair scraped carelessly into a high bun. She swiftly re-tied the scarf and joined the other parents, a huddle around the school gate.

The school bell chimed loud and discordant. Ellie crossed the road in time to see the doors open. She merged into the clash and embrace of parents and children, and reached Shirani just as she released her small daughter from a hug, both of them laughing and breathless.

Ellie touched Shirani gently on the arm. The other woman looked up, startled. She pulled the child into her body, tense and poised to run, but was trapped by the crowd around her.

Ellie leaned in to murmur quickly in Shirani's ear. 'My name is Ellie Harper. You've been hanging up on me. There's nothing to be afraid of. I'm a friend of Sathyan's. Come with me, please.' She looked down at the little girl. 'Come on, honey. It's Renu, right? I like your shoes.'

The child smiled. 'I'm not supposed to wear them, but they're my favourite.'

'I like sparkles, too,' Ellie replied. She pulled out the High School Musical pencil case she had bought at Dali Butler and waved it in front of the child, then took her hand, leading Shirani and Renu back into the school building.

'Do you need anything, madam?' A teacher stopped Shirani and looked from the child to Ellie.

'It's all fine,' Shirani replied. 'Renu just forgot her hat. We'll be out in a moment.'

'Thank you,' Ellie said as Shirani led her into a classroom.

'Don't thank me, I have nothing to say to you. There's a reason I don't take your calls.'

'I know. You're being followed. I saw the van,' Ellie replied.

'Not just followed. The phones are tapped. I don't trust my computer. I don't trust anyone.' The door to the classroom rattled and Shirani jumped as though she'd heard a gunshot. 'I can't do this.' She murmured something to her daughter in Tamil. Renu tried to argue but Shirani raised her voice and insisted. 'This was a mistake,' she said to Ellie. 'Leave me alone. Please don't do this again.'

'After the shooting, you went back to the newsroom,' Ellie said desperately. 'You didn't run to the side of your lifelong friend and professional partner. You knew it was coming. You were prepared.'

'Of course I knew it was coming! Everyone knew it was coming. Even Ameena.' The anger in Shirani's voice subsided, the grief breaking through. 'She wrote that obit months ago. I just did what she asked me to do when it happened.'

'And what would she ask you to do now?'

'*She* isn't here to ask me anything.'

Ellie tried again. '936/8 Araliya Place. We know it's a brothel and we know Ameena visited it often. Did she have an illegitimate child she was hiding there?'

Shirani looked at her sharply, opened her mouth and then closed it abruptly. The reaction prompted Ellie to push on.

'She paid for a large shipment to this address—children's books.'

'Ameena wasn't hiding a child. She never hid anything.'

'How about a lover?'

Shirani laughed bitterly. '*That's* your theory?' Shirani asked disdainfully. 'That she was killed by a lover? Ameena loved Sathyan, and before him, her husband, Anil. There was no one else. There was never anyone else for her.'

'Not even your husband?' Ellie asked quickly. 'We have records, Shirani. Phone calls between them over the last six months. Too many phone calls.'

Ellie didn't actually think Sachin Dennis had anything to do with Ameena's death. This wasn't a crime of passion. It was a well-planned, well-funded and well-executed assassination. But there were aspects of Ameena's life that didn't add up.

'You're so stupid.' Shirani pulled her handbag across her chest. 'They were planning my surprise birthday party.'

'And your divorce? Thirteen years ago, your husband filed for divorce but you eventually reconciled.' It was a stretch, but the maths worked with the secret child theory.

'Sachin and I were having problems. All couples do. We worked it out. We're happy now. *I'm* happy now.' Shirani's eyes strayed to her daughter. 'He's in Canada, waiting for me. He wasn't even here when it happened. He loved Ameena. We all did.' Tears began to fall down her face.

Ellie knew love and grief when she saw it. But she also knew deception. Shirani wasn't telling her everything. 'Please sit down. Help me understand. The brothel—why did Ameena spend time and money there?'

'She was meeting a source. It was a safe place to do it.' Shirani pulled a tissue out of her handbag and sat down, reluctantly. 'It wouldn't serve the government to surveil that location. The owner and the President have an arrangement of mutual discretion.'

'The name of the source?' It was worth a try.

'I honestly have no idea. Confidentiality is standard practice for safety, mine as much as the source's. Ameena never told me more than their code name—Narada.' Shirani watched her daughter play with the pencil case in the corner of the room. 'Ameena's key focus was the arms-for-infrastructure deals that are being made with the Chinese government and their contractors. Her source had primary evidence: lists of weapons, paperwork on the money trail, emails confirming the exchange.'

'The exchange of what?' Ellie asked.

Shirani shook her head, irritated. 'The exchange of weapons for the privilege of building infrastructure here. The terms of these contracts are ridiculous—they include ninety-nine-year leases and military landing rights for the Chinese. The right to bring their naval ships into our harbours, planes into our airports. That kind of thing.'

'You mean like the new port at Hambantota?' Ellie asked. Solomon's briefings to Washington about the port had been troubling. He said China's foothold on the island had become a stronghold with this port.

'The port, the airport and others.'

'What other infrastructure projects—highways?'

'Of course. Think about it. Everything China needs from the outside world has to sail past Sri Lanka, most importantly energy. You invaded Iraq and made nice with Saudi tyrants to secure your energy supply. China is taking a different approach, creating allies by investing in them.'

'The Belt and Road Initiative,' Ellie said. China had been securing land and sea routes for the last decade as part of its String of Pearls strategy.

Shirani nodded, looking at the door again. 'I've got to go.'
'Who pays for all this?' Ellie asked.

'The Sri Lankan people pay. We always do. Either we take out loans with the Chinese and become more indebted, or the Chinese fund the projects directly. Either way, debt becomes equity very quickly.'

'And China owns a piece of Sri Lanka,' Ellie finished. Solomon was right to be alarmed; station chiefs usually were. 'What is the Sri Lankan government getting in return for the contracts? Money?' Politicians here were known to skim a transaction fee for every contract they touched.

'It's more complicated than that, but yes, that's essentially it. The government gets the weapons it needs to finish this war and the politicians get the cash they need for their retirement or exile plans, depending on which way things go.'

'You mentioned primary evidence—'

'Most of it was confiscated after we ran the first two articles. The rest was taken after her death.' Shirani talked faster now, moving over to her daughter. She swiftly packed up the pencils, whispering instructions to Renu.

'Wait, please.' Ellie grasped Shirani's arm.

'No, *you* wait. Wait here and let me go. Do your job and get your own answers.' Shirani jerked her arm away knocking a chair over. 'How dare you come to my daughter's school and ambush me. I—' Her eyes still glistened. 'I'm done with this place. I'm taking my family and we are getting out. I don't want any trouble, not now. We're so close.'

'Where are you going?' Ellie put some distance between herself and Shirani. Renu huddled into her mother.

'Canada. We have family there. Sachin has taken our older two. I'm joining him . . . soon. An extended holiday.'

Ellie understood. 'Canada's beautiful. Peaceful and progressive.' Tenby had already confirmed that Shirani had moved her flight to leave tonight.

'Ameena said the same thing. All her favourite authors were Canadian: Shyam Selvadurai, Michael Ondaatje, Michael Clayton. She should have gone while she had the chance.' Shirani reached for her daughter's hand and led her to the door. 'Take care, Ellie. I know you mean something to Sathyan and he's lost enough. Don't follow me out. They'll be waiting.'

Renu raised the pencil case, offering it back to Ellie.

'Keep it, honey. It's yours.'

The little girl smiled and followed her mother.

Ellie exhaled deeply. She had more information, but not enough. There were not enough data points to see the trajectory she was looking for.

Almost too late, she registered something Shirani had said. She ran after her, past the empty school yard and gates. Everyone had collected their children and gone. A car screeched to a halt as Ellie reached Shirani, who shuddered and turned at the noise.

'The first two articles,' Ellie said urgently. 'You said, "the first two articles". Was there another one planned?'

Shirani looked around the road reaching for the door handle. 'Please go.'

'Was there another?'

'Yes,' Shirani bundled Renu into her car, then moved around to the driver's side door.

'Where is it?' Ellie asked.

'It's gone. They took everything, I told you.'

'Could Ameena have been killed for it?' Ellie's mind raced. She used to be better at this.

'Absolutely,' Shirani replied. 'She was going to publish it on the fourth of February.'

'Sri Lanka's Independence Day?' That was soon.

'Yes, poetic justice and all that. I think it was almost ready. Ameena was on the verge of . . .' Sudden fear on Shirani's face made Ellie turn.

The van was approaching slowly. A large lens peered over the top of the window. Could they have heard their conversation? Ellie pulled the frayed edges of her scarf forward, tucking her hair under its olive-green silk. Her eyes scanned the road for the motorcycle. The van was predatory but predictable. The man on the bike was different.

'Leave me alone, I beg you,' Shirani hissed as she started the car. 'There's nothing I can do for Ameena anymore. Now I have to do this for my family.' She shut the car door and sped away. The white van pulled out and followed her.

16

THEN (2005)

The waiter hovered, checking on her glass of iced water every few minutes. Ellie took several gulps and the young man rushed forward to refill it. She had developed a reputation for tipping well and was always given the table at the back near the service exit. It was noisy but secluded.

Sathyan's message had been brief. She exhaled with relief when he walked into the Hare Krishna cafe. He sat down, reached for her water and drank deeply.

'Thank you for meeting me.' He looked around nervously. He smelled of sandalwood soap.

'You don't need to thank me.' She touched his leg. He jerked, like a startled animal.

'Sorry, I'm so stressed.' He tried to smile. He reached under the table and held her hand tightly and briefly. 'I don't know who else to turn to. I don't even know what to do.'

'Talk me through what's happened. I'll do everything I can,' Ellie said.

'The Tigers will be back soon. The Army came to our village and killed a boy, a child, right in front of our eyes.' He shuddered, remembering. 'After that, more of our people want to join the movement. Of course they do. Gajan is determined to go with the Tigers when they come.' He took another drink of water, wiped the tears that fell down his face. 'I thought I had more time. There's a field group going to Jaffna Hospital next month. I was going to bring him back with them. The Anti-Landmine Lobby said they would pay the bribes at the checkpoints. But now, it's too late.'

She wanted to take his face in her hands and comfort him. But he had been very clear. In public, they were friends and work colleagues.

He leaned towards her. 'Could your friends at the Embassy bring both of them out? If Gajan disappears, the Army will kill Amma.'

'My friends?' she echoed.

'Yes, your friends. There are soldiers at the US Embassy—could they help?' He stopped as the waiter placed two cups of steaming tea on the table. 'If *you* asked them, they might listen. I know they don't care about us, but they might do it for you. Could they get my brother and my mother out?'

'I'll ask,' she replied. She wanted to promise him she could fix this. She wanted to be the one who would do that for him.

'I don't know why I waited so long. It always seemed like there would be more time. I should have known, after Appa . . .'

'Don't think like that. I'll talk to the Embassy and see if they can help us.'

'Us?' he repeated.

'Yes, us. We're an us, aren't we?' She held his hand again under the table.

He clasped her tightly in answer. 'I've never really been an "us" before. Thank you,' he smiled. 'I bought you something.' He reached into his bag and pulled out an olive-green scarf with soft lace trimming.

•

Ellie sat across from Redmond, watching him read her submission. It would be harder for him to say no this time. She had come straight to his office from JFK Airport.

There was a map of the island behind him, with pins stuck in the main cities. Red and blue wool connected them like arteries and veins across the body of the country, delineating which side controlled which pieces of land. The vital organs of a body distributed between two parasites.

He pulled out an envelope and handed it to her.

She flicked through surveillance photographs of her and Sathyan. Nothing particularly incriminating unless you knew what to look for. They were careful. They always met at the Marbury. Once a small colonial manor, it was now a cheap hotel tucked away in Havelock Town, a quiet outer suburb of Colombo, far away from the diplomatic scene. 'I never lied to you about the relationship,' she said. 'It's all there in my submission.'

'Those aren't *our* surveillance photographs. Solomon has no interest in following you. These belong to the CID,' he replied.

Sweat prickled under her shirt. 'Why are they watching me?'

Redmond raised his eyebrows. 'They're watching *him*. He comes and goes between Jaffna and Toronto, a fundraising hub for the Tigers.'

She tried to remain impassive. She had worked for Redmond for a long time and, although they were on the same side, she knew better than to give him leverage. He couldn't know how much she cared for Sathyan.

He placed her report on the table. 'I don't think this boy is a worthwhile source of intel.'

'I told you what he saw in his village, the execution of an unarmed combatant. That's a violation of the Geneva Conventions.' Even as she said it, Ellie knew Redmond didn't care.

'Everyone violates them. All the time.'

'He has value to us,' she insisted.

'Yes, I've discussed it with Solomon. He has value to us, but not outside the war zone. He has value if he stays. This is what we've been waiting for. Think like an agent. Not like this guy's girlfriend.'

'It's not like that,' she argued.

'I think it *is* like that and I'm happy for you, Ellie.'

She scoffed and turned away.

'God knows it's a lonely job and we take comfort where we can find it,' he continued. 'But don't get distracted. You're there for a reason. You're digging up Muslim bodies for the Arabs as a cover to access the eastern province. You're *actually* tracking Semtex for me. We need to know who's selling it and who's buying it. We need to know how it ended up on the USS *Cole* in Yemen, killing seventeen American sailors, and a bus in Colombo, killing two American tourists. *That* is your mission in Sri Lanka. That has *always* been your mission.'

She was desperate. 'I understand, Redmond. But Gajan's testimony is direct evidence of summary executions.'

'You have one kid who maybe saw one killing who will say anything to get out of the war zone,' he countered.

'Do you doubt him? Do you doubt me?' she asked.

'No. But a UN Special Commission will. Even *they* will want more than this. Despite their lack of commitment to evidence-based policy decisions, they will want a big fat dossier of evidence that the Sri Lanka Army are executing unarmed combatants and threatening their families.' He leaned forward. 'I want the Tigers and I want the Semtex. I want to know where they're being trained and where they're building bombs.' He stood up and walked over to the map of Sri Lanka. 'The reports we're getting indicate that it's somewhere in this region.' He touched the jungle that no one had penetrated yet. 'The recruits are all taken there. If we can find the camps, we can free all of them, not just the one who's lucky enough that his brother is sleeping with the right agent.'

'So, you're a humanitarian,' she replied.

'You know, Ellie, you act like you're the only one who cares about what's going on here. I care. I just have to make the harder calls. I have to choose between which lives we protect and which ones we—'

'Which ones we hang out to dry?' she interrupted.

'It won't be like that,' he said. 'If this kid can deliver, then we'll get him out.'

'You can't promise that. If we get him out now, we know he'll live.' She persisted even though she understood the bigger picture Redmond was defending.

'If we get him out now, he's of no value to anyone except his brother. If he stays in, he could do something really important.'

'Please don't make it sound like we're giving him an opportunity to be a hero,' she retorted.

Redmond wouldn't back down. 'His father was a hero. His brother works for the Anti-Landmine Lobby. You think *he* doesn't care about the others in the camps?'

'I think Sathyan has lost his father and his sister. He's desperate to get his little brother out.' Her hand strayed to the scarf around her neck.

'Then this is the only way.' Redmond shrugged. 'The boy stays. He gives us the location of the training camps. *Then* we get him out. I'll petition State myself to get them moved to DC. They can come live with you, happy families and all that.'

'Shut up.'

'I'm serious. To show you how serious I am, I'll share the best surveillance resource I've got with you—Scott Barnett—as long as he does all my work first.'

'Jesus Christ,' Ellie sighed.

'Excellent, you're set,' Redmond replied, hearing the resignation in her voice. 'Now say thank you. If you weren't in love with the brother, you'd run this kid like the asset we both know he is. Do what you've been trained to do and recruit him. Promise him a better life at the end of it. Promise him he'll be watched and protected, threaten him that his family is in danger. Do what you usually do.'

'I usually manipulate people to get what you need under the guise of serving the rule of law.' She did what her psychometric testing in college had promised.

'You do it very well, Ellie. That's why you're here.'

17

NOW (2009)

Ellie folded away the scarf as she called Tenby and requested immediate surveillance on Shirani Dennis' home.

'Surveillance? Ellie, this is Sri Lanka, not India or Pakistan. I'm sorry, I can hear you're worried, but we just don't have the resources for that. We can't even keep an eye on *you*. Where are you? Solomon is livid. He's asked Scott to keep your Personal Locator Beacon activated at all times from the Frontal Lobe *and* update him every hour.'

'Great use of Bureau resources,' she replied. The station chief *was* pissed.

'It is if it keeps you out of trouble. We're starting the next session at 1400 hours. I'm sending a car.'

'I need to follow up a lead,' she replied, looking down the busy street for a tuk-tuk.

'No, Ellie. No leads. You made a deal with Dilshan, and whether you meant it or not, Solomon intends to enforce it. The investigation is done. Ameena Fernando was killed by an unknown assailant. It was very sad. We'll pay for *The Lanka Herald* to name an award after her, and if Sathyan wants a visa to the US, I will do that for him—for *you*.'

'Thank you, Tenby, that means a lot to me. He hasn't accepted it yet, but he's not safe here either. Just give me a little more time,' she pleaded. 'You've got this afternoon's session with the Chinese under control. You don't even need me—' She stopped. The black SUV pulled up fast in front of her. The car window slid down and the cool air from the air conditioning washed over her. 'Asshole,' she said.

'Part of the job description. I'm keeping you safe whether you want me to or not,' Tenby replied, turning off the hand-held tracker that had located her phone.

•

Dilshan Perera looked at Tenby quizzically when he chaperoned Ellie into the meeting. The US and Chinese delegates were sitting in the velvet boardroom of the Cinnamon Grand, mired in the finer points of village sanitation.

Ellie sat next to Tenby, turning Shirani's words over in her mind. Ameena was working on a third article with a fourth of February deadline. Confiscated and dangerous. Where was it? She had to get to the brothel. Fucking Solomon. She looked at her watch. 14.50.

'Ellie?' Tenby prompted her.

'Sorry, what?' Ellie asked. The room was waiting for her to say something.

'You were going to update us on the Pakistan maternal health programs. USAID is interested in funding similar clinics here and we'd all benefit from your experience. Talk us through it.' Tenby smiled tightly at her, then at the other delegates.

'I'm not sure we have time, Tenby. There are lots of agenda items to get through, so let's focus on the contentious ones. We can talk about best practice at drinks tonight.' She adjusted her watch.

'The delegates from the PRC do not attend the nightly drinks.'

Ellie turned to face the familiar voice. It was Su Lin Kwan, the cultural attaché's daughter. She looked even lovelier in a suit.

'Is that company policy?' Ellie asked.

'It's common sense. There's a lot of work to do.'

She was right, there was a lot of work to do. Ellie needed to fast-track things or flee the building, whichever she could achieve first. She checked her watch again. Brothel, Shirani, then Sathyan. She wanted to talk to the journalist one more time before she left Colombo. Maybe brothel, Sathyan, then Shirani.

'Do you have somewhere else to be, Dr Harper?' Dilshan asked. He shook his head at Tenby, as if completing some prior conversation.

'She's fine,' Tenby replied, clearing his throat nervously. He nudged Ellie under the table with his foot, and pointed to the screen at the front of the conference room, where her Pakistan report had been projected. 'Ellie, your presentation, please?'

Ellie sighed. 'You all know how a maternal health clinic works. The ones in Pakistan are based on the "Hub and Spoke" approach pioneered by WHO in East Africa. The problem in Sri Lanka is access. We won't be able to transport the prefab clinics through the jungles and landmine zones in the north.'

'We can transport them for you,' Su Lin Kwan replied. 'We have the technical capacity to clear mines and build highways across terrain like that. The World Trade Organisation has challenged all of us to move away from a donor culture and ensure that twenty per cent of the aid we give to developing countries is in the form of trade.'

'I'm familiar with the Aid for Trade Policy,' Ellie replied. It was such a stupid slogan but an important paradigm shift.

'Then you'll know that rather than making Sri Lanka dependent on aid, we want to help it create sustainable economic outcomes,' Su Lin said. 'To engage in trade with the rest of the world, Sri Lanka needs highways, ports, airports and economic infrastructure.' Su Lin smiled. 'That's what we're doing here, Dr Harper. We're building a port in Hambantota that can receive those pre-fab clinics and a highway that can deliver them to people in need. The same ports and highways will take produce from Sri Lankan farmers and sell it to the international market. When the *New York Times* writes about the Belt and Road Initiative, they don't mention that we have raised four hundred million people out of abject poverty in China over the last twenty years. That statistic doesn't work with the Yellow Peril motif of Western journalism, does it?'

'Maybe not,' Ellie replied. 'But that four hundred million averages out to only two per cent of your population per annum. If you're *not* lifting two per cent per annum, then you're just not trying hard enough.'

Su Lin burst out laughing. 'You're right, unlike you Americans, we don't just read the briefings that reinforce our respective worldviews,' she said. 'The newspapers *here* will tell you how Chinese investment in Sri Lanka is improving people's lives. Even *The Lanka Herald* wrote about it.'

Ellie turned to Dilshan Perera. 'We make highways too, sir. We might not match the Chinese concessional loans but, unlike them, we *will* use local labour. That's a guaranteed vote winner for you, Mr Under Secretary, given the national unemployment rate is at an historic high. Let me talk you through the rest of our presentation,' she said, setting her shoulders back and clearing her throat to reclaim the room's full attention. If she had to talk the delegates through the benefits of investing in maternal health, she'd do it quickly but properly.

•

At the end of her presentation, Ellie left the room quietly and without an exchange of the usual tedious pleasantries. Tenby caught up with her as she exited the hotel lobby.

'Thank you for doing that, Ellie. It was fast but thorough. You excel at development policy, even if Redmond thinks you're better at other things. Reminded me of old times. Stay for the next session, please,' he implored. 'I'm struggling in there and I need your help.'

She shook her head. 'Tenby, I know Solomon wants you to mind me, but please, let me get on with what I'm here to do.' She raised her hand, trying to flag down a tuk-tuk, but they passed her, full of passengers. 'Look, check the ancillary agreements to the Mine Ban Treaty. Look for a bilateral agreement between Germany and us—I'm sure we can get those mine sweepers for less than the Chinese. You can leverage that.'

Tenby touched her arm. 'I can't convince Dilshan that you're part of these talks if you skip most of them, you know. Please, Ellie.'

'Tenby, you're an accomplished diplomat. You're First Secretary, for Christ's sake. These people like you. Convince them for me.' She hugged him briefly and then turned back to the road. She finally hailed a tuk-tuk, its bright red and black carriage like a whirring ladybird.

She held on to the railing of the tuk-tuk as it weaved through the traffic. The prayer beads on the rear-view mirror swung violently with every turn. She looked in the man's side mirror and recognised the plates of the vehicle behind them. It was the same white van from Ameena's crime scene, coming closer.

She made sure the GPS tracker was on her phone, then texted Arjuna and Scott to let them know her destination. The tuk-tuk stalled in traffic, horns honking around it. Children ran up to the open side-door to offer her tired plastic toys.

Ellie shook her head at the little vendors. The white van inched closer to her. She could see the driver and passenger now.

The tuk-tuk driver turned onto Horton Place, the clotted arterial road that carried smaller streets to the elegant homes of Colombo 7. Ellie leaned forward to shout in the driver's ear.

'Turn left here,' she instructed.

'No, no, madam. It is further along.'

'Doesn't matter, turn here—now.' She looked behind. The passenger had rolled down his window, his arm hanging out of the van.

The tuk-tuk driver noticed him too. 'You have friends?'

'I do, and I don't want them. You understand?' She reached out with a twenty US dollar note in her hand.

'I understand.'

'Fast as you can.'

'Formula One madam, but main road is safer for now. More people.' He shifted the gears and the tuk-tuk engine spluttered angrily. She could smell smoke from the exhaust as the driver revved a few times, then mounted the curb. People screamed and shouted at him. The driver waved his hands, yelling in return. She grabbed the railing tighter as the tuk-tuk lunged back onto the road and flitted between cars. The driver shifted gears again, stalling it behind an Army truck.

Peppered with numerous embassies, Colombo 7 was a high security neighbourhood. Ellie checked her location. The US Embassy was twenty-five minutes away in the wrong direction. The nearest ally was the French Embassy, three blocks north. The British High Commission was four blocks southeast. That was her contingency plan. The white van was four cars behind them now. The door opened.

'Go, go, go,' she shouted. 'We've got to go.'

The driver reached up and kissed the prayer beads. 'Don't get out madam, trust me.' He wriggled the tuk-tuk forward so he was once again on the pavement, but this time he held on to the side rail of the Army truck. The soldiers in the back shouted at him. 'Hold on,' he ordered.

She held onto the tuk-tuk.

'No, hold on, madam,' the driver repeated. 'Army truck— own lane.'

She transferred her grip onto the truck. With the tuk-tuk in neutral, it pulled them forward, sandwiched between the truck and a wall, riding caddy with soldiers who were now waving their rifles at them.

'Few blocks only, madam,' the driver reassured her. Soon enough, he directed her to let go and did the same, pushing off the side of the truck. He turned left down a narrow lane, wide enough only for tuk-tuks and motorcycles.

She turned back to see the white van skid to a halt and the passengers jump out. Two Sri Lankan men, in civilian clothing so they could blend into the streets more easily. One tall and athletic, the other stockier, with sweat dripping down his bald head onto his puffy cheeks.

The tuk-tuk entered the heart of Colombo 7, surrounded by colonial mansions rising above the stucco walls. The driver took three more turns and braked suddenly at the top of a stone stairwell. He kissed the prayer beads again. 'We end here, madam, this is tuk-tuk, not jeep. You go downstairs, three doors on right. You have a very relaxing time after journey here.' He smiled happily, as though this was a perfectly normal drive. 'I wait for you?' he asked.

She took out another twenty dollars from her wallet. 'No, thank you. I'll make my own way back.'

'Are you sure? Goondas looking for you. Not far behind.'

'I'll be okay. Maybe lead them away for me?' she said, smiling at his delight.

'Aaah,' the old man winked. 'I understand. Go quickly.' He doffed an imaginary cap and took off.

•

Ellie knocked on the battered wooden door, checking all sides of the alley. There was a small opening in the door at eye level, and a man stared out through the metal bars.

'Ameena Fernando sent me,' she said.

The opening slammed shut. She waited, hearing nothing after the receding footsteps. She pounded the door again.

'Please, I was followed,' she hissed.

The main door opened. The man stuck his head out, looked around, then ushered her in with a gun. He was dressed in expensive jeans and a tight t-shirt. She pulled the remnants of a tissue from her trouser pocket, wiped the grime off her face and pushed her thick hair back into some semblance of order.

She was led through a shadowy corridor into an open courtyard. She looked up at the shaft of sunlight. As her eyes adjusted, she saw that the courtyard was an atrium that rose three storeys high. Each floor had an internal verandah that circled the atrium, and doors that led to other rooms. Each floor also had a similarly clad man pacing the verandah.

'Sit. Madam will be with you in a moment.' The doorkeeper pointed at the silk cushions of a rattan sofa.

A young boy brought her out a glass of chilled avocado juice.

She took one sip, then another. She finished the glass quickly, to the boy's amusement. He was about to offer more when an immaculately made-up woman glided towards her on the marble tiles.

'Please, don't stand up,' the woman said. 'Rest. You've had a busy trip already, Ellie.'

'I'm sorry, do we know each other?' She looked at the Madam closely. She had thick, arched eyebrows that framed her large eyes. Her kohl was artfully smudged underneath, and plum-red defined the soft abundance of her lips. The bridge of her nose was perfectly formed, as if it had been drawn with a ruler. She was stunning.

The Madam laughed a rich, throaty laugh at Ellie's scrutiny. Her coquettish elegance gave way to an edge Ellie now remembered.

'Manisha?' she asked incredulously.

Manisha assembled her features back into studied sophistication. 'I've aged a little.'

'Not at *all*,' Ellie disagreed.

'Liar. It's been a long time since you were in Colombo. Four years, no?'

'Yes, four years. You were still the night manager at the Ceylon Cricket Club.'

'I was more like an entertainment agent. Respectable men came in the front door of the Club and I discreetly brought the less respectable ones in the back door to service their needs.'

'And here? What do you do now?'

'The same thing, but with a little more honesty. We are still hidden away, of course. A private and safe space. But I don't have to pretend that my clients are genteel old boys who've come for a gin and tonic and a chat about better times.' Manisha adjusted her robes. 'People come for what they need and I provide the skilled artisans to give it. Why are you here, Ellie? I don't remember you as someone who used my staff.'

'I'm looking into the death of Ameena Fernando.'

'You mean the murder of Ameena Fernando. We can speak freely.'

'Was she a client? Or a friend?'

'If she was a client, I couldn't say. I can tell you that she was a friend and a good person. We had a certain mutual respect.'

'I know she came here. I have diary records of meetings she had with someone. Perhaps you? Perhaps one of your staff?' Ellie suggested.

'Again, I couldn't say.' Manisha rang a small bell and a young woman emerged from the wings, placing a silver tray down on the table between them. A plate of dumplings, a tea set and a bowl with small cubes of jaggery.

'Tea?' Manisha offered. 'You know it's rude to refuse in Sri Lanka. We cater for all tastes here.' She picked up a piece of fudge and put it in her mouth.

'Sugar, madam?' The servant lifted a square of the fudge with delicate silver tongs. She dropped it carefully into the hot liquid when Ellie nodded. It bobbed to the surface, melting quickly like a small, brown iceberg.

'Palm sugar. It sweetens everything,' Manisha observed. She raised her cup to her lips, leaving a smudge of lipstick on the rim.

Ellie continued. 'Although I didn't know Ameena, I don't think she came here to utilise your staff either. I've met her partner, and I don't think she needed this place.'

'Oh, you'd be surprised who needs this place, but please do continue.' Manisha reached for another piece of palm sugar.

'I wonder if she came here to meet her source. I'm just thinking out loud.' Ellie didn't want to reveal the conversation with Shirani. She had already exposed the journalist to danger. More danger.

'And I'm enjoying listening to you think out loud. But I couldn't offer an opinion. Another refreshment perhaps?'

'No, thank you. There's a lot going on in Colombo at the moment.' Ellie walked to a mural on one wall of the courtyard. 'People are negotiating the spoils of war. Are your clients Sri Lankan politicians or Chinese diplomats and businessmen?' She motioned to the mural. It was a geisha girl flying through the air, carried by a flock of cranes. It looked like a commissioned composite of cultural stereotypes.

'My clients are entirely none of your business,' Manisha answered.

Ellie returned to her chair. 'Ameena was investigating a story that got her killed. Let's just agree she was meeting her source here and paying you for the privilege.'

'It was my privilege to know her,' Manisha replied.

Ellie added Manisha to her list of suspects. The brothel could have been the subject of Ameena's investigation and it was too valuable to too many people to be exposed. She couldn't see Manisha as the mastermind behind the murder, but she had learned the hard way not to assume innocence.

'Ameena wasn't the sex-gate kind of journalist, unless it impacted on good governance. Although when has sex not impacted on good governance?' Manisha sniggered.

'I'm trying to work out what those payments were for if she wasn't compensating you for the use of a discreet room. Was she hiding a child? And were you blackmailing her because of it?'

'Hidden children and *blackmail*?' Manisha threw her head back and laughed again. 'Oh Ellie, you watch far too many crime dramas. I keep secrets. I don't trade them.'

'Then why would Ameena send schoolbooks to this address, Manisha?' Ellie's eyes scaled the floors spiralling up to the light.

Manisha's tone didn't waver. 'An administrative error. It happens.'

'May I take a look around?'

'Absolutely not,' Manisha smiled. 'May I take you to the door?' She stood up and reached for Ellie's arm, linking hers through it. 'This way, if you will.'

She didn't take Ellie back to the discreet entrance, though, rather led her up the stairs and onto the first floor. At the third door, she stopped and led Ellie inside.

'This is my favourite room,' she whispered.

It was dark, thick curtains drawn. A large cloistered cupboard with carved wooden screens stood to the side. Two lamps dangled above an altar, and as Ellie approached them she could smell the remnants of heavy incense in the air. It reminded her of her father's neighbour at the nursing home, The Pray-er, and his holy oil.

'Some of our clients have various issues with God and religion,' Manisha murmured. 'This room is called the Chapel. Some people come here to be punished by God. Or by me. Some people come here simply to confess and be forgiven.'

She stood by the wooden lattice that Ellie now realised was a confessional. Someone could enter either side and not see the person opposite, but they could hear them through the screen. Ellie walked around the room and then up to the confessional, opening a door to look inside. Ameena might have sat there and received confession after confession from her source without ever knowing who he or she was.

'Some people come here to pray,' Manisha continued. 'What would *you* like to do, Ellie?'

'I don't pray anymore, Manisha. Not for many years.'

'Me neither,' the older woman confessed. 'God left this island to its demons a long time ago.'

•

Manisha accompanied Ellie down to the courtyard. Arjuna was waiting for them. The Madam greeted him with the comfortable embrace of old friends.

'You're keeping well?' She raised a hand to Arjuna's scarred cheek and kept it there. He didn't flinch or move away.

'I am, thank you. I didn't know you worked here. You look beautiful. The place suits you.'

Manisha twirled in a slow pirouette, showing off her satin robes and curves. 'Any time, Arjuna. I'm always here for you.'

He smiled and shook his head.

'Take good care of her, won't you, darling? She barely survived Sri Lanka the first time. Both of you. Perhaps she needs a stiff drink at the usual place?' Manisha suggested.

Arjuna nodded. 'Yes, I hear their whisky selection is the best in Colombo. Thank you.'

Manisha turned back to Ellie. 'Stay safe. This is a terrible place to die.'

'I've seen worse,' she replied.

'No, you haven't.' Manisha kissed her deeply on the lips. She tasted like palm sugar.

•

As soon as Ellie and Arjuna left the brothel, Manisha made the call.

'She just left, heading towards Colpetty,' she lied. 'No, I don't think she's armed. Will I be seeing you this evening?'

More questions about Ellie instead of an answer.

'*Of course*, I didn't tell her anything about you,' she replied. 'You know that's not how I operate.' She listened, bored, as the other person's questions became increasingly frantic. 'You knew this would happen,' she said eventually. 'She's investigating Ameena, and Ameena came here. There was nothing we could do. She came here but she doesn't know why or what for.'

She didn't tell the man about Ellie's theories.

•

Ellie wiped the plum lipstick from her mouth, put her seatbelt on and turned to Arjuna. 'Thanks for picking me up.'

'Solomon sent me. He's pissed at you. Apparently, you arrived at a negotiation late and left early.'

Ellie dismissed Solomon's criticism, which had undoubtedly been more colourful than Arjuna's summary. 'You and Manisha seem pretty friendly,' she observed. 'You know she was more than just the night manager for the Ceylon Cricket Club?'

'Everyone knew. She was their fixer. Whatever clients needed, she got it for them. Whatever messes they made, she cleaned it up for them. She knew all their dirty secrets.'

Manisha knew but wouldn't tell.

'Where are we going?' she asked.

'Manisha said "the usual place"—the Cricket Club, of course. She was trying to help you. You need to listen more.'

'You obviously understand her subtext better than me.'

'It's a guy thing. We also have higher emotional intelligence.'

She laughed. 'Shut up.'

'Have you added her to your suspect list?' he asked.

'Yes, for now. She has motive if Ameena was investigating her clientele. It just doesn't feel right . . .' She was missing something at Manisha's. 'Shirani talked about a trade that happens here—the Sri Lankan government receives weapons and kickbacks from China in exchange for awarding infrastructure projects.'

'Like the Hambantota Port,' he said, reaching out to wipe the dust off his side mirror.

Hambantota—where Su Lin Kwan said the Chinese could warehouse the pre-fab health clinics. She said even *The Lanka Herald* wrote about it.

She called Scott. 'Did Ameena Fernando report on the benefits of Chinese investment in Sri Lanka?' she asked.

'Hey Scottie, how are you?' Scott answered. 'Thanks for tracking my phone and noticing that my route to the brothel was unusually circuitous and my speed was exceptionally fast. Thank you for demanding that Solomon send out a team to cover me.'

'Thank you, Scottie,' Ellie said. She hadn't seen the team but she didn't doubt that Scott had sent them, or that Solomon had balked. 'I mean it. Thank you.'

'You're welcome. I've also upped your security status to HKR.' High Kidnapping Risk.

Ellie knew he was right to do so. 'Thank you.'

'And I'll have a look out for China-friendly pieces by Ameena.'

'If you can't find anything on the internet, talk to the archives department at the Carter Center.'

'Those Commie-lovers? Sure.' Scott clicked off.

'I'll take you to Hambantota.' Arjuna rolled his sleeve down to cover the scars on his right arm and buttoned the cuff. 'We can visit my sister. Namalie talks about you all the time. She wants to cook for you, say thank you for all the gifts you send the boys.'

'She doesn't have to. It's nothing.' The gifts didn't make up for what had happened. Forced together at the hospital, watching over Arjuna, Ellie had got to know Namalie well. If Namalie knew Ellie better, she would hate her.

'I told her that, but she insists. Let's get that drink at the Ceylon Cricket Club and work out a plan,' he said.

'Can we stop at Sathyan's place first?' she asked. The last time she had seen him, Tenby had been with them. There was so much more she wanted to say.

'So you can traumatise each other again? Tenby said the visit to the Anti-Landmine Lobby was painful for everyone, including him. He's worried about you. I don't think seeing Sathyan again is a good idea. You need to stay on mission.'

'He's an important part of the mission. I have questions.'

'I'm sure.' Arjuna shook his head and turned left at the lights.

18

NOW (2009)

Ellie stood at the gate, which now had a heavy metal chain wrapped around it. She rattled it. Arjuna had refused to come in with her.

'It's too painful to watch the two of you together,' he'd said. 'I'll be at that fancy cafe we passed on the way here. Call me when you're done, and I'll come back for you.'

She had checked the crime scene photos and coroner's report in the car one last time. Something was missing.

Sathyan appeared on the other side of the gate.

'I'm sorry to disturb you,' she said. The familiar squall of pain in her chest gathered itself slowly.

'It's not a disturbance. Have you found something?' he asked.

'I've lost something.' She checked the street as he unlocked the gate. It was empty, but she wasn't naive enough to think this was good news. She followed him inside the house and went straight to the bookshelf, to the family photograph she had returned to Sathyan.

'Did Ameena wear a ring?' she asked, picking up the photo. Ameena's hand was raised to her eyes, shielding them from the sun. In the CCTV footage, when Ameena had reached out for the cashew nuts, Ellie thought she had seen something.

The coroner's report had revealed that Ameena's right-hand ring finger had been broken, as though someone had carelessly pulled a ring from it and then dropped her hand, leaving behind the incongruously placed bloodied handprint on the body of the car.

Post-mortem. It had to be. The second-last bullet would have shattered Ameena's window. The last bullet would have killed her. The force of it would have thrown her back into the seat, but not more than that, not enough to fling her hand out of the window.

Someone had reached in and *pulled* it out.

'She wore two rings,' Sathyan said. 'Her wedding ring on her left hand, even after the separation. And a navarathinam.'

'I thought Ameena was Buddhist,' Ellie said, surprised. Navarathinam rings were studded with nine small gemstones, and typically worn by Hindus, who revered the nine planets.

'She was, but she liked to cover all religions and all superstitions,' he tried to joke but his words caught in his throat.

'Were any of her personal effects returned to you?'

He bit his lip and then released it in pain and shook his head. 'Nothing. Does that help you?'

'I don't know. I'm just thinking.' The navarathinam ring wasn't listed in the inventory from the crime scene.

'I gave Ameena the ring,' Sathyan confessed. 'My surname, Navaratnam, has the same meaning—nine gems. I wanted it to keep her safe. I wanted the planets to protect her. Silly, isn't it? As if any of it's real.'

Ellie didn't know what to say to him. She sifted through the books on the bookshelf and stopped at one. '*Every Day Proofs?*'

'Ameena's undergraduate degree was in pure mathematics. She loved number problems,' he explained. 'She liked the logic of them. She said mathematics was complex but understandable, unlike human nature. One clear meaning, not ten confusing ones.'

She nodded. 'Did Ameena ever write any good pieces about Chinese investment in Sri Lanka?'

'What do you mean, "good pieces"?'

'A positive piece rather than a negative one?'

'You really don't understand Ameena yet, do you? She didn't write positive or negative pieces—she wrote accurate and honest ones. She did a series years ago that you're probably thinking of. It had a catchy title: *Crouching Investor or Hidden Dragon?*'

'That *is* catchy. Do you have copies?'

'The office might. She didn't keep back issues here. It talked about how Sri Lankans are benefiting from China as a regional partner. We need hospitals, schools and roads. Every country has to align itself with a benevolent superpower. China is ours.'

A benevolent superpower. The US was an ageing one that had not looked after Sri Lanka.

'I met Shirani today,' Ellie told him. 'She said she couldn't help me. Do you know her husband, Sachin?'

'Yes, of course. He's great; works at the Borella Preparatory School. It sounds fancy, but it's a public school in the suburbs. He's overseas at the moment.'

'Did you know they were having marriage problems?' She didn't think either of them were responsible for Ameena's death, but there was more to Shirani's story, and it might explain the textbooks.

'That was years ago, before I knew Ameena. What does that have to do with anything?' Sathyan asked. 'I haven't seen

Shirani since the hospital. Neither of us could say much. The last time before that was at Shirani's birthday party. Ameena gave her a book, something to read on her next holiday.'

Ellie walked along the length of the bookshelf, studying the guidebooks. There were small gaps, the books tilting against each other where some had been removed.

'Did Ameena have a briefcase?' she asked suddenly. The passenger seat next to Ameena had been protected from the shattered windscreen by something large. Something that was also missing. The killers were after very specific items.

'No briefcase. She had a leather satchel. Her father gave it to her when she graduated from university. I was going to get that buckle fixed. She could do mathematical proofs, but she was shit at personal admin.'

'It's possible Ameena was planning another piece about the arms deal,' Ellie said. 'I think she might have been close to publishing it. It was planned for Independence Day.'

Sathyan shrugged. 'She never knew when to stop. Like you.'

She stood opposite him but didn't look him in the eyes. 'How is your mother?' she asked.

'Surviving. She moved to Colombo, lives with her sister here. Too many memories up north. How is your father? Surya?'

'He's okay, thank you for remembering. I had to move him into a nursing home. He didn't like that. Started quoting Article 9 of the ICCPR.'

'That's a good one,' he smiled.

'He's a biologist,' she said. 'With access to Google. He put up a fight, but not much. He can see where the Parkinson's and dementia are going. It's a lovely nursing home,' she reassured herself as much as him. 'There are a lot of Sri Lankans there. Although I suppose here, you'd never use a nursing home.'

'Perhaps. We do look after our elders better. But we tend to eat our young.'

'All cultures do that.' Neither of them smiled.

'Why did you come here, Ellie?'

'I don't know. I want to say I'm sorry.' She had never looked him in the face and told him how his brother had died. Four years ago, she had sat in a hospital cafeteria, looked down at her hands, and spared him the details.

'You said sorry already,' Sathyan whispered.

'I wanted to say it again,' she replied. The guilt that had kept her away had now drawn her back. The guilt that had kept her silent then, kept her silent now.

'Why did you come here, Ellie?' he repeated. 'To my home. To Ameena's home.' He shook his head. 'Helping Ameena won't give you the redemption you seek.' He took the photograph from her hands. She had forgotten she was still holding it. He put some distance between them. 'It's been so many years. Seeing you brings back the memory of love. But that's all it is.' He swallowed hard.

'You loved her very much,' she said.

'I did. There is no justice for her as there will be no justice for my brother. But I'd like to know who killed her and perhaps even why. I'd like to know why someone thought they had the right to take her from me, to take her from her family. I'm sick of living with the memories of my dead. Can you understand that, Ellie?'

'I can,' she whispered. She kissed him on the cheek and finally said the words. 'I'm sorry, Sathyan.'

There were other words she held back. *I'm sorry I left. I'm sorry I never came back. I'm sorry I never told you the truth.*

'Me too,' he replied.

Both of them meant it, but neither of them felt better.

•

Ellie tugged on the padlock. The security camera hadn't been replaced, but the glass on the ground had been cleaned up. The sunlight was fading and the Arabian jasmine released its sweet perfume into the air.

She checked her phone for a message from Arjuna. It wasn't like him to be late, so she started walking towards the main junction she expected him to take. She heard a low rumble to her left and turned, seeing the motorcycle approach her slowly from the top of the street. The rider's helmet visor was down but his build and his bike were familiar to her. It was definitely the same guy as before.

She reached for her phone and elevated her status on its Personal Locator Beacon to 'Distress' for the High Kidnapping Risk team. Then she hastened in the direction of Pettah markets where she could either disappear safely into the crowds of hawkers or grab a tuk-tuk easily.

She heard the motorcycle narrow the gap behind her and quickened her pace, ducking down the first lane towards the street hawkers calling out to locals and tourists alike, the crescendo of their pitch competing with the honking of the delivery trucks.

At the flower market, elderly ladies with gnarled hands wove roses and chrysanthemums into thick garlands for weddings and temples. Ellie moved quickly among them, then turned into the nearest alley, heading towards its exit, but stopped suddenly when she saw the motorcyclist was already there.

He had anticipated her escape route and circled around; waiting for her again. She remembered Pettah markets from her last mission in Colombo, but this man knew them better.

She turned quickly and ran into the tailors' quarter. A little boy rushed towards her with a kaleidoscope of scarves draped over his arms and shoulders.

'Madam, madam, for you,' he smiled. She shook her head but he opened his arms like a magnificent tropical bird, colours flashing iridescent.

'Just look,' he thrust his small hand into hers and pulled her to a rusted mirror. He dumped his goods on a rug and then rifled through them, finding an embroidered shawl.

He cast it around her shoulders and positioned her squarely in front of the mirror. Despite its rusted patina, she caught the reflection of the men from the white van. The taller man was ahead, closely followed by the other one, the shirt across his barrel chest now fully soaked in sweat.

Adrenaline surged faster through her veins, giving her more clarity and more speed if she needed it. She was in a crowded place. It could go either way. She couldn't see the HKR team she had called but she trusted they were nearby. Station protocol dictated they deploy within four minutes of receiving her call. However, now that she'd been forced deeper into the labyrinthine markets, local knowledge outweighed Special Ops training.

The tailor's boy looked at her in the mirror and then behind her reflection, to the two men approaching slowly.

'Time to go, madam?' he asked quietly.

She nodded, unwrapping the shawl and returning it to him.

'Go Mosque. More people,' he said, pushing her in the direction of another alley.

The boy called out to his friends who were folding shawls together. They looked up and then towards the men.

The boy winked at her. A group of boys swarmed up and surrounded the two men, shoving shawls in their faces, offering different prices and tightening the circle around them while Ellie raced towards Main Street and the Jami Ul-Alfar Mosque, its red and white striped minarets rising above the narrow lanes.

She glanced back for a second. The men were still coming for her, lunging through angry, shouting tailors. She could not see the motorcycle anywhere. She ran into the path of a tuk-tuk that swerved to miss her. The driver honked ferociously as she turned down an alley into a shaft of waning light. She let herself breathe. Measured, deep and slow breaths. She was adrenalised but in control. She could run and she could fight. She had options.

Bradfield and Sharkey used to say it was all about having options.

She heard shouting again and turned. Both men had almost caught up to her. She looked up between buildings, trying to find the mosque, but saw only slivers of pink sky. She exhaled. She would find it.

She set off again, feeling stronger and faster. One more turn and she was back among the thrum of vegetable and dried fish stands. She darted down an aisle. The men ran after her. In front, she heard the rev and roar of a motorcycle. The rider was waiting for her again, his shoulders hunched and ready. He revved once more, but this time, pushed his bike too hard. Its back wheel spun out twice before he steadied it. She recognised its tailpipe and saw the whole sticker now, the blood-red, gaping lips and outstretched tongue of the Rolling Stones.

With no way forward or back, she turned down the first alley, weaving between stalls, knocking crates over as she went, jumping over others. She saw the exit to the market, which would take her to Front Street where she'd find an empty tuk-tuk easily. She raced out into the falling light of day and was hit by a flash of red.

19

NOW (2009)

A red Mercedes Coupé braked and skidded to a halt. Ellie fell across the bonnet and rolled on the ground.

She jumped up, bruised and covered in dust. She looked for the man on the motorcycle, but he had gone. The door to the Mercedes opened and a familiar face smiled at her.

'Can I give you a lift?' Dougie Vanderstraaten asked.

She scrambled into the car, nearly landing her face in his lap.

'That was quite an entrance.' The old man eyed her dishevelled state. 'I see you're still as elegant as always.'

'Thank you, Dougie. That was close.'

'It was. Where would you like to go? Let me take you there,' he said warmly.

Ellie thought for a moment. At the brothel, Manisha had recommended Arjuna take her for a drink at 'the usual place'.

'The Ceylon Cricket Club please, Dougie,' she replied, trusting her gut and following the clues.

'How fortunate, I was already asked to get you there,' he replied. 'I assume you had a good reason to be running through the streets of Colombo. Where is your man?'

'Arjuna's at work,' she said, wondering the same thing about her friend. 'Other projects.'

'Keeping you safe *is* his project. I'm turning you over to him after my next drink. Rumour has it you've been seen at all the wrong places since our breakfast cocktail this morning.'

'I'm investigating Ameena Fernando's death. I'm going to the places she went to.'

'As I said, all the wrong places. Why can't you be like other aid delegates? Pretend to work and take advantage of the beaches, the grand hotels and the wildlife.'

'I've encountered the wildlife.'

'The *other* wildlife. Those thugs are CID. They've been following you from the moment you landed and triggered a red flag. So far, they've been gentle with you. But you've obviously touched a nerve.'

'I can still trigger a red flag here?'

'You *are* a red flag here and you always will be. You shouldn't have come back.'

'I was instructed to return. Redmond sent me.'

'Well at this rate, Solomon will be sending you back earlier than Redmond may have expected.'

The car turned into the long driveway of the Ceylon Cricket Club. It was flanked by lush stretches of lawn as manicured as Dougie's fingernails.

Above the portico, the Sri Lankan flag fluttered alongside the Club's flag, its crossed cricket bats flying in the wind. A bank of black SUVs parked around the curve of the driveway, shining like polished coal in the last rays of the sun. A valet dressed in a crisp white uniform and gloves opened the door and welcomed them both out.

They were ushered into the foyer, its teak floorboards and panelled walls making it look like an East India Company ship that had run aground.

They walked past walls of sepia-toned photographs entombed in glass cases. Young men with their starched cricket whites, consumptive grins and lacquered hair parted sternly down the middle.

Dougie stopped at one photograph.

'My grandfather,' he pointed proudly to a young man. 'He went mad in the end, refused to take his whites off, and started chasing the staff with his Gradidge Imperial Driver.'

'I'm sorry to hear that.'

'I'm not, it was a fine bat. We buried him with it and bought a membership at Lords with some of the estate. Seemed fitting.'

'Yes, that was very respectful of you.'

Dougie chuckled, leading her deeper into the Club to a pair of embossed wooden doors. These opened onto an antechamber where they were greeted by soldiers wielding security wands.

Without speaking, one of them scanned her body. The other searched her bag.

Dougie briefly clasped her arm. 'I'm not invited to this party, Ellie. You have a friend in there. Let him do the talking, if you can.'

'Thank you for finding me this afternoon, Dougie, I mean it.'

'I didn't "find" you, Ellie. Your Personal Locator Beacon told your people where you were, and *they* told *me*. I was just following instructions from your friend, Scott Barnett.'

'You say that, but I know you care,' she replied, surprised that Scott had called on Dougie to rescue her. The old man was resourceful and had survived Colombo for decades by following instructions, but he was no High Kidnapping Risk team.

He patted her on the cheek. 'I'll call Arjuna and wait for you at the bar.'

He pushed her gently into the cavernous hall and left. It was empty except for a group of people in an alcove at its far end, sitting by open glass doors with soft muslin curtains billowing around them, disguising them in a diaphanous shroud.

As she approached, she saw cultural attaché Eric Kwan stand up and shake hands with Dilshan Perera. He exchanged final words before he turned and walked towards her.

'Lovely to see you again, Dr Harper. My daughter enjoyed the opportunity to engage with you today.' His eyes wandered over her dishevelled appearance.

Dilshan Perera was sitting with Tenby, who looked relieved to see her.

'You shouldn't have dressed up for me,' Dilshan laughed.

Ellie took a seat opposite him.

'We were just continuing this afternoon's talks,' Tenby explained. The rash around his neck was getting worse. He really needed to see a doctor about it. 'Your help was invaluable, Ellie, thank you. The US will provide the Sri Lanka Army with those landmine sweepers you mentioned.'

'Great. There's a lot more we could do together,' she replied, looking for a waiter with a cold face towel.

'Perhaps,' Dilshan said. 'But perhaps it's time for you to go home.' His features arranged themselves into an expression of mourning. 'I see you are still looking into Ameena Fernando's death. Ameena's family and mine were—are—lifelong friends.

Her father was even on my cricket team. I was devastated by her death. We are conducting our own inquiry and your presence here is getting in the way.'

'We understand, sir,' Tenby said smoothly. 'Ellie's mandate is simply to write a report for the family. I'm sure she will reassure them that you have everything in hand.'

'Historically, Dr Harper has always exceeded her mandate. Much like Ameena.' Dilshan didn't take his eyes off her. *The Lanka Herald* was unnecessarily provocative. Not that provocation justifies such a response. Who do you think murdered her, Dr Harper? She made many enemies for you to choose from.'

'I don't know yet, sir. Who do you think did it?' she asked, daringly.

Dilshan sneered. 'Some people say it was me. Can you believe a minister murdering a journalist? Do you suppose I threw my hands up in the air and exclaimed, "Will none rid me of this turbulent priest?" I resented Ameena. I was enraged by her and disappointed with her. But I did not kill her.' He did sincerity so well. 'My religion tells me to forgive her, so I forgive her.'

'What does your religion tell you about the Tamils in the north, sir?' she asked. The latest US satellite imagery did not show forgiveness from the Sri Lanka Army. They were pulverising the Tamil civilians as well as the Tamil Tigers. This latest military campaign was clearly intended to be the last of its kind, a final solution.

Tenby shifted uncomfortably in his chair, turning to call the waiter and gently nudging her with his foot at the same time. Annoyed, she nudged back harder.

'The planets and Lord Buddha's blessings are on us,' Dilshan declared, as if that explained everything.

'The planets,' Ellie repeated. She thought about Ameena's missing ring.

'Yes. They have aligned auspiciously and we are ready to deal with the problem once and for all.'

'That would be a wonderful achievement sir, where so many others have failed. What is your plan, if you don't mind my asking?'

A military miracle seemed a lot, even for the planets and the Enlightened One.

'That would be revealing military secrets,' Dilshan replied.

'Like the military secrets Ameena Fernando was investigating?' she asked. 'She was about to publish an exposé on it. I've seen the evidence and I know there's a foreign power out there who will not be happy.' Her heart raced. She had nothing, but she had to put some chips on the table. She had to give him something to fear, something worth bargaining for.

'Spurious allegations, Dr Harper. We bought arms using state funds, as we are entitled to do.'

'Ameena's article referred to heavy artillery and cluster bombs—'

'More lies. Although you're hardly in a position to judge us if we *were* using cluster bombs.'

He was right. The US hadn't signed the convention on cluster bombs. Nor had China.

'As you know, we maintain a Zero Civilian Casualty Policy,' Dilshan continued. 'We would never use these kinds of weapons on our own people. China will help us end this war, and then educate our people and export our goods. It's time the US was challenged. There is a new world order and all places are up for grabs.'

'The old-world order could still serve you well, Mr Under Secretary,' Tenby said tentatively. 'We could help you serve your country's interests. We're just asking that you to talk to us more; perhaps talk to us first before you talk to . . . others.'

Ellie chimed in with her support. 'We have the largest aid budget, defence force and surveillance network in the world,' she said.

'You do indeed. Are you willing to trade for it?' Dilshan asked.

'We are willing to *share* it,' Tenby replied.

'Share?'

Ellie made eye contact with Tenby, and he nodded his encouragement. 'Yes, that's what we do with our friends,' she replied. 'Perhaps USAID and the Defence Department could talk to your people about what that might look like. I've worked here before. I know which tickets need to be clipped.'

Dilshan shrugged. 'Perhaps. It's nice to be wanted. To be taken seriously. All we want is to rebuild our country. Ameena saw it differently. She saw it incorrectly and published it inaccurately. For which we were suing her in the Supreme Court of Sri Lanka.'

'Why respond at all? You didn't have to answer to her or refute her.'

'Justice.' The word was grotesque coming out of the man's mouth. Dilshan looked past her shoulder. Solomon was walking towards them. 'Ah, it's time for my weekly security briefing. We work closely with the CIA here, all partners in the war on terror. The axis of good.' He held his hand out, dismissing her.

Ellie stood and turned to Solomon. 'Bill,' she nodded.

'Ellie,' Solomon replied. 'I trust you've not been making trouble.' He looked to the Under Secretary.

'Nothing I couldn't handle,' Dilshan answered. 'She's a little insubordinate, but I'll allow it given her history in Sri Lanka. I'm surprised you let her return.'

'She's been useful in her own way,' Solomon replied. He would never admit that Redmond had overruled him.

'She's been a great help to us,' Tenby said more warmly. 'We've made good progress this afternoon, thanks to her.'

'You guys get together a lot, do you?' Ellie asked Solomon.

'The US is always welcome at my table,' Dilshan answered for him.

'It's business,' Solomon said.

'Funny,' she replied. 'I thought it was politics.'

'If you find out who did this to Ameena, I want to know,' Dilshan declared. 'I am your first call. Do we understand each other?'

'We understand each other,' Solomon replied on her behalf. He took her by the elbow and guided her out.

Through the antechamber, Solomon pulled at his collar, sweat from his neck sliding down into the crevice he'd created. 'Last night I requested your immediate return to the States,' he told Ellie without ceremony.

'I'm still here. I guess you were denied?'

'Redmond asked for forty-eight hours, which is all the Sri Lankans need to assassinate you and hide the body.'

She nodded. 'So not really a stay of execution?'

As soon as her diplomatic immunity was revoked, she would become like any other Sri Lankan citizen—fair game. She had forty-eight hours to get the truth and get out. Thank God Scott had changed her status to High Kidnapping Risk, although the team's recent failure at Pettah troubled her.

'It's expensive and logistically complicated for us to protect you,' he said. 'But even harder to locate and ship back your body.' Solomon exhaled deeply. 'So, set your watch, Ellie. There's a flight scheduled for you in two days. Monday, 2100 hours.'

He adjusted his tie and returned to the hall, leaving her alone in the antechamber.

She walked out past the wall of photographs again, then remembered something Dilshan had said. She did some quick math in her head and walked up and down the walls until she located the photographs from 1965. A much younger Mahinda Rajapaksa, Dilshan Perera and Chaminder Fernando smiled for their team photograph.

'The President and Dilshan and Ameena's father, Chaminder, were childhood friends,' Dougie said, behind her.

'So Ameena would have grown up knowing Dilshan.'

'Like an uncle. Dilshan was once a human rights lawyer who advocated for the land rights of villagers. I know it's hard for you to imagine. You prefer your villains black and your allies white.'

She raised an eyebrow but didn't disagree. 'So how does Dilshan Perera go from human rights lawyer to—'

'Please save your descriptive nouns for the safety of the American Embassy. Power is corruptive and corrosive in Sri Lanka. He wasn't always like that.'

She turned back to him, surprised.

He blushed self-consciously. 'I know—very poetic for an old drunkard?'

'No, I was thinking that it's a very intimate insight into the murder suspect. Do you know everything about everyone?' she asked.

'Often, yes. But in this case . . . come, come,' Dougie beckoned her back through the ages to another photograph. 'There,' he pointed a crooked finger.

She read the names of the cricket team of 1948, the year of Independence. There was Dougie, aged twenty-three and a recently recruited spy for His Majesty George VI. His hair was jauntily parted on the side, unlike everyone else.

'There are generations of ties in Sri Lanka,' he said.

'Generations of power,' she remarked. The surnames in the photographs looked familiar: Bandaranaike, Dissanayake, Jayawardene, Senanayake. The names of presidents, politicians and judges. An inner circle in Sri Lanka that one could only be born into. *Generations of bloodshed and secrets too*, she thought.

They stepped out onto the tiled landing, under the shadow of the Sri Lankan flag. The lion held its sword and slashed away at the glow of the moon behind it in the wind.

Arjuna's car pulled out of valet parking and glided around the driveway.

She thought about the white van that was almost certainly parked outside the gates of the Cricket Club and would follow her back to her hotel. She saw the motorcycle in the parking bay, though not its rider. He was never far behind. He was tracking her effortlessly, unhurried, often without her awareness, until he decided to show himself. She didn't know which was more threatening—empty streets and unseen enemies or the white van and motorcyclist that declared their intentions.

Arjuna's car stopped in front of her. She was grateful she was not alone but also annoyed.

'Where were you? I waited for you at Sathyan's,' she asked.

'I was told the HKR team would pick you up,' Arjuna replied, looking confused. 'Solomon's EA asked me to take him from a meeting at Mount Lavinia to the Cricket Club; something about his usual driver being unwell. What the hell happened to you? You look awful.'

'Thanks so much. The HKR team never came. And that motorcycle—that's the one who's been with me since that first day at Ameena's office. He chased me into Pettah today.'

Arjuna reached over and pulled his camera with its heavy telephoto lens from the glove box.

While he took photos of the motorcycle, she reached for her phone and made a call, then several more. No one answered, so she left messages on voicemail.

Arjuna glanced at her, listening to her urgent words. He put the camera away and took his phone from his shirt pocket. 'Control,' he said to the Embassy switchboard, his voice tense. 'I'm sending two addresses to you—get a couple of teams to both. Now.'

Ellie made another phone call as Arjuna finished his message and started the car.

'If you're hearing this,' she said to the voicemail, almost praying. 'Please get out of the house. Please.'

•

The motorcyclist stood in the shadow of the drivers' quarters. He watched the American woman through the haze of cigarette smoke and pall of the early evening light. She was pretty. Black hair that framed delicate features. Light brown skin that looked like it bruised easily. She had started to notice him too. He liked that.

He pulled his earpiece out and called his contact.

'Did you hear all of that?' he asked. The surveillance in the Club was extensive. Many people had heard the conversation between the American and Dilshan Perera.

'I did. She's still fishing.'

'She has evidence,' the motorcyclist said.

The man cleared his throat, a tic the motorcyclist recognised now. He sneered, waiting for the man to frame his next instructions carefully.

'Not all of it.' The man didn't sound convinced. 'But she's questioning the right people. She'll piece it together soon enough.'

'Do I have the kill order?' The motorcyclist tried not to sound too enthusiastic. He knew enough about the man to recognise that he was morally conflicted about the jobs he ordered. But he was getting better. He had ordered the second hit more confidently and it was the right call. The motorcyclist had been impressed. 'Do I have the kill order?' he repeated.

'No,' the man replied at last. 'No kill order, yet.'

Yet.

'A hurt order. Just hurt—do you understand?' the man asked.

'Yes, of course,' the motorcyclist replied. He had time. And now, so did the American woman. He dropped his cigarette into the dirt and let its embers burn out.

•

'Any word?' Arjuna asked, belatedly pulling his seatbelt across his chest.

'Nothing. No one's answering,' she said, hitting redial on her phone. Still no answer. She left another message.

'Where to, Ellie?' he asked, accelerating hard, the car hurtling down the Cricket Club's long driveway.

She rapidly made her choice—she just hoped she could live with it. 'Colpetty, quickly,' she said, tersely, expecting to see the motorcyclist follow them. She knew he couldn't be far away.

Arjuna nodded, heading fast in the direction of the middle-class suburb. 'Do you think Dilshan did it?'

'Hard to tell. He's had a hand in so many crimes here, it wouldn't be surprising. He's unapologetic and entitled by birth, but I didn't sense the usual dilemma that narcissists have when they've done something wrong.'

'When they need to hide it but they really want to boast about it?'

'Exactly. Have you been inside the Cricket Club lately?' she asked, her fingers hitting redial on her mobile phone.

'It's invitation-only, an elite crowd. I'm afraid I don't cut it.'

'I'm relieved you don't cut it. A lot of familiar names.'

'Sri Lanka,' Arjuna shrugged. 'The same offenders every time.'

She tried to remember where she'd seen a name before. 'Dissanayake? Do you know him?'

'Sure, everybody knows the Dissanayakes. There's more than one. Plantation owners in the hill country. They were tight with the British but switched sides in the 1940s when the independence movement looked successful. Mostly lawyers and judges now.'

Arjuna honked at the bus in front of him and then swerved into the opposite lane, swerving back skilfully before oncoming traffic got anywhere near them.

Ellie was thrown against the car door and then back again. Unfazed, she took the encrypted laptop from her bag and scrolled through documents.

'Lawyers and judges. Judges . . .' she muttered.

'What are you looking for?' Arjuna asked.

'Cyril Dissanayake. He was in the photograph with Dilshan . . .'

'Which photo?'

'On the wall of the Cricket Club.'

'Cyril Dissanayake is a Supreme Court judge. His younger sister is a QC in London, or something fancy like that. I don't remember the exact family tree, but they're all famously upstanding members of the legal community,' Arjuna said.

She finally found what she was looking for in her files. 'Here it is. Supreme Court Justice Cyril Dissanayake authorised a warrant for police to search and seize anything from Ameena's house and office. It was issued the day she died, Sunday eleventh January.'

'That's unusual for three reasons,' Arjuna said, weaving in and out of traffic. 'Firstly, courts are closed on Sundays. Nobody gets a warrant, even the Under Secretary. Secondly, Justice Dissanayake is a pedant for procedural fairness. That warrant is too wide.'

'And thirdly?' she asked.

'Thirdly, in Sri Lanka, the police don't bother with warrants. Anti-terror laws allow them to do whatever they want.'

'This is a little different,' she pointed out. 'If you've been accused of killing a high-profile journalist and the right to free speech with it, you don't want to violate the right to privacy before her body has hit the morgue, do you?'

'Makes sense. You might want the technical permission of a warrant, but I wonder what brought on Dissanyake's change of judicial heart? Blackmail, bribery, or the threat of violence?'

Ellie nodded. 'Perhaps the judge was one of Manisha's clients.' Perhaps he was just a friend of Dilshan's, like Ameena had been once. She thought about Ameena's missing satchel. The warrant and all the searches. Dilshan Perera was looking for that third article. She needed to find it first. After Colpetty.

20

THEN (2005)

Ellie cleared security and entered the Frontal Lobe. The monitors twinkled, every piece of data analysed for patterns and aberrations, for risks and threats.

She sat down across the table from Scott and Tenby and exhaled deeply.

'That kind of day?' Tenby asked.

'That kind of life,' she replied. 'Please tell me you have something that will make my life better.' She looked at the gadgets Scott had assembled on the table.

'I have a range,' he replied.

'Start with the best, Scottie,' Tenby suggested.

Scott used tweezers to hold up a small wire with a knob on the end. 'We could insert this into something that won't get confiscated from him. I'm thinking one of those religious pendants.' He opened a box on his table and took out a small silver cylinder. Inside it was a prayer scroll. 'Here's one I made earlier.'

'For me?' she asked.

'For Solomon; another job. Do you know if the kid wears one of these? Or we could put it into the cyanide capsule he'll be given.'

'The capsule's too risky. What about his inhaler? Could we put a second tracker in an inhaler?'

'A second one? Ellie, I'm not even sure you can have the first one. I'll have to steal this for you as it is. It's state-of-the-art, for high value assets only.'

'He is high value. He's only a kid.' She picked up the pendant and draped it over her wrist.

'Half our assets in the Middle East are kids,' Tenby said. 'Militants aren't the only ones that recruit them. He's not high value until he gets access to something we need. Scottie, can she take this?'

Scott nodded. 'I can spare you one because you're a good guy and the inventory fellas owe me a few favours. Solomon doesn't need to know.'

'Thank you, Scottie,' Ellie said. 'I'll return it to you, I promise.'

'No, you won't. These are never returned. They usually get buried with the body of the asset. Solomon told me you've got a thing with the brother, Ellie. If this goes wrong, I hope you've got a good story for him.'

'It won't go wrong.' She thought about the promise she had made to Sathyan.

'In our line of work, it always goes wrong,' Scott replied. 'We're not running a bakery here. A good day is when the body count is more of them than us.'

•

They took their usual table at the back of the cafe. Ellie cleared her throat, as though something was stuck. She coughed and felt the airway open. She looked Sathyan straight in the face and lied. 'I'm so sorry. We can't do it. I tried every connection I've got. USAID's mandate is humanitarian not political.'

Sathyan's face crumpled. 'This *is* humanitarian. You would be bringing two refugees out of the war zone. I've read the definition of asylum; they meet the standard. They are in genuine fear for their lives if they stay.'

'That case has to be made once they apply to a foreign government for asylum.'

'They will never live to do that. If you can get them to Colombo, the Canadians can help us.'

'The Canadians always promise more than they can deliver. There's another way.' She took a deep breath. 'We can watch him.'

'What?' Sathyan wiped his face and folded his arms across his body to stop shaking.

'Give him this.' She slid the envelope across the table.

'I don't want money, Ellie—'

'It's not money. It's a tracker. One of the tech guys at the Embassy, Scottie, gave it to me for Gajan. Tell him to wear it on his wrist and we will know exactly where he is.'

'What good will that do?'

'USAID will follow him. As soon as he nears the coast, we'll get a Red Cross boat to pick him up. We'll be watching the whole time.'

'Why not pick him up now?'

She coughed lightly and lied again, 'I told you. I'm not allowed to.'

She couldn't tell if he believed her, if he wondered how a USAID employee had access to trackers like the one he was now turning over in his hands.

'Why doesn't the Red Cross just pick everyone up?' he asked.

'They're not allowed to either. The Sri Lankan government doesn't acknowledge that there's a crisis happening in the north. Therefore, according to them, there's no need for the Red Cross to enter domestic waters to make food drops or pick up refugees. I'm surprised any UN ships still manage to get through for food drops, but then again, their remit is slightly different.'

'The government just pretends there isn't a problem and you all go along with it?'

'Pretty much. The Red Cross has to maintain a neutral distance to ensure they can enter conflict zones. It's the only way they can do anything at all.'

He pushed his chair back, jolting the table. 'What about your government? Do you maintain "a neutral distance"?'

'Please keep your voice down.'

'Well?'

'We're doing what we can.' She held his gaze the way she had been trained to do. The way she had done to countless others. 'Please, Sathyan. Give him the tracker and trust me. As soon as he's near a drop zone, I'll send word to the Red Cross and they'll get him out.'

•

Ellie sat next to Scott as he manned the drone. She watched on the large screen as the camera tracked and then hovered over the camp. The camera zoomed in once, twice, then a third time.

'I've been watching this for days now,' Scott yawned.

'Thank you,' she said. 'I know you've got a lot on.'

'It's okay, it's important to you.'

'How many drones cover the region?' she asked.

'More than you'd think. Twelve dedicated to India, plus five for border patrol and the neighbours.'

'Pakistan.'

'The ugliest one of many.'

'It's a rough neighbourhood.'

'Very rough. Karachi is harder to comb than the mountains of Afghanistan. Rumour has it Bin Laden is hiding out there.' He swivelled the camera around and pulled back a little. 'This is addictive. Like some weird reality show where you get a God's-eye view on things.'

'Thank you, Scottie. I mean it,' she repeated.

He nodded. 'Your boy is there. They picked him up five days ago and marched day and night, to here. I think this is a central training hub. I've identified five caches of munitions already.'

She watched the dots move across the screen. Tigers, guns and children. 'Put me through to Redmond.'

Scott dialled the codes, acknowledged Redmond and handed the phone to her.

'Let's take the camp,' she said to her boss.

'It's too early and you know it,' Redmond replied. 'The kid gives us eyes and ears on the ground. I want to know who's in charge and who they're talking to. I want their suppliers. There's an arms trade route that runs from Asia all the way to the Middle East, Africa and then back again. If those assholes are selling to the Tigers, they're selling to the jihadis too.'

She felt sweat trickle down her body despite the air conditioning in the Frontal Lobe. 'He's a kid, not an undercover operative. He isn't trained to extract information.' Sathyan's brother couldn't spy for them. This was getting out of control. She should have known it would.

'Make contact with him and recruit him. Give him a wire.'

'They'll find it.' She said it with certainty. 'There's no privacy in a terrorist training camp. This isn't a restaurant front for the mafia. They'll work out he's spying on them in five seconds and, if he's lucky, they'll execute him immediately.'

'I want the network, Ellie. Talk to Scott about what he can give you. Maybe a response call device so the kid can alert you when he sees something useful. Then you find a way to make contact and get the intel.'

'You're talking about years of cultivation here. Years of setting up a cover. Redmond, the deal was that I put a tracker on him, he leads us to the camp and . . .' her voice trailed away, as she realised the truth. 'You knew all along where the camp was?'

Redmond showed no remorse. 'We had a general vicinity of two thousand square miles but no pinpoint location and I don't get a lot of playtime with the drone to scan the entire Vanni region. So, he saved us a lot of time and money.'

'But you always wanted more,' she replied.

'Yes, *we* always want more. The war on terror is a long game, you know that. We can wipe them out in Afghanistan, but each time we cut the head off this monster, it grows back more powerful and more amoral than before. Every asset in every region counts.'

'Some more than others,' she snapped. 'We will move mountains to keep some safe. This kid's got nothing.'

'This kid doesn't need anything. The Tigers are training him to be a suicide bomber. They won't suspect a fifteen-year-old boy whose biggest crime until now was some culturally unacceptable masturbation in a paddy field.'

'He's too young, too green to learn.'

'We have ten-year-olds in Baghdad noticing the movement of unmarked crates and calling it in. Everyone can learn, especially if they want to live. His chances aren't good with the Tigers. Promise him we'll get him and his family out.'

'I've already promised that to his brother.' The floor was starting to feel closer to her than it should.

'And you're not lying. The timeframe is just different. The quicker you get in there and make contact, the more likely he is to stay alive.'

Redmond was right about that part. She hated him for being right. Ellie knew this negotiation was over before it began. Redmond would get what he wanted.

'Take a team with you,' he continued. 'Whoever you want, as long as they're already in-country.'

'BS are here,' she replied. Barry Sharkey and Shane Bradfield had first worked with her in Pakistan. Collectively, and accurately, they were known as BS. She had requested them for the exhumations in Sri Lanka because they respected the chain of command that came from Redmond and above, adhered to it, as did she, but also understood that everywhere they went, choices were made. Rights and values were traded just as easily as lives. If they could, BS were prepared to do more than the mission scope, without ever compromising the mission itself.

'Fine. I don't know why Sharkey and Bradfield agreed to your Muslim mass grave project in the first place. They're overqualified.'

'What can I say? I'm persuasive. And even ex-Black Ops need a break. I'll take them and Arjuna Diwela. He can pose as my translator again—my Tamil isn't good enough for the north. He has clearance for this.'

'That's a lot of highly trained manpower for one kid.'

'One kid being taken to one camp full of a lot of militants.'
'Terrorists, Ellie.'
'Right.'

The line went dead. She held the phone, listening to the silence. Scott took it from her and returned it to its cradle.

21

NOW (2009)

Arjuna parked the car outside the house in Colpetty and killed the engine. None of the lights were on. When Ellie had left the Cricket Club, her first call had been to Sathyan. No answer at home, work or his mobile phone. Her next calls had been to this house, with no answer either. She kept trying until they pulled up outside the gate.

The gate was open, its lock broken.

Arjuna removed the gun from his ankle holster and chambered a round. He gave it to her, then took his primary weapon from his shoulder. 'Can I depend on you?' he asked.

She took three deep breaths. 'I'll take the front.'

He nodded and broke away from her, heading down the side of the house.

The front door was open. She nudged it wider with her foot, both hands on the gun to keep it steady, her arms tight and outstretched.

The corridor was lined with suitcases, packed and waiting like sentries in the darkness. She walked down the corridor and pushed the first door open. Moonlight cast a milky film over the study. Drawers were open, books and papers piled in haphazard columns.

The study had been searched.

She kept walking. A sudden noise made her turn, gun ready, hands shaking. Nothing. The living room was large and empty. A few paintings had been taken down from the walls and wrapped, resting on each other.

She left the living room and headed down the main hallway towards the staircase.

A shadow appeared at her flank. She swung around again.

'Careful,' Arjuna said. 'Bottom floor clear. Nothing in the kitchen or servants' quarters. The message bank is full. Diary on the kitchen table says the taxi is booked for seven pm—in half an hour. Upstairs?'

'I'll go.' Three deep breaths again, and this time she let her body relax. There was power and strength in the state, if you trusted it.

'I'm right behind you.' He followed her up the stairs. The first door opened into the master bedroom. The bed was covered in clothes, one last suitcase open and half filled. The air held a distant scent, frightening in its familiarity and consequences.

There was another door at the far end of the room. Its lock had been shot through. She pushed it open.

Shirani's body was collapsed in a corner of the bathroom, her head turned away as though she was burrowing into the unforgiving walls for safety. Blood poured from three bullet holes in her back, soaking her shirt and fanning onto the tiles, channelling into the floor drain.

Shoes sparkled under Shirani's body.

'Oh God,' Ellie cried. She tucked her gun into her belt and ran to pull Shirani back. The journalist's eyes were open and frozen.

Ellie let her slide to the floor, her head hitting the tiles with a dull thud.

She lifted Renu's jaw and desperately felt for a pulse. Her skin was still warm but there was no heartbeat.

'Call an ambulance!' she screamed at Arjuna. Her hands were slick with blood. She wiped them on her trousers and checked for a pulse at the child's wrist. She put her ear to the small, still face and listened for breath, but couldn't hear anything over her own ragged breathing.

Arjuna touched her shoulder and she jerked around, slipping in the pool of blood. Shirani's blood—and Renu's.

'We need to keep moving. I've called it in but we need to get out. There's nothing left here, Ellie.' He pulled her up and steadied her.

She looked at him. His face was contorted by grief as well as the warp and weft of damaged skin on his face.

She focused. She had seen something else in the room.

The open suitcase on the bed had a Canadian guidebook in it. Ellie opened the first page. It was inscribed.

> *Dearest Shirani,*
> *You are my best friend.*
> *All my love, Ameena.*

She flicked urgently through the book. The pages fell open at a photograph of the two women. Younger, arms around each other, unguarded and unconditional.

She kept flicking through it and stopped on a receipt used as a bookmark. She crushed it into her pocket and returned the guidebook to the suitcase.

'Ready.' She followed Arjuna out the door, back down the staircase and into the corridor lined with bags. Her eyes blurred.

A screech of jeeps and police cars pulled up outside the house.

'That was fast,' she said to Arjuna.

'Too fast,' he returned, troubled. 'Put your hands high in the air, Ellie. No sudden movements. Not one.' He followed his own instructions and walked out slowly with his hands up. He spoke clearly in Sinhalese and English. 'Do not shoot. My name is Arjuna Diwela. I am US Embassy security. I am carrying a weapon that is holstered. Above us,' he pointed to the sky, 'is an American drone. They are watching me, my colleague Ellie Harper, and you. Do not shoot,' he repeated.

Ellie kept her arms raised. The soldiers circled them. Arjuna told them where their weapons were in Sinhalese. Two men stepped forward, confiscated their guns and then searched them roughly for more.

Behind them there was shouting in the house as the bodies of Shirani and Renu were discovered. The soldiers turned back to Ellie and Arjuna, rifles poised. There was a blow to Ellie's back, the sharp stab of a rifle butt. She sank to her knees and focused on pulling air into her lungs. The receipt was still in her pocket.

The soldiers cuffed her hands in front of her and dragged her with Arjuna to the waiting jeep.

•

The vehicles stopped at the gates of the Criminal Investigation Department. The soldiers spoke to the guards, repeatedly motioning to Ellie and Arjuna. The guards flashed torches in their faces and waved them through.

She still had her phone, which meant that Scott knew where she was. He had found her once before, he could do it again.

There was supposed to be an HKR team on her twenty-four seven and extraction teams on standby at the Embassy, loaded up and ready for this exact situation. Solomon didn't like her, but he would have scrambled a rapid response unit immediately and woken up the Ambassador. Standard response time was three minutes to exit the Embassy, and at this time of night, eighteen minutes to intercept, max. They should have arrived at the CID building by now.

The jeep doors flung open. 'This doesn't look good,' she said to Arjuna. She was dragged out and shoved against the bonnet of the car.

'No talking,' the soldier commanded, before he drove a fist into her gut. She fell to her knees, gasping. Something rose from her stomach into her mouth and she swallowed it back down, gagging. She dropped onto her side on the dusty cement of the car park, knees curled up to her chest.

He jeered and said something in Sinhalese to the others who laughed. Ellie caught the words *American* and *lawyer*. The soldier grabbed her arm and tried to lift her, but she was heavy and slipped out of his hands. He tried again but she lay still and unmoving on the ground.

He retracted his foot, ready to deliver another blow to her gut. The shiny black boot came towards her. She caught it in her cuffed hands, lifted her body into a sitting position and twisted his foot around at the same time, using his own momentum to topple him next to her.

Another soldier cocked his rifle and pushed it into her face.

'I insist that you call the US Embassy,' she said calmly. 'Ask for Bill Solomon. He's the Embassy's Head of Security and a friend of Mahinda Rajapaksa.'

The soldier pulled Ellie's cuffs roughly towards him. '*President* Mahinda Rajapaksa,' he said. 'Your embassy has been called. We'll see if they come.'

They would come. She was still under Solomon's protection and he left no one behind.

Ellie and Arjuna were dragged through several corridors, past locked doors. Soldiers came in and out of the cells. In one, she saw a naked man tied to a chair, his head hanging forward against his chest. His skin was striated with long, thick welts. A soldier stood over him, a leather belt slung over his shoulder. The buckle glistened with blood.

The soldiers stopped at a cell door and Ellie and Arjuna were pushed inside. Ellie was forced into a chair, her cuffs unlocked, her arms twisted behind her back and re-cuffed painfully. Arjuna was shoved into the seat beside her. He laced his feet around the legs of his chair.

'I'm not very good with torture anymore, Ellie,' he said to her in Spanish. It was one of their shared languages, alongside English and Hindi.

'Todo va a estar bien,' Ellie whispered rapidly in return. 'No te preocupe.' *Everything will be all right. Don't worry.*

A soldier stepped forward and punched him.

'I'm an American citizen—' she shouted.

A voice behind them. 'You're an American spy.' An older man emerged from the shadows wearing the markings of a Sri Lankan general. 'And you've been investigating the death of Ameena Fernando.' He walked around them as he spoke.

She willed herself to keep her eyes forward.

He leaned down behind her. 'We've learned the science of enhanced interrogation from the CIA, Dr Harper. What shall we extract from you first?'

She closed her eyes and braced for the pain but it didn't come. He stood up and gave instructions to the soldier, who rolled up his sleeves and undid his collar.

'Tell me about your illegal investigation.'

She thought about Scott, and the team that was on its way. If she could just buy him some time. 'I'm here to help USAID draft the terms of our aid package. Once the war is over, you'll implement a transitional justice program. There are many parts to that program that we can fund, but we need to be sure what that funding will be used for. I'm reviewing your existing aid infrastructure so we can build on it.'

Please, Scottie, she thought.

The general nodded to one soldier, who punched Arjuna in the face. His head snapped back, rocking the chair back. The soldier put a foot on Arjuna's knee, steadying it. 'You need to understand something, Dr Harper. While I can't hurt you just yet, I can hurt him. And look at him.' The general put his hand in Arjuna's hair and pulled his head roughly back, inspecting the distorted skin. 'Look at this monster. What's a few more scars? Would anyone notice them?' He dropped Arjuna's head and walked back around to her. 'You were saying?'

'I . . . I'm investigating the death of Ameena Fernando, on the instructions of the State Department.'

'On the instructions of State, or *outside* the instructions of State?' he asked.

She swallowed hard. Who had he been speaking to? Would Solomon betray her? He had told her to stay alive. 'Ameena has family in the US. They petitioned our government to look into it.'

'The Sri Lankan government is already looking into it. Any American investigation has no jurisdiction or authority. *You* have no jurisdiction or authority.'

The soldier flexed his hand and balled it into a fist again.

'Wait,' she shouted. 'I wasn't supposed to do a full investigation. I was supposed to confirm the findings of the government's investigation and reassure the family that every effort was being made here to identify her killer.'

'And why have you disobeyed your orders?'

That was a good question. In the past, she had never disobeyed the CIA. She had gone beyond what was required of her, but never against it. This was different.

'I'm not sure why,' she answered honestly.

The general nodded and the soldier hit Arjuna again. He groaned and spat blood on the floor.

'Ameena's partner Sathyan was . . . is a friend of mine,' she offered reluctantly.

'Sathyan Navaratnam. You were lovers once.'

'Yes.'

'Are you lovers now?'

'No, not now.'

'You've been diligent for your ex-lover. And what have you found out? What has your investigation yielded? Was it the Sri Lankan government? Perhaps the Chinese? What did Shirani Dennis tell you before you killed her?' He motioned to her bloodied clothing.

'I didn't kill her,' she replied, knowing this to be a lie. The woman had been thirty minutes away from a cab ride to the airport, to freedom and safety. Shirani and Renu, with the sparkling shoes and the High School Musical pencil case. It was Ellie's fault.

She was conscious of the receipt in her pocket. The soldiers had ignored it when they searched her for weapons.

'I didn't kill her,' she repeated. 'I went there tonight because I thought she was hiding something. I wanted to talk to her again before she left.'

'It's a shame she never made it.' The general pulled a chair in front of her and sat down. 'Shirani Dennis and her daughter, sweet little thing. What did she tell you?'

'Nothing, nothing useful.'

Another soldier stepped forward, swinging his rifle at Arjuna, this time a blow to the side, sending his chair toppling into Ellie. His bloodied face against hers, his breathing ragged in her ears. She pressed her lips to his scarred face in silent apology, tasting sweat and tears. Tasting his blood.

'Try harder, Ellie,' the general suggested.

The first soldier grabbed Arjuna by the shirt and pummelled his face with three quick blows to the nose. She heard bone crack as blood gushed down Arjuna's shirt.

'Stop it, please,' she cried. 'Shirani thought Ameena was working on another story—a secret story. Ameena hadn't told her about it, at least that's what she said. I thought if I could find out what it was about, I could work out who killed her . . .' Her mind was racing. Where was Solomon? Where was the HKR team? They'd let her down twice today—something was horribly wrong. She needed more time and she needed the soldier to stop hurting Arjuna.

'It's too late now,' she said. 'I don't know much more than when I started. Ameena was investigating the Sri Lankan and

Chinese governments. Maybe they killed her, but I have no proof. The only person who might have known more is dead.'

The general nodded to the soldier, who lifted Arjuna's head again. A purple bruise radiating across the smashed bridge of his nose, his face sticky with blood. He pushed Arjuna's head back with one hand and curled the fingers of the other.

'Wait!' she cried. 'Wait! I've told you everything I know!'

The soldier raised his fist high.

The door opened.

'That's enough, gentleman,' said Tenby. 'Jesus Christ.' He looked at Arjuna and shook his head. 'You'll hear from the Embassy about this.' He extracted a folded piece of paper from his pocket. 'I have a release request from the Ambassador.'

The soldiers huddled around Tenby's paperwork.

He signalled to two US soldiers behind him, who stepped forward and lifted Arjuna, dragging him easily to the door.

Ellie felt the cuffs fall from her wrists. She brought her trembling hands to her lap and rubbed them hard.

Tenby offered her his arm but she shook her head.

'Where the *fuck* were you, Tenner?'

22

THEN (2005)

Ellie gave the soldier a pile of passports and papers. He slung his assault rifle over his shoulder and opened the first passport. The gun slipped forward and hit the WHO emblem on the door of her jeep.

Her papers showed that she was setting up mobile clinics in the region. WHO's work gave her a legitimate opportunity to enter the militarised zone, track Gajan and use the clinics to move around while staying close to him. It was safer and more effective than her usual USAID cover.

'Out,' the soldier motioned to her and the others.

'It's all there,' she smiled and pointed to the papers. She had the right documents for Arjuna, her translator, and the WHO employees, Barry Sharkey and Shane Bradfield. They were the last vehicle in the four-car convoy that was headed for Mankulam, eighty-seven miles from the location of the Tiger training camp.

'Out,' the soldier repeated, pulling the handle on Sharkey's side. Two more soldiers stepped forward and started a cursory search of the vehicle. She wasn't worried. Bradfield had hidden four 9-mm and sixteen rounds of ammunition deep in the chassis of their jeep, as well as three light vests. He knew exactly where to put it, but that was all he could fit. They couldn't risk more.

'Sure,' Sharkey replied. 'No problem, chief.' He got out of the jeep, unfolding his six foot five frame very slowly. The early morning sunlight picked up the red flecks in his curly brown hair and beard.

The soldier stepped back, dropped the papers and fumbled with his weapon, hauling it back into place.

Arjuna emerged from the driver's side, arms raised, and spoke rapidly in Sinhalese, explaining that Sharkey and Bradfield were there as sprayers with the dengue fever eradication program.

The soldier shouted at them again, moved his hand in a circular motion and then returned it to his weapon, steadying the gun in his hands and lifting it so it was angled up towards Sharkey's chest.

'No problem, chief,' Sharkey repeated. He turned around slowly, hands in the air. Tucked into the back of his pants was an *Empire* film magazine from a few months ago. The soldier pulled it out. 'You can take that, I've finished with it. Although, may I?' Sharkey tentatively reached for the magazine and flicked through its pages. He stopped at a picture of Aishwarya Rai, Bollywood goddess and star of the recent *Bride and Prejudice*. He kissed the picture and gave the magazine back to the soldier, who laughed.

'Papers.' The soldier kicked at the papers on the ground. 'You go.' He gave the magazine to another soldier.

Sharkey picked up the papers and passed them through the window to Ellie. He got back in the car and said, 'Take good care of Aishwarya.'

The soldiers saluted him with the magazine and let them through.

'I can't believe you gave them Aishwarya.' Bradfield shook his head. 'I wouldn't give her up for anyone.'

'No choice, mate,' Sharkey shrugged. 'Plus, I have more in my kit. *Vanity Fair* did a nice spread after the Oscars. I'd like to see what choices Hilary makes after *Million Dollar Baby*.'

'Agreed. That was a helluva performance,' Bradfield replied.

'Okay enough BS, thank you. Sharkey, nice work with the magazine,' Ellie interrupted. 'We've got an hour's drive to the WHO clinic. The medics will rotate. Four teams in, three teams out. Arjuna and I will do basic field patch-ups and vaccinations. Any serious medical issues will have to be seen by the real medics. Arjuna will handle the triage and send critical patients to the other teams. I'll identify the asset.'

'You better get that triage right, Arjuna,' Bradfield teased. 'Don't want sir here to have to do surgery.'

'My surgical skills are better than yours,' Ellie retorted.

'Post-mortems don't count. My field surgery is excellent, never lost a soldier or a limb.'

'It's true. He's pretty good with a medi-kit,' Sharkey confirmed. 'And he's actually been, you know, in the field.'

'I've been in the field,' she said.

'You've been *near* the field,' Arjuna corrected. 'Or you go into the field after we've cleared it for you. You and the other report-writers.'

'Not to disrespect you, sir,' Bradfield soothed her. 'Your intel is always the best and I trust the plays you call. There's no one I'd rather have in my earpiece than you.'

'Me too,' Sharkey echoed. 'You've got a great brain, sir. And a uterus of steel, if you don't mind me saying. You ask for the jobs other agents wouldn't dare.'

'Thank you, Sharkey,' she said, looking out the window.

They were right. Ellie was trained for the field as all agents at her level needed to be. She could defend herself, but she wouldn't kill unless she had to. Sharkey and Bradfield killed first and read movie magazines to avoid thinking about it later.

They were a good team. She could go into the field, interview survivors and piece together what had happened. She could evaluate which broken bodies meant broken laws, and which laws were worth defending. But she needed these guys to go in first. On this mission, Sharkey, Bradfield and Arjuna were there as her protection detail and the extraction team if necessary. She didn't have the authorisation to exfiltrate Gajan, but—as BS always said—she needed options.

The key to staying alive in the field was having options.

•

The local Tiger leadership had agreed to allow their cadres to come to the clinic for tetanus boosters. Arjuna was in the tent at the other end of the clinic, giving a group a public health session on dengue prevention and management in Tamil. Ellie had a small window of opportunity, and she had to make it count.

Ellie wrapped the used sterile kit in its packaging and threw it in the bin like a basketball.

'Good shot,' the boy said in English, almost smiling.

'Thank you. I have three younger brothers who think they coach me,' she replied, re-gloving her hands and then opening another sterile kit. She unfurled it on the table beside her. 'Take off your shirt please, I want to listen to your chest. Let's see how your lungs are doing.' She pulled the stethoscope out of her pocket and placed it around her neck as the boy moved to comply. 'Gajan,' she began quietly.

The boy jumped, startled. 'How do you know my name?'

'I know your brother, Sathyan. We're good friends. We work together.'

'Is he okay? Is my mother okay?' he asked.

'They are absolutely fine. They miss you and they're really worried about you.'

'Are you the lady that's going to get me out?'

'I am. But not yet. This isn't the right time. How are you?'

'How am I?'

'Yes, how are you?' she repeated.

Gajan finished removing his shirt in answer. The skin on his stomach had been stripped off in patches, as though rubbed with steel wool. He lifted his elbows. The skin around them and on the underside of his forearms was raw.

'What were you doing?' she whispered, lifting his arms gently. She didn't know which ointment would soothe this.

'Training. Getting ready to fight when the war starts again.' He pulled his elbow away and clasped his hands in his lap. He looked so young. He *was* so young.

'Are you allowed to keep things, Gajan? Like personal items?' she asked.

'A few, not a lot.'

'Okay. This is your asthma inhaler, a new one, but not a real one. If you turn the internal canister like this, it turns it on. And then, if you want to meet, you press it three times. It emits a signal on a frequency I'll be monitoring.'

'Are you a spy? That looks like James Bond,' he said.

'It's better than James Bond, actually. If there's something you need to tell me, you can effectively call me. I can meet you at the clinic. Tell them you're having trouble with your asthma.'

Gajan stared at his hands. She tried to reach out to him again. 'Sathyan said you like electronics, that you're good with your hands. You like making fish traps and Lego robots?'

'Yes. Now I make bombs.'

'Hang in there, Gajan. I want to get you out. I'm trying. But until I can do that, while you're still at the camp, I'd like you to help me.'

'Are you an American spy?' he asked again. 'Sathyan said you help refugees. But you sound like a spy.'

'No, I'm not a spy. I'm trying to help you. But I need you to help me first.'

'You want me to spy on my friends for you?' he asked.

'No. I don't want you to do that. I just want you to keep watching and thinking about what you're seeing. Pay attention without looking like you're paying attention. Can you do that?'

'You mean spying.'

'I mean paying attention to the details. Like who's in charge, who's bringing your weapons. Who's bringing your bomb parts. Listen out for words like Semtex.'

When he didn't say anything, she touched him on the arm and he recoiled from her. His scrawny arms were covered in bruises. His eyes were filled with fear.

•

Arjuna shut the door behind him. 'How many did you see today?'

'Forty-three. Some with fever but not as widespread as I expected. A lot of tetanus shots, and I'm almost out of antibiotics.'

'We're lucky we were allowed to keep any at all,' he noted.

She had worked with Arjuna and BS on two tours in Pakistan over the past eighteen months. They had been embedded with health units in other countries before and understood the currency of medication. On previous missions, their meds had been confiscated by the Army or the militia, depending on which region they were in. She had handed out vitamins and interviewed civilians; Arjuna and BS scoped the cities and countryside for terrorists.

'Good to know the WHO still have some clout. They'll clear out when the fighting starts up again. Properly,' Arjuna qualified, when Ellie raised her eyebrows. 'In-fighting between Tiger factions doesn't count. I mean when everything goes to complete shit again.'

'Won't be long now,' she predicted. 'Both sides have rested well during the ceasefire. They've re-armed, replenished their human cannon fodder, that kind of thing. They've had some time to plan a genocide or a futile secessionist movement.'

'It's not futile, Ellie. The Tigers control one-fifth of the island. They are a state in all but international recognition.'

'Yes, and international acceptance of their methods has changed. 9/11 took care of that. The question is, which superpower will fill the Sri Lankan government's begging bowl with the arms they need to finish this?' She suddenly felt exhausted. How many of the people she had seen today would survive the next conflict?

'Your intel is telling you another big offensive is coming?' he asked.

'Don't need any intel or a crystal ball. Just a history book. The two-state solution won't work in Israel and it won't work here for much the same reason.' She sprayed down the table and wiped it clean. The astringent smell of disinfectant filled her nostrils. 'It's inevitable. They'll fight to the death.'

23

NOW (2009)

Ellie gently tilted Arjuna's head back in Tenby's car and packed his nose with tissues to staunch the flow of blood. He winced, tears streaming down the small gullies and crevices of his skin. She wiped his face and neck with more tissues.

Solomon had sent two extraction teams and Tenby. She watched the two black SUVs overtake them and enter the US Embassy first. Once they had passed through the security portals, Tenby's driver took them into the underground car park.

Ellie helped Arjuna stand properly. He needed a doctor and painkillers. She needed her medication, too.

'Solomon's waiting for you in the Frontal Lobe,' Tenby said, leading them through the bowels of the building to the surveillance room where Scott was at his computer screens, looking suspiciously like he hadn't moved for days.

Solomon was standing over him, reviewing information on Scott's screens. When he saw her, his face flushed an angry red. Arjuna must have seen it too, because he tightened his arm around her shoulder which was holding *him* up. She helped him over to the nearest chair and braced herself.

Scott grimaced when he saw Arjuna's face. He called for a medi-kit.

'What the fuck happened out there?' Solomon growled. 'Once again, you've left behind a trail of bodies, and then you wind up at the CID. You could have been killed.'

He paused, his arms folded across his chest. Tenby shifted uncomfortably on his feet, eyes down. The only sound was Arjuna's heavy breathing through his blood-clotted sinuses and smashed cartilage.

'Well?' Solomon demanded, taking a step towards her. Tenby moved back instinctively.

'Sorry, sir, I wasn't sure if you'd finished,' Ellie said, her body still trembling with rage. Tenby had placed Arjuna and her in grave risk; when she confronted him, he'd mumbled some excuse about delays at the Cricket Club and Colombo traffic. He was wise to move back. She wanted to kill him.

'Don't you fucking give me cheek, Harper.'

'Honestly, sir, I don't mean to. You're right, I could have been killed, or worse, Arjuna could have been killed.'

'Damn straight,' Solomon said, looking over at Arjuna who was collapsed in his chair. '*He* would be a great loss to us.'

'At the Cricket Club, I saw the same man who's been following me in Colombo,' Ellie said, her brain trying hard to shift gears, calm the adrenaline and give Solomon the briefing he wanted. The faster she could brief him, the faster she could get out of the Embassy. She knew where to go next. With that single receipt in the Canadian guide book, Ameena Fernando had helped her one last time before she died. 'Arjuna and I called

Shirani Dennis and Sathyan Navaratnam repeatedly to alert them to potential danger. Arjuna called it in to the Embassy as well. Then we proceeded to Shirani Dennis' home first—'

'Why *her* home first?' Solomon demanded.

Ellie swallowed hard. The pain that was balled in her chest from the moment she had seen the sparkling shoes on the bathroom floor, unfurled itself and crept up her body, threatening to choke her.

Solomon nodded and then tilted his head, as if choosing his next words carefully. 'For the rest of your life, that will feel like your fault. For *now*, I need to know what to say to the Sri Lankan government, and to Redmond, given you were almost killed.'

'Tell them I was doing my job. The investigation into Ameena Fernando's death led me to her colleague Shirani Dennis. We were devastated to find her . . .' Ellie hesitated and pressed on. 'The CID picked us up at her house and understandably thought we were responsible. They did exactly what I would have done. They interrogated us with reasonable force.' She did not look at Arjuna as she continued. 'We're grateful you intervened when you did, but there's something wrong with the HKR team's comms, sir.'

'Excuse me?' Solomon said. Communications with Special Ops were critical to the safety of their people.

'I've called them twice today, and twice they were either a no-show or delayed.'

'That's ridiculous—'

'It's true sir,' Arjuna said, his voice muffled by the tissues and clotting blood.

'We need to look into it,' Ellie said. A breakdown in comms or command would land on the station chief's desk.

'I know what we need to do, thank you, Ellie,' Solomon said curtly, turning to Scott. 'I'm sure there's a reasonable explanation.'

'On it,' Scott said, swinging his chair back to one of his computers.

'Thank you, sir,' Ellie said. 'I'm done here. Please tell the Sri Lankan government that I'm going home soon and I'm using my remaining time to say my goodbyes.'

Solomon exhaled loudly. 'I'm not the enemy here, Ellie,' he said. 'We've all got a job to do and at the end of the day, it's about protecting US interests.'

'I know that, sir, and I'm grateful for the time you've given me.'

'I told Redmond I'd give you time and I keep my word with him—*generally*. You've got thirty-five hours left and then you get on that plane, or you accept that I can't protect you. No matter how much Redmond cares about you. Do you understand?'

She nodded.

'Clean yourselves up and then let's run down the clock without losing anyone else, shall we? I'm going for a smoke. Yes, I know I've got cancer.' Solomon didn't wait for a response. He turned and left, the others silent until he'd cleared the door of the Frontal Lobe.

Ellie turned to Scott. 'What have you got for me?'

'Not what you want. The HKR team comms will take some looking into and I haven't cracked the Tardis yet. I don't even know where its off-site is. Could be anywhere. All I can tell you is that it's made in China.'

'I could have told you that. Isn't all technology made in China?' Arjuna said, every word making him wince.

Scott tossed the box of tissues to him. 'No, I mean the encryption was designed in China. They have a certain laconic programming style. Their own vernacular, if you will. The Tardis was programmed to copy all data from the smartboard and whatever it was synced to. Presumably Ameena Fernando's computer, her phone and the server of the newspaper.'

'Could the Tardis hold that much data?' she asked.

'It can *pull* that much data. It downloads and transfers quickly and continuously, too.'

'Meaning?'

'Meaning that once you insert it, it senses new data being added to whatever it's leeching off, and it will mine that too. It's a proactive device. Once it's programmed properly, it just executes its mission without further instruction. A bit like Arjuna here.'

'Thank you.' Arjuna nodded, the movement making his eyes water. The tissues were soaked red.

'If the encryption is Chinese, are we looking at the MSS?' Ellie asked.

'I think so,' Scott nodded. 'The Ministry of State Security is very well equipped.'

'We know that Ameena was investigating Ming-Na Wu, ostensibly a Chinese agri-business with some interesting product diversification. Could they have planted this to find out what Ameena knew about their arms deal?'

'Yes, if they could get it in there,' Scott said. 'They could pay anyone to do that. A cleaner, maybe.'

Tenby cleared his throat nervously. 'What do you know about this deal, Ellie?' he asked. 'Do you know who her source was?'

She was still angry at her friend, but now that Arjuna was safe and Solomon hadn't marched her to the airport, she was calming down—a little.

'No, no idea about the source, Tenby,' she replied. 'And nothing more on the deal than what was published by Ameena.

I lied to Dilshan, back at the Club. All of the evidence, the hard drives, even the scraps of paper are gone.' She didn't tell Tenby about the last notebook. Or the receipt she had taken from Shirani's home. She tried again not to think about the child on the bathroom floor. 'What did you come up with on Ming-Na Wu, Scottie?'

'Not much. China doesn't have the same public disclosure requirements we do.'

'Yes, because you're so honest about everything,' Arjuna said.

'I can see you're in pain, so it feels inappropriate to make fun of you, but you sound like Kermit the Frog,' Scott said.

'I *am* in pain and I'd like to share it with you.'

Scott smirked, then returned to Ellie's question. 'China doesn't have an equivalent of the SEC, nor can I just make a request under the Freedom of Information Act, which they also don't have. The company isn't listed on the Shanghai Stock Exchange. I eventually identified its board of directors—which includes Kwan.' He tapped away on his computer. 'Its agribusiness is legitimate, by the way. It's a key producer of farming equipment, fertilisers and pesticides. Kwan's daughter runs its charitable foundation, which works with impoverished rural communities in China.'

'What about its transaction history?' Tenby asked. 'That should give us some clues.'

'Good question. It's telling by its absence. I can't find anything, no sales outside of China,' Scott replied.

'And inside China?' Ellie probed, without much hope.

Scott shook his head. 'Its main client is the PRC, but there was nothing noticeable. No transactions marked "Illegal Weapons for Export", sorry.' Scott closed down two windows and opened up a new site. 'As for its lineage—MNW didn't exist before 2003, and its holding companies still barely exist.'

'Who's behind the curtain?' she asked.

'No idea. Someone who doesn't want to be seen,' Scott replied.

'Could Ameena have taken a peek and died for it?' Tenby asked.

'Maybe,' Ellie said. Ameena, Shirani and Renu. The last two were on her. There was a husband and two children waiting in Canada. The pain continued to spread through her chest. 'Scottie, keep working on the Tardis and MNW for me if you have time.'

'Sure, there's a civil war raging in the north but I'll crack on with this,' he sniped.

'I thought we weren't engaging in the war in the north. We're sitting this one out, aren't we?'

'We are,' Tenby replied. 'But we still like to keep an eye on things. Our drones fly a grid over the South Asian quadrant, right down to the third parallel north in the Indian Ocean. We're always watching the Thoroughfare. With China rising, it's more important now than it ever was.'

'And the north? Are you watching that too?' Ellie asked.

'Yes,' Scott replied. 'Although it's the east we're more interested in.'

'Show me.'

Scott zoomed in on the north-eastern quarter of the island. 'Troops moving this way—those purple patches are a convoy of refugees.'

'How many?'

'Easily three-hundred thousand,' Scott replied. 'Moving slowly that way, towards the coast. Red Cross ships stationed here, here and here.' He pointed to spots in the Indian Ocean. 'They're waiting.'

'Can you identify the weaponry?' Ellie asked.

'I can. But I need Solomon's approval to play with the satellites. I'm not allowed to just harness the Frontal Lobe's toys at will. What are you looking for—any weapons in particular? Chinese ones perhaps?' he asked.

Ellie shrugged.

'It's not illegal to sell weapons to another sovereign nation. American arms companies do it all the time,' Tenby said. She saw a flicker of something in his face but couldn't be sure what it was. Once an agent, always an agent. Even one who'd left the Agency for Embassy life remembered his passionate defence of American foreign policy.

'Immoral, perhaps, but not illegal,' she said.

'It's not immoral to help a country defend itself,' Tenby replied.

'That's the grey area, isn't it?' Ellie replied. 'The Sri Lankans might buy legal weapons, but we're powerless to stop them from using those weapons illegally on their own unarmed people. The Tamil people are still citizens and, in most cases, *civilians*, of Sri Lanka.'

'I don't know what you expect me to say, Ellie. I'm a diplomat trying to influence tyrants. I'm not the buyer here.' Tenby pulled at his collar to scratch his neck.

'True, we're *sellers* in this scenario. And we are bound by international law *not* to sell weapons that have an indiscriminate effect—such as cluster munitions. What if we know what our weapons are being used for and we sell them anyway?'

'We're not here to debate the morality of the arms trade,' Tenby argued. 'It exists whether we like it or not, and we have to participate in it as buyers, sellers and regulators. The security of the United States depends on our ability to engage in that market in an informed and empowered manner.'

'"An informed and empowered manner"? Jesus, Tenby, who taught you to say that—Bell Pottinger? You should go to confession and atone for that bullshit immediately.'

'Ellie, I'm trying to help the US *and* you, but you make it really fucking hard. Has anyone ever told you you're a sanctimonious hypocrite?' Tenby replied.

'I *have* heard that before, yes. You know that UN Weapons Inspectors will eventually get hold of this information.'

'And *you* know, Ellie, that UN Weapons Inspectors only ask questions if they are pushed by a foreign government to do so,' he snapped. 'They don't initiate inspections out of concern for public safety and human rights.'

'And cinnamon isn't as valuable as oil, I get it. I've got work to do and Arjuna needs to clean up.'

'I'm fine.' Arjuna replaced the bloodied tissue in his nose with a fresh one. 'Nothing a double shot of morphine won't fix. Scottie, my car is back at Shirani Dennis' house. There's a camera in the glove box, with photos of a Person of Interest. The one who's been stalking Ellie. He's got all the makings of a hired gun and maybe even a suspect in Ameena Fernando's shooting.'

'I'll send a team,' Scott said. 'Let's see if the car or camera is still there.'

'One more thing,' Ellie said.

'Just one?' Scott retorted.

'Okay—a few things, please Scottie. Let me know if you work out what weapons the Army is using,' Ellie asked. 'The more detail the better. And the Tardis—I presume it pulled the newspaper's entire server as well as her personal docs. Let's see if you can do better than the Chinese security service.'

'I'll do my best,' Scott replied. He flicked between the screens in front of him faster than her eyes could track.

Tenby stayed her departure with one hand. 'I don't know what this has to do with Ameena Fernando's death, Ellie. You're going far beyond your mandate now. You've upset the Sri Lankan Under Secretary and irritated the Chinese cultural attaché—'

'That's your concern about my conduct? I've upset a despot and irritated a diplomat?'

'He has a point, Ellie. You've alienated high-ranking officials of two countries, one whose soil we're standing on, the other who's a key threat to our security,' Arjuna said.

'Sorry, Arjuna. Scottie's right, you do sound like Kermit.'

'Kermit is a superstar,' Arjuna replied.

Sharkey had loved Kermit. He used to do a note-perfect rendition of 'Rainbow Connection'.

'Ellie, we want a seat at this table.' Tenby shook his head. 'You've been arrested once and it wasn't pretty. We've only got so many Get Out of Jail Free cards, and I'm not sure Solomon will play another on you. Don't fuck everything up because you still feel guilty about the little brother.'

She thought about Gajan. Like him, Renu would be a child forever. Ellie would have to live another day.

'That's not what this is about, Tenby. Not anymore, anyway.'

•

Ellie signed three sets of papers for the new car, took the keys and went outside, walking across the compound to the Embassy's open car park. She'd been given a small sedan with local plates. The early morning sun filtered through the reinforced steel gate. She realised she hadn't slept or eaten. She looked at her watch. 0600 hours. She had twenty-nine hours left before what little diplomatic protection she had in Sri Lanka ended. Arjuna joined her at the car.

'You ready?' she asked him.

His face was swollen, with bruises spreading across the bridge of his nose, but the bleeding had stopped. 'What are we waiting for?' he asked.

'A smoke break.'

'You don't smoke.'

The back door to the building opened and Scott stepped out. He walked casually over to them, his eyes avoiding the cameras all over the compound.

'You're still here,' he said, flipping open a pack of cigarettes and offered it to both of them. Arjuna declined but Ellie reached for one. She used the lighter Scott held out, shielding the flame with her hands.

'I'd like you to check one more mobile phone for me, please,' she whispered. 'Calls made, between him and Ameena, over the six months leading up to her death.'

'Whose phone?'

She drew the smoke into her mouth and then breathed it out. She repeated the act, creating a screen of smoke around her lips. She dropped her voice again and said the name.

He lit a cigarette for himself. 'Solomon won't like it.'

'He doesn't need to know.' She had a hunch. Was it a hunch? More of a growing fear. 'Cross-reference it, please.'

'"Please"?' Scott raised his eyebrows. 'Okay, sure. Just so you know, Solomon's running down the clock.'

'Then what? He washes his hands of me?'

'Don't be so dramatic. Then he has a team prepped to exfiltrate you, with or without your consent. It's for your own protection.'

'He's done a stellar job of that so far.'

'You're still alive, aren't you?' Scott threw the cigarette stub on the ground.

'He could exfil me right now—lock the Embassy gate, take my passport and put me on a plane back home.'

'He could, but Tenby pleaded your case.' He exhaled. 'It's a beautiful country, Ellie.' Scott said. 'So much potential and goodness. Light within the darkness. Light despite it. I've been here a long time. There's a reason you're drawn back, and it's not just the men.'

Ellie smiled sadly. Maybe it was the dead women. 'Did you get everything I asked for?'

He nodded. 'The gear's all in the boot. I put in a few extras, just in case. Meds too—for Arjuna and your anxiety and hemostatic gauze for gunshot wounds.'

'Thank you, Scottie. I never . . .' She stopped and tried to frame her words properly, more words that were four years overdue. 'Before. You found us in time. You saved us.' She floundered. 'I never thanked you for what you did for me; for us.'

'You didn't have to. It's my job, Ellie. I wish I'd got there earlier.'

She did too.

She turned to Arjuna as Scott left them to walk back towards the Embassy's back door. 'Do you think you can drive?' The bruising across his face was becoming visible under his dark skin.

'Are you serious?'

'Yes. I need to get somewhere without being followed. I don't know who's outside waiting for us.'

'Let me tell you who's there—a white van, the CID and that motorcycle we can't shake.' Arjuna peered into the car's side mirror. 'God, Ellie. Look at my face. My Miss Universe days are well and truly over.'

'I know and I'm sorry. You had such a bright future in that competition.' She pulled out the receipt from her pocket and straightened it, but kept it covered from the CCTV positioned strategically in the Embassy car park. 'We need to go here . . . and I need you to come with me.'

'I suppose a hit of morphine is out of the question.' He took a bottle of tablets from Scott's medi-kit and put it in his pocket. 'How did you know it would be there?' he murmured. 'In the *Lonely Planet*?'

'I think I'm getting to know Ameena a little. I'll explain on the way.'

24

THEN (2005)

Ellie helped the boy onto the examination table despite his protests. His hand looked like a club, wrapped and rewrapped in a makeshift bandage. It was soaked dark red. Gajan exhaled deeply. She could see him swallowing the urge to cry out. The wound was a mess, but she wouldn't be able to talk to him if she called in a doctor.

Arjuna took one look at it and left the tent, returning quickly with Bradfield.

'Hold onto the side of the table with your other hand, kid,' Bradfield instructed, ripping open a medi-kit. 'And try not to kick me. This is going to hurt.'

'What happened?' Ellie asked.

'Doesn't matter,' Gajan muttered. He held onto the table, his knuckles white.

Bradfield peeled away the strips of torn t-shirt with efficient resolve. The translucent layer of new skin ripped away with it, blotches of fresh blood appearing underneath.

'This flesh here,' he said to Gajan. 'This is infected. If you don't look after it, it will get worse, and we'll have to remove it.'

He gently pressed the perimeter of the wound where smelly pus oozed out. He wiped it and more returned. Arjuna opened three packets of gauze.

'What happened?' she asked again.

Gajan looked at her resentfully. 'I was building an IED. The trigger switch caught. I disconnected it from the explosive, but I must have missed something. Could have been worse.'

'The bombmaker's creed,' Arjuna commented.

'Are you any use to the Tigers now, like this?' She motioned to the deformed hand.

'You mean, am I any use to *you*?' Gajan asked.

She looked sharply up at the boy's face. 'Is that what you think—that you're just being used by me?'

'I *am* being used by you. At least with them, there is some reason, some purpose to it.'

'There is no purpose to this war, there is only a brutal and tragic end. Look at me.' She gripped his face. Arjuna and Bradfield stopped tending to his wounds, but stayed where they were, within restraining distance. 'Think about your brother and your mother. They love you and they want you back. Follow the plan, and don't give up hope.'

The boy laughed bitterly. 'Hope. Nampukiren.'

Bradfield dressed the wound and wrapped it up again. 'This is for the infection. It's a double dose.' He passed Gajan a packet of antibiotics and more dressings. 'Keep the wound dry and clean if you can. If the infection gets worse, insist on medical help. You can't serve their purpose if you're dying of sepsis.'

He tried to help the boy off the table, but Gajan pulled away from him and walked out of the room without looking back.

•

Ellie brought her tray of food over and sat with the team. Sharkey and Bradfield spent their days with the mosquito units, spraying the open waterways with DDT. It gave them access to the small villages and settlements that cropped up around the region, where they could gather intel. They returned each evening for a quiet briefing in the WHO's mess tent.

'Boys.' She took a seat opposite Arjuna. 'Good day?'

'Long day,' Sharkey replied. 'Bradfield and I were just talking about making a change.'

'Oh?' She mixed the usual daily ration of yellow dhal with rice. Yesterday they had gotten fried okra as a treat. 'How so?'

'There are more NGOs entering the field,' Bradfield explained. 'You know, because the new prime minister seems promising. The NGOs are building demountable healthcare clinics, toilets and water pumps. They need labour. Strong labour.'

'You want to build toilets?' She picked a small stone out of the dhal.

'We want to be closer to you,' Sharkey replied.

'That's sweet,' Arjuna said.

'Shut up. You know what we mean. We're here on a protection detail, not a reconnaissance mission.' Sharkey leaned forward so he wouldn't be overheard. 'You've got Scottie in the sky for that, and us on the ground to keep you safe.'

'We are safe,' Ellie replied. 'You said so yourself. The NGOs think everything's fine.' She didn't want to share her own doubts about it. She wanted Sharkey and Bradfield out in the field, crossing paths with Gajan as his unit moved through the region.

'There's nothing you can do for the kid, sir. I know you're frustrated. Until he gives you real intel, you have to keep him in play. You know that,' Bradfield muttered. 'This is a long game, and you don't control it. The kid does.'

She stared at her food. Gajan had no real control. He had to be in the right place at the right time, and recognise that he was learning something valuable. Something he could bring to Ellie, that she could use to release him.

'He's just a kid,' she said.

'A kid with a gun and a bomb-making skill set.' Bradfield scraped the remnants of food on his plate into a pile and finished it. He pulled out a protein ration from his pack and squeezed the paste into his mouth, grimacing.

She slid her plate towards him and took the ration.

'You're sure?' He didn't wait for her answer and started eating.

She squeezed the paste onto her finger and licked it.

'We've made a decision about your security, sir.' Sharkey reached over and helped himself to a spoonful of Bradfield's food. 'It's better served if we stay in close proximity to you. Our weapons are hidden in the base of a crate at the back of the tent, covered by humanitarian crap. We couldn't even get to them fast in a firefight.'

That troubled all of them. The Tigers made regular checks on the clinics under the pretext of ensuring staff safety. Sharkey and Bradfield couldn't even carry the few guns they had smuggled in.

'There won't be any firefights, guys. Come on. We're the WHO,' Ellie said with false bravado.

'You obviously haven't seen *Black Hawk Down*,' Sharkey replied.

'It's a cinematic masterpiece and an important lesson for all of us.' Bradfield said. 'Those boys had no options, that's why they died. If we stay with you, you've got options.'

'And,' Sharkey added, 'if you watch the movie, you'll get a better feel for what real combat is like, sir.'

'Shut up,' she replied. 'That's the last time I share my dhal with you.'

'It's decided then,' Sharkey said. 'Enough spraying mosquitoes. More building toilets.' He took her plate from Bradfield and finished it.

•

Gajan's infection had spread. Bradfield cut the bandages and pulled back the dressing, releasing a putrid odour into the room. The nub of the missing finger was swollen with pus. The tips of the remaining three fingers were black, the darkness creeping towards the knuckles. Where the black stopped, an angry red took over.

'He's going to lose the other fingers, sir,' Bradfield said. He tenderly lifted the hand and turned it over. 'I can do it, maybe at these joints here,' he motioned to the knuckles. 'But I'd prefer not to. We need to get a surgeon in here.'

Gajan pulled his hand away. 'You're not a doctor?' He struggled to get off the table, tipping forward. Bradfield caught and steadied him.

'Take it easy, kid,' he soothed. 'I'm a field medic, but a surgeon will make sure you can use that hand properly.'

Ellie placed a hand on Gajan's forehead. He was burning. He growled and jerked away from her. Her hand came away damp.

Bradfield opened his bag and pulled out a vial. Both Bradfield and Sharkey carried enough morphine to get them through *some* field surgery, but not all. 'This is the good stuff. Top shelf. I only use it on special occasions.' He injected it into Gajan's arm, then lifted the hand again and slowly dipped it into a metal bowl of warm saline. The boy clenched his jaw, his nostrils flared. He refused to make a sound. Tendrils of blood and pus drifted into the water like seaweed.

Arjuna refilled the boy's empty water canister and handed it to him. 'The morphine will kick in soon. Drink. It will help the fever. Take at least six of these a day if you can.' He thrust a packet of morphine tablets into the boy's other hand. 'Keep it on you at all times. Get ahead of the pain and stay ahead of it.'

Gajan's eyes started to glaze and his breathing slowed. He finally relaxed on the table.

'How are things at the camp?' Ellie asked.

He shrugged. 'I'm training the others to make the bombs. Until I heal.'

'What materials are they ordering?'

Gajan paused, remembering. 'High explosives: nitroglycerin, C-4, Semtex, acetone peroxide and mercury fulminate. Also, ammonium nitrate. It improves the explosive yield.'

'The explosive yield?' she echoed.

'Yes, it's the—'

'I know what it is, Gajan.' It was unsettling to hear the words come out of a child's mouth.

'What else can you tell me? What about detonation?' she asked.

'Mostly remote detonation. Some self-detonation, victim-operated IEDs.' He shifted on the examination table, gasping when he had to move his hand.

'Remote detonation? Mobile phone?'

'And others.'

'This isn't a word game, Gajan. What are the other triggers?' she asked.

'Key fobs, walkie-talkies and garage controllers. These are harder to engineer, but they give us more control. We need electronic parts from China. I give the spec list to Commander Seran and then he talks to his people.'

'How long does it take for the parts to come?'

'For the electronics, a week on eBay.'

She shook her head. Fucking eBay.

'The explosives take longer. Two weeks, but if we plan ahead, it's very efficient. No time to stop. Must keep building.'

'Do you know who Seran uses for the explosives?' She needed a name for Redmond. Even better, a name and a photo he could use to track the seller.

'No.'

'How does he make contact? Mobile phone, sat phone, email? How is he communicating the orders and setting up the meets?'

'I don't know. He's always on his mobile. He's planning something. He asked me what I would need to make ten suicide vests. He's been pushing us, like there's a deadline.'

'Ten vests.' Her heart raced.

'Yes. He wants everything ready by August twenty-seventh.' He was babbling now, words tumbling out fast, delirious with fever.

'August twenty-seventh,' she repeated. That was two weeks away. 'Any idea of targets?'

'No, just numbers and specs.'

'Gajan.' She put a hand carefully on his arm. 'I need you to find out more for me. I need targets, locations and dates.'

He shook his head.

'Innocent people like your father and sister will die,' she persisted.

'Innocent people always die. Here, we die with purpose,' he repeated his indoctrination. 'I'm not afraid to die.'

She tried again. 'I am. I think you are, too. I think you're a boy and you are being made to do a man's work. Men are killers, not children.'

'Men, women and children—we're all capable of killing.'

'Yes, we are all capable of killing. But you are not a killer, Gajan. Not yet.'

'You don't know me,' he replied, tears in his eyes. 'You don't know what I've done.'

25

NOW (2009)

Ellie rapped loudly on the door until the small hatch opened. A face peered out, then shut the hatch before she could speak.

She rapped again. She heard running footsteps and the bolts of the door slide open.

The same guard as before let her in and asked her to raise her arms. Arjuna did the same, wincing as the man touched his bruised side. They were led into the atrium where Manisha was waiting.

'He's looking for surveillance, not weapons,' she said.

'I'm not here to expose you,' Ellie told her. 'Not yet, anyway. I like you.'

'Thank you, Ellie. That's kind, but you shouldn't let it get in the way of doing your job. What is it you want? I've told you everything I know.'

'Not at all. You've told me everything you're willing to tell me. I can't subpoena a list of your staff, but I'm going to make a wild guess. About eight months ago, Ameena Fernando started coming here to meet her source. A few months later, she made a large order of books for your brothel. The books are schoolbooks, Manisha, for some of your staff. Your under-aged staff.'

'You don't know what you're talking about, Ellie.'

'Let's find out, shall we?' Ellie broke away from Manisha and ran up the stairs, three at a time. Behind her, Arjuna grabbed the guard and threw him against the wall. Another guard shouted and followed her. She kicked open a door. The room beyond was empty. The guard reached her and grappled her from behind, arms tight around her chest. She pushed back hard, slamming him into the railing of the balcony, nearly toppling over it herself. Then Arjuna was at her side, pulling her back from the edge, steadying her and driving an elbow into the man's nose.

Another guard approached from the other side of the verandah. He tackled Ellie and pushed her down on her stomach, smothering her with his body. She shoved her elbow sharply into his gut and jerked her head back, stunning him enough to throw him off, but before she could get up, he gripped the railing and levelled a kick at her belly. She absorbed it, and used the man's force to bring his leg down towards her and twisted his knee. She heard the nauseating pop of the patella disconnecting.

She wasn't here to fight. She pulled away from the tangle of limbs and sprinted down the corridor, kicking open more locked doors. Each one was the same, empty.

She heard Manisha shouting instructions to her men as she reached for the next door. Manisha had climbed the stairs by then and spoke as Ellie was about to kick it open.

'Don't,' Manisha said sharply. 'Locksmiths are expensive in Colombo. Just knock and open the door—you'll find what you're looking for. My men aren't coming.'

'You won't have them shoot me?'

'Upholstery is difficult to clean.'

Ellie knocked and opened the door. There were three boys huddled together on the floor, a game of cards scattered, forgotten around them.

'You're scaring them,' Manisha said behind her.

'*I'm* scaring them?' She left the boys and walked down the corridor.

'I have clients in those rooms, Ellie. Please respect their privacy.'

Ellie shook her head in revulsion. 'I think all other rights are forfeited, Manisha, when you decide to violate a child.'

The guards had finally hobbled up the stairs, one with his face covered in blood, the other with his knee already ballooning up. Arjuna stood behind them, a piece of the railing hefted in his hands.

'If they touch me, I will kill them,' Ellie said.

'I know,' Manisha said softly. 'I'm glad you can still feel outrage, Ellie. I feel so little these days. Come downstairs, please. Let's start over.' She stretched out a hand. The other was in the pocket of her silk gown.

'Put your gun away, please, Manisha. There's a drone above us catching all of this, and an earpiece your men missed.'

'Arresting me achieves nothing. I want Ameena's killer, too.'

'Do you? This is motive. Did she threaten to uncover this?' Ameena would have accepted prostitution, but not child prostitution. Ellie didn't want to think about what had been done to those children. If she let herself think about it, she would have to squeeze her hands around Manisha's elegant neck. 'Did you set up the hit?'

'I don't need to kill her or anyone. People need me, Ellie. I am the most protected person in this city, more than Mahinda Rajapaksa and his cousin. They have power and soldiers, but I have what people need.'

Ellie turned away, disgusted. 'What was she doing here? I'm sure she wasn't a deviant.'

'No, she was terribly straight. Something about all that righteous indignation is so attractive. You have it, too.'

Ellie ignored the comment. 'You sent me to the Cricket Club, Manisha. Why?'

'I was trying to be helpful. What did you find there?'

'A lot of photographs of dead brown people who wished they were white.'

Manisha laughed. 'That's particularly funny—and accurate—coming from you. Internalised racism is the most innocuous part of our colonial heritage. What else?'

'I crashed a conversation about the spoils of war.'

'Gruesome, isn't it?' She took a step towards Ellie.

'Stay right there. I want to see both your hands.'

Manisha smiled and placed both hands on the balcony railing, turning into the morning light in the open atrium. A red dot appeared on her forehead like a potu, and then moved down her body, towards her heart. Too late, Ellie shouted, lunging forward to knock her down.

A shot rang out and blood gushed from Manisha's chest. She looked at Ellie, confused. Her guards shouted and stumbled forward.

Ellie turned to the rooftop the shot had come from. The shooter was masked, but she knew who it was, the shape of his body, the assurance of his stance, the way he waited for her to spot him. He saluted her and ran.

Ellie reached inside Manisha's pocket and threw the gun to Arjuna. She pressed hard on the wound in Manisha's chest. A small boy pushed a towel at her.

'Don't move,' she said to Manisha.

'Come closer,' the woman whispered, flecks of blood merging with her lipstick. Ellie brought her face closer to the dying woman, breathing in the scent of her perfume. 'You should pray. God answers those who seek forgiveness.'

'Christ, Manisha, who did this to you?' The towel was fully soaked. 'Please tell me. Before it's too late.'

'I'm sorry, Ameena. Forgive me.' Manisha focused on Ellie's face. 'Forgiveness is the key,' she whispered. Then her eyes closed.

Ellie felt for a pulse. There was nothing. The blood pooled around them, thick and shining. It spread out like a fan, unfurling towards the edge of the balcony and dripping onto the tiles below.

•

'You didn't need to come, Tenby, we were handling this,' Ellie said to her old friend. Seeing him triggered her anger again. Tenby knelt by the body and lifted the sheet from Manisha's pale face.

'If by "handling this" you mean "being in the vicinity of another murder", then yes, Ellie, I see you're *handling* this.'

'Pretty cocky for a man that doesn't leave the Embassy without a bulletproof vehicle—and then continues to arrive late to the scene of every crime.'

'Now, now children, this is getting tiring,' Arjuna said, nudging Tenby out of the way. He straightened Manisha's hair and returned the sheet over her body. He whispered words of a Buddhist prayer. 'Forgiveness? She said forgiveness is the key?'

Ellie nodded. 'She didn't have time to be more specific.'

'She was right, I suppose,' Tenby said. 'Everyone makes mistakes, everyone wants to be forgiven. Nobody wants to end up like this.' He backed away from the corpse.

She looked around at the crime scene and then back to the rooftop. 'Have you checked that out?' she asked Arjuna. 'It was a sniper rifle with a laser pathfinder.'

'Nothing up there. He was long gone. Not a lot of policing happening here,' Arjuna motioned to the two policemen who had come to remove the body.

Tenby wiped the sweat from his face and neck, his hand lingering at the back of his neck, pinching the tension there to release it.

'You don't need to be here, Tenby,' Ellie repeated.

'You told Solomon you were just going to say some farewells. Someone has to explain why you're leaving a trail of bodies behind you.'

She flinched.

'Sorry, I didn't mean—'

'It's fine,' she cut him off.

Tenby grimaced. 'I expect we'll see someone from CID shortly, to make sure Manisha didn't keep any records.'

'She was a professional,' Arjuna pointed out. 'One thing that doesn't make sense to me is why *Ameena* created records. She made her payments to the brothel electronically. Why not just withdraw cash and hand it over?'

Ellie smiled sadly. 'Because Ameena was a professional too. She created a trail of crumbs that led us here.' She marvelled at the mindset of a woman who knew her days were finite but lived them fully anyway. 'I was hoping Manisha might do the right thing by Ameena and give me a last confession,' she said. 'You know how it is.'

Confession. You must confess to be forgiven.

The chapel.

'Come on.' She bolted down the stairs, Arjuna shouting 'What, what is it?' behind her.

She found the door she was looking for. Arjuna held his hand on his weapon when Manisha's guards tried to stop them.

'Step away, gentlemen,' he advised. 'We'll be quiet and fast. Just step away.'

Ellie closed the door and looked around the room. The familiar fragrance of incense was strong in the air. There was a hairshirt for the penitent hanging on a hook behind the door. She touched its abrasive surface and high collar. She felt guilt for her sins, but wearing a hairshirt would only give her a rash.

She opened the carved doors of the confessional. It was empty, of course. Two booths divided by a screen. She wasn't sure what she had been expecting. There was a Bible on the seat.

She picked it up. Underneath it was a ring; a slender, dull gold band with nine gemstones set in a square. Nine stones for the nine planets.

'Ameena,' she whispered.

Arjuna came to stand beside her. 'There's only one way this ring got here. Manisha must have ordered the hit and claimed it as a trophy.'

'Perhaps,' she said.

'Perhaps? *Definitely*, Ellie. I don't know who just killed Manisha or why, but how else would Ameena's ring get from her dead body to a confessional in a brothel?'

'There's one other way. I just need to think . . .' She was almost there. She had most of the pieces, but she needed a few more. Ameena had always been committed to the evidence that proved and told the story. Ellie put her hand in her pocket and felt the receipt. She needed more evidence. And a change of clothes. She was wearing layers of other people's blood. Nothing truly washed it away.

'Where to next?' Arjuna asked.

'Let's go home. Pack your things and let Namalie know we're coming to Hambantota,' she replied.

26

NOW (2009)

Arjuna checked Scott's gear one last time. In addition to Ellie's encrypted laptop, Scott had given them radio earpieces, wire cutters, tactical goggles with night vision, Kevlar vests and a combat medi-kit. He wasn't taking any chances. Ellie had pocketed Scott's personal handheld, and he had reluctantly agreed to reconfigure the small device to her biometrics.

Satisfied they were properly equipped, Arjuna set off. He took them away from the highway as quickly as he could, and onto village roads, through the rice fields, blankets of green that swirled around them. Each portion of the patchwork was divided by narrow canals. Ellie saw a man walking behind a bony bullock attached to a plough. He pushed the animal with one hand, and swatted it with the other, urging it out of the rut. Eventually the bullock freed the plough and moved on, churning the muddy, drowned earth. In the distance, Ellie could see a row of houses.

'Are we there already?' she asked.

'No. I want to show you something.' He pulled over. 'Take your shoes off and roll up your trousers.'

She followed Arjuna along the thin ridges that separated the paddy fields from each other. He balanced easily, his feet finding the solid ground and avoiding the softer parts that fell away.

The row of houses she had spotted was actually a train carriage. It sat in the middle of the paddy, red and rusted, surrounded by green. It had been rolled upside down by the tsunami of December 2004, its wheels in the air. The glass from its windows was no longer in place.

When they reached its entrance, the smell of sandalwood incense drifted out towards her.

'Come,' Arjuna said. Water pooled inside the carriage, lapping gently at his ankles. Someone had attached a rudimentary pump, ensuring that the water circulated instead of stagnated, but mosquitoes still clustered in its bowels.

The seats were made of slatted wood and vinyl, suspended from the ceiling of the upside-down carriage. People had hung garlands from the seats and they fell like jasmine stars from the ceiling, brushing her face as she walked through the aisle.

'This was the Southern Express. It took people, mostly workers, from Hambantota to Tangalle. It survived the tsunami's first wave. It was derailed and ended up on an embankment next to the tracks, and toppled over. Survivors say that no one was killed, just injured and scared.'

'The second wave?' she asked. Her voice was quiet but it echoed inside the watery cave. Blades of sunlight fell on the flowers and peeled the swollen vinyl off the seats.

'The second wave . . . that embankment was seventy-five miles south of here.'

She shook her head as she walked through the rest of the tomb, unable to imagine the power and fury of the hand that had picked up this carriage and hurled it across the land, bringing it finally to rest here. 'Survivors?'

'Five, out of an estimated eight hundred passengers. There were three other carriages just like it, never found.' He stopped at the last window, the wisps of sandalwood fading. He opened the bag around his shoulder, extracted a long, thin stick of incense and lit it.

'How many people from your village?' she asked.

'Too many. My family was in Colombo for a wedding. We got lucky that time. Thirty thousand dead: twenty thousand in the south and ten thousand in the east, although the eastern numbers aren't accurate. I think it was much more there.' He murmured a prayer, then stepped back out of the carriage onto the muddy bank. 'It was like the earth shuddered and then sighed. I think it was a message. A reminder that we are only temporary visitors on this planet, even though we behave as though we own it.'

'I think it was the tragic movement of tectonic plates, Arjuna,' she whispered. 'I don't mean that disrespectfully. I just don't think there were deeper forces at play. If there were, then those forces are so cruel to kill the innocent like that.'

'Innocent?' He turned to her, his face more beautiful in the light than in the shadows. 'Every religion speaks of an epic cleansing that happens from time to time. Noah and his ark. Nataraja and his cosmic dance of death. There is always a purging of evil. None of us are innocent in this country. We are all complicit in great crimes against each other. The tsunami was a reminder that we are being watched and there are consequences for our actions. We think we can escape our crimes, but we can't. There is always a reckoning.'

•

Ellie followed Arjuna up the narrow stairwell. He pressed a button at each landing, setting off a fluorescent light that flickered and ignited half-heartedly. She grasped the railing, then wiped the grit and stickiness from her hand onto her trousers.

'Hands to yourself,' he said. 'It's not much, but the plumbing works and this suburb doesn't get blackouts. It's a pretty good grid to live on. Mostly families of teachers and soldiers around here.'

'Why so much enlistment from this neighbourhood?' she asked.

'From this region, from the whole south. It's different down here. More farmers, more poverty, more religion.'

'Therefore, more patriotism?'

'More nationalism,' he corrected her.

They stopped at the third floor and he opened the door, calling greetings loudly in Sinhalese.

A woman with Arjuna's almond eyes and wide smile came out to welcome him. She held him tightly as he lifted her into the air. When he put her back down, she started scolding him, taking his face in her hands and turning it this way and that to get a better look at his bruises.

'Yes, yes.' He pulled her hands away and stepped aside so she could see Ellie hovering in the doorway.

'Ellie! Come in, come in!' Namalie cried. 'It's been a long time.' She hugged Ellie. The last time they had seen each other was in the ICU of Colombo General, where they both sat vigil by Arjuna's bedside, watching him through a plastic bubble as nurses changed his sterile dressings, debrided his charred skin and kept him sequestered from infection.

'Thank you for having me,' Ellie said, letting go of her finally. She pulled out the chocolates and fruit she had brought. 'Some books for the boys too. Arjuna mentioned they were into programming? I thought they might like the Steve Jobs biography.'

'Thank you, Ellie. That's lovely. Come, sit down. You're just in time for dinner.'

Ellie excused herself and went to the small bathroom. She bent over the sink to splash water on her face and the back of her neck, and took her medication. Leaning on the sink, she breathed deeply, in through her nose and out through her mouth, looking at her face in the mirror.

Namalie depended on her brother. She loved him, and Ellie had almost taken him away from her.

'I thought you might need this,' Namalie handed Ellie a towel as she left the bathroom. Namalie looked around self-consciously. 'It's not much.'

'It's home and it's lovely. Thank you.' *It's home when your brother is here, safe with you*, she wanted to say.

Namalie smiled. 'Come and eat.'

•

Ellie took the dirty plates from the table and placed them in the shallow sink. Namalie joined her in the kitchen with the empty pot of rice.

'How is he?' Ellie asked her.

'He's okay, I think. His body recovered a long time ago. The scars have healed as much as they ever will. They might fade a little more over time, but not much,' Namalie replied.

'There are other surgeries overseas. I looked into it and sent him information. I could organise it. We would cover it. We owe him that. But he never replied to my emails.' Ellie picked up the scrubbing brush in the sink.

'Please don't,' Namalie remonstrated, taking the brush away. 'You're our guest.'

'More like family,' Ellie said. She reclaimed the brush and began washing the plates.

'Thank you, Ellie.' Namalie allowed her to continue. 'Arjuna told me about those surgeries. He says he'll keep his scars. Says he's grown attached to them. I think the scars are his way of punishing himself.'

'He doesn't need to punish himself,' Ellie said.

'There are scars on the outside, but it's the ones on the inside I worry about more. He still has nightmares. Not as many as before, but still.'

Ellie had nightmares too. She didn't say anything.

'He refuses to meet anyone. I've tried, my mother has tried. There are plenty of women who would be interested. He earns a good living, it's a respected job with the Embassy. He's a hero with the Hambantota division of the Army after what happened. He could get a job here, if he wanted. People still remember my father too, with love.'

Arjuna had told her that story. Namalie's husband had been killed alongside their father by the Marxist uprising in the south twenty years ago. The Marxist JVP had dragged them from the post office where they worked together, taken them to the playground across the street with others, garlanded them with rubber tyres, poured petrol on them and then set them alight.

The Sinhalese called it the Time of Great Fear, the time of silent killing, when Sinhalese people had killed Sinhalese people instead of Tamils.

Namalie took a clean plate from Ellie and began to dry it. 'He says he's driving diplomats around, providing security, like an armed tour guide. Given the state of his face, I think he does more than just drive people around, but he won't tell me. He doesn't want to worry me.'

'He can take care of himself,' Ellie tried to reassure her.

Namalie stopped working and turned to face her. 'He wants to take care of you too. You know he volunteered for your assignment? He's been happier since you returned. It's given him a sense of purpose. Like he was waiting for you.'

27

NOW (2009)

Arjuna took his clothes off and folded them neatly. Before he was recruited by the Agency, he had worked in the Sri Lanka Army. His father had also taught him to be neat. Cleanliness is next to Godliness. A Christian homily that had pervaded their Buddhist home.

He pulled out his small toiletries bag from under the sink. Namalie kept it there for him when he returned the first weekend of every month to see her and the boys. Everything was there, including the expired painkillers. He hadn't needed them for years, but he liked to carry them just in case. Just in case of what, he didn't know. The nerve endings were dead; they would never feel pain again.

He looked at himself in the bathroom mirror. Four years ago, when he had returned to Namalie's home to recover, she had removed all of the mirrors in her small apartment. Only faint shadows remained on the cupboard doors and walls where they had once been.

The boys never complained and the mirrors never returned, even years later. Now, one new, small mirror had been placed in the bathroom.

He closed his eyes and remembered. He opened his eyes, looked at his face, and remembered. He closed his eyes and tried to forget.

Four years ago, Gajan had led them deep into the jungle. He had found the weapons seller that Redmond wanted, that Ellie had been sent to Sri Lanka for, who had traded in Semtex which had killed American sailors and American tourists. The whole team were hungry for success: Ellie, Sharkey, Bradfield and him. Missions went sideways all the time. Sharkey and Bradfield's families were told they died bravely. Arjuna had survived, his body wracked with fear and ravaged by fire.

He twisted his body in the mirror.

Only here did he look at himself.

The slash across his chest had formed a keloid scar, a shiny, thick ridge like a ceremonial sash.

He turned, fascinated by the way his skin rippled across his body like the waves of the ocean, cresting and falling. It had its own topography of damage. The pigment had never returned, and his skin was mottled pink in places, white in others.

He traced the path from his left shoulder, where the lighter had been held, to the right side of his hip. From the place where the fire had started to devour his body, to where it had stopped when a US Black Hawk circled overhead and bullets ripped into the earth around him, killing almost everyone.

When Ellie had dragged him down and rolled him over and over again in the merciful earth that was red and wet with the blood of the others.

28

NOW (2009)

'Where to now?' Arjuna asked, passing Ellie another canister of water. They had two in the back and a small crate of food from Namalie. She had been baking butter cake from dawn.

'I've made you fish buns, too.' Namalie handed her a warm paper bag. 'He's not allowed to eat those mutton rolls. They're bad for him.'

'Thank you.' Ellie kissed her.

Namalie held her and whispered, 'Don't let him do anything foolish. Take care of him, please.'

'I will,' Ellie promised. She climbed into the car and accessed the new map she had downloaded.

Arjuna drove them in the direction of the highway. 'I assume we didn't come all this way for a family visit.'

'No, although it would have been worth it just for that. Namalie's really special,' Ellie said. She opened the window and let the cool morning air in. Her diplomatic immunity would be revoked in eight hours.

'She is. So where are we going next?' Arjuna asked again.

'Where Ameena is guiding us to go.' She showed him the address on the receipt she had found hidden in Shirani's *Lonely Planet*.

•

Arjuna parked the car outside the Alston Copy shop in Hambantota. The early morning traffic had picked up, but offices hadn't opened yet. They walked a block down to a small street vendor and picked up a deep-fried mutton roll.

'Where can I get some coffee with my cholesterol?' Ellie asked.

'Enjoy it, life's short. Particularly if I keep hanging out with you.' He doused his mutton roll in chilli sauce. 'How did you know the receipt would be there?' he asked.

'It was something Shirani said at the school. She said Ameena loved Canada.'

'Everybody loves Canada,' he replied, wiping the sauce from his chin.

'Apparently Ameena's favourite authors were Canadian: Selvadurai, Ondaatje and Michael Clayton. Clayton is not a Canadian author, though. He's a character in a movie.'

'The one with George Clooney?' Arjuna asked.

'Yes, there's a scene in that movie—'

'We're here because of a scene in a movie?'

'Not just any scene. And not just any movie. It's an excellent film, one of my favourites.' Sharkey and Bradfield would have loved it. Bradfield more so, he always appreciated the quiet, cerebral thrillers.

They returned to the copy centre as the security grill rolled up. A young man took his position behind the desk next to a computer. He was surrounded by self-service photocopiers.

Behind him, young men and women in striped uniforms were loading reams of paper into industrial-sized copiers.

'I'd like to collect this, please.' Ellie handed him the receipt.

'Just a moment, madam. The computer is warming up.' He tapped a beat on the desk with his pen. 'Sorry, madam. Very slow.' He typed the receipt number into his computer. 'This is for collection by Ameena Fernando or Shirani Dennis. Passport ID is required, madam.'

'Ameena sent me,' she said.

'I'll need to see a letter of authorisation, madam,' the man replied.

'Right. No problem.' She took a step back, unsure of what to do next.

'Malli,' Arjuna addressed the young man as little brother. He spoke to him in Sinhalese, telling him that freedom of speech was at stake in the authoritarian dictatorship they lived in. The man looked from Arjuna to her and back to Arjuna again. He looked behind him to see if anyone was watching. He answered Arjuna earnestly, so rapidly that Ellie missed it, and nodded.

'One moment, please.' He went to the back storeroom.

'I can't believe that worked,' Ellie muttered.

'You'd be surprised how many people feel that way. He can't release the boxes, but he'll do what he can.'

'Boxes?'

'Boxes—twenty of them, stored at the back. Ameena left a mailing list with them, too. And specific instructions: if Shirani Dennis didn't pick up the boxes by February fourth, Sri Lanka's Independence Day, they were to be posted to all local civil society activists and international media.'

The man returned. He placed an envelope on the counter and passed it over.

'Thank you, malli.' Arjuna took the package and a copy of the mailing list. He led Ellie out the door and back to the car.

She opened the envelope. It was a special edition of *The Lanka Herald*, detailing the arms deal. It included copies of crucial primary correspondence between Dilshan Perera and Cultural Attaché Kwan, agreeing to the purchase of legal and potentially illegal weapons, including short-range heavy artillery.

There was something else in the envelope. Ellie tipped it into her hand. It was a USB stick. She plugged it into her laptop to find digital copies of the magazine and supporting evidence—lists of chemicals and weapons, purchase prices and sale dates.

'Back to the Embassy now?' Arjuna asked. 'Please? We have a USB stick, her article and a mailing list.' He took his jacket off and unclasped the strap on his holster.

'Were there any embassies on Ameena's list?'

He checked the papers and then shook his head.

'She had lost faith in the international community,' she said. 'This still doesn't tell us who killed her, Arjuna.'

'No, but it gives both the Sri Lankan and Chinese governments compelling reasons to. This is a story worth killing for. Let's take it to Solomon. He doesn't like you, but he'll help.'

'I'm not ready for the Embassy yet.' She checked the mirrors, expecting the man on the motorcycle to be there.

'We're a target now, Ellie. The Sri Lankans and the Chinese will want this. The longer we hold onto it, the more danger we're in. We're wide open here. We've evaded one motorcyclist so far, but what happens if there are four?' His eyes were also on the mirrors. 'We need to get it to the right people.'

'I'm just not sure who the right people are.' Ellie exhaled. Ameena no longer trusted governments but she had backed herself the whole way. She had made sure the article would survive, even if she didn't. Ellie wanted Ameena's strength; she wanted to be held in the other woman's certainty.

'Let's get out of here,' she said. He started the car.

•

The motorcyclist circled the block and parked in the alley next to the Alston Copy shop. He took his helmet and jacket off and put his sunglasses on before crossing Mayfield Road—recently renamed Huihuang Avenue—and ordered a mutton roll. He watched the American woman and the burned man come out.

She held an envelope tightly to her chest.

His employer was right about her. She had found what they were looking for.

She looked deeply tired, had ever since the mother and the child. He was sorry about the child, but there had been no other way. He would be sorry about the American too, she was pretty.

•

Ameena's research showed that all transport routes for China's illegal weapons led to the new airport and seaport at Hambantota that had been financed by the superpower. As Shirani had explained to Ellie, when Sri Lanka defaulted on the massive debt it owed to China, all of these debt-funded strategic bases would become Chinese equity-funded assets.

Hambantota's new airport was graced with an impressive five-storey car park. It was empty and dusty, sand blowing in from the ocean.

Arjuna pulled into a car space.

The airport was a monolith of glass and concrete, a large neon banner proclaiming it Mahinda Airport, after the President. The tarmac was devoid of planes. As they walked across the sky bridge, approaching the terminal, they could see into three floors of solitude.

At the entrance, a soldier stopped them and asked for their identification papers. He looked at the papers and then at Arjuna's face, then handed the papers back, speaking rapidly in Sinhalese. He pressed his hands together in the traditional greeting and then shook hands with Arjuna, until Arjuna pulled away.

'Thank you, malli.' Arjuna urged Ellie into the airport.

'You *are* a local hero. I thought your sister was exaggerating.'

'Shut up. Check out the boards.' The signs were all in Sinhalese, English and Mandarin. The Arrivals and Departures boards were empty save for one plane arriving in four days and leaving thirty minutes later. The check-in desks were numbered optimistically from one to thirty. Each was manned by Sri Lankan girls wearing a modern version of the traditional Kandyan skirt and blouse, meticulous makeup, and slightly robotic smiles.

'What do you think?' Arjuna surveyed the vast emptiness and opulence that the Chinese had funded and the Sri Lankan people would pay for.

'I think, Vanity, Thy Name is President Mahinda Rajapaksa.'

•

Arjuna drove them to the outskirts of the airport, to the eastern side of Hambantota Port. The airport backed onto an unfenced national park. He pulled off the highway into scrubland. They took their backpacks from the boot of the car.

'It's too exposed between here and the warehouses. We need to hike the rest of the way,' he said, handing Ellie her earpiece and helping her with the wire transmitter. He inserted his own and lifted his shirt so Ellie could thread the wire down under his shirt to his phone.

'Scottie, can you hear me?' he asked, adjusting the earpiece.

'Affirmative. I can hear you and I can see you. Drone CJCK128 is overhead. Move northeast, two clicks towards that small ridge. You can see out over the port from there,' Scott said to them.

When they reached the vantage point, they stopped for water and reconnaissance.

'Third warehouse from the left.' Ellie took the binoculars from her face and wiped away the sweat.

'That's a lot of military vehicles for a domestic warehouse storing everyday imports and exports.'

The vehicles were marked with Sri Lanka Army signatures—and PRC Army ones.

'I knew Su Lin Kwan was full of shit,' Ellie said.

'You did not,' Arjuna scoffed. 'Tenby told me you thought she was cute, so you bought her whole "I'm here to bring food and medicine to the people" routine.'

'Enough bickering, children,' Scott said in their earpieces. 'The Chinese Army seems to have access to all the runways.'

'Airport plus port plus warehouse plus PRC military vehicles. What does that equal?' Ellie asked. Through her binoculars, she could see crates being loaded onto Sri Lanka Army trucks. 'I'm going to get closer.'

'Don't be ridiculous, Ellie.' Arjuna looked at her incredulously.

'Scottie will cover me.'

'Cover *you*? What am I supposed to do? Wait here? You're running out of time,' he reminded her.

'Yep. I'll have a quick look around. Back in an hour. I need to know what's inside the crates. Ameena had government correspondence and payment records but no photographs of the actual weapons. Her exposé is pointless unless we have some hard evidence to prove what's going on here.'

'This whole exercise is pointless if you die.'

'There won't be any trouble.' She had promised Namalie she would take care of her brother. Years ago, she had made the same promise to Sathyan, too. 'Just stay here please, Arjuna.' Her heart rate quickened and the familiar tension coiled and then uncoiled within her. She could do this.

'You weren't responsible for what happened,' Arjuna replied fiercely. 'How many times do I have to tell you, Ellie? I wanted to be there. It was my job, as much as yours.'

She shook her head. It was his job, but her responsibility. Her debt. 'Stay. Do that for me.'

She adjusted her earpiece and pulled out Scott's encrypted handheld, placing her thumb on the screen and lifting it to her eye to read her biometric data markers. 'Okay Scottie, I'm ready—are you in?'

'I'm not comfortable with this, Ellie.' Scott's anxiety was loud and clear in her earpiece. 'You should call it in. Solomon can send a team. You can search and document the warehouse together, under the cover of darkness and surrounded by heavily armed Special Ops guys. Bravo 3 is on standby.'

'I don't want a team. I'll be in and out, without making a sound. Are you in?' she asked again.

'Yes, I have you on the drone and I'm in your—excuse me, *my* handheld. If you get caught, I'm wiping it from the inside. Everyone knows we have a drone overhead, but we don't like to get caught spying on the neighbours, it's not cool.'

'Definitely not cool.' She put on her tactical goggles and tightened her cap. The midday sun was beating down hard. She took the dirt road as Scott instructed and followed it through light scrub for a kilometre.

'Half a click east and then one due south and you're at the fence.'

'Got it.' She ran until she came to the wire perimeter. She crouched, took the cutters from her backpack and was about to cut the fence when she heard Scott shout.

'Stop!'

'Jesus, what is it?'

'The fence is electrified. Judging by the electromagnetic radiation I'm picking up, the shock is supposed to damage rather than deter.'

'And you're only picking this up *now*?' She shuffled back from the fence, pulling her backpack with her.

'Yes now, because I switched the drone scope from telescopic to EMR vision, so you're welcome.'

'What do I do, Scottie?' She surveyed the fence doubtfully.

'Take the defibrillator out of the bottom of your pack,' he instructed.

'That's encouraging.'

'Just do it. Get your cutters ready. Turn the dial on the defib right up. You're going to shock the fence to momentarily shut down its local generator. You should have about ninety seconds to cut an Ellie-sized hole in the fence. Even if the generator restarts, you can get in and out of the hole.'

'As long as she doesn't touch the sides, right?' Arjuna said, absorbing the whole plan. 'What happens if the generator restarts while she's still cutting the fence?'

'Then *you* have about four minutes to get down there, turn the defibrillator back down to normal, and shock Ellie's heart. Position the pads at ten o'clock and four o'clock.'

'Failing that, you can dig an Ellie-sized hole in the ground,' she added.

'That's not funny,' Arjuna warned.

'It'll work, Ellie,' Scott reassured them both. 'Remember, turn the dial right up, cut the hole fast and big.'

'Wait,' said Arjuna. 'Won't the Army register the perimeter breach?'

'No, the circuit will still be complete. From what I can see up here, it's not that sophisticated.'

Ellie wiped her palms on her trousers. She put the cutters on the ground next to her, flexed her hands, braced herself with the defib on high, and shocked the fence.

The impact threw her back hard, sparks darting into her hair and face like a swarm of fireflies. A thunder crack in the distance told her the generator had overloaded.

'Now, Ellie!' Scott shouted. She trusted his reading of the EMR. She attacked the wire, both hands on the cutter, clamping hard.

She crawled through the hole head and shoulders first, trying not to touch the sides. 'I'm heading to the warehouse.'

She crept down to the building through the scrub. At the warehouse wall, she pulled out a small, extendable mirror from her pack and raised it to the window to see a group of soldiers seated around a small table, playing cards and watching a Chinese television show.

'I need a way in. Are the doors alarmed?' she asked.

'I'm a surveillance hack, Ellie,' Scott replied. 'Not a psychic. If you head left along the wall, there's a garage door at the back.

A loading dock. No heat signs, I think everyone's off duty. I can't imagine they're expecting trouble. But Ellie . . .'

'Yes?'

'I was looking at satellite footage for the last week. It doesn't have drone clarity but the sat's pretty good. Two days ago, a convoy of black SUVs drove into the facility and didn't drive out. I'm getting into the facility's own surveillance right now to see if I can tell you who arrived, but I think they were important. The SUVs were souped-up to the max.'

'Government?' Ellie asked.

'Yes, but which one? I couldn't get plates. Key figures from the Sri Lankan government are still in Colombo, locked away in their war room. They come out occasionally to say something inspirational to the nation or abusive to the foreign press. I don't think it's them.'

'The Chinese?'

'I can't find any chatter on Kwan's movements.'

'Okay, I'll keep an eye out.' She found the open garage door and entered the warehouse. Scott was right. The building was stacked with large reinforced fibreglass crates. It was dark inside, she could see that each crate was sealed and marked with numbers and Hànzì characters.

Ameena's notebook had contained a list of numbers they hadn't been able to decipher.

'Scottie,' she whispered. 'Remember those numbers I gave you before?'

'Vaguely.'

'Run a Number Nine algorithm on them. Something a pure maths boffin like Ameena could do in her head, under pressure, if she was hand-copying a list of numbers but trying to encrypt it as she wrote.'

She heard him typing. She waited as long as she could. 'Anything?'

'It's a match. Chemicals and weapons. The first two numbers you gave me are dual-use chemicals that have civilian and military applications. I've got ID tags for white phosphorus, phosgene, and chlorine gas.' Scott went silent for a moment, then she heard him exhale. 'Look, Ellie, these chemicals are precursors to chemical weapons, but they're also used in agriculture and other legitimate industries. How many more numbers do you have?'

She looked at the towers of crates around her. 'A warehouse full, I think.' She heard more typing.

'The weapons are heavy artillery,' Scott told her. 'Multi-barrel rocket launchers, thermobaric weapons and cluster munitions . . .'

This was Sri Lanka's Zero Civilian Casualty Policy. She sank down on the floor of the warehouse. She felt ill.

'Shit,' Scott muttered. 'Do you think MNW was selling these to the Sri Lanka Army and Ameena was about to blow the lid open on that?'

'Yes, but where did she get the list from?' she asked.

She had hidden the copy of Ameena's report in the chassis of their car, just the way Bradfield had taught her. Now she knew it contained the same list of chemicals and weapons from the journalist's notebook. Ameena had sat down with someone, somewhere private, who gave her the time and access to scribe a very specific list.

Somewhere like the confessional box at Manisha's brothel.

Ameena had an inventory of legal-but-excessive weapons and illegal weapon components in her notebook. Ellie had

Ameena's report, the only evidence showing that these were sold by MNW to the Sri Lanka Army. All other evidence had been 'removed' from the public or private domain.

Except these crates. 'Scottie, are you recording this? What's your picture quality like?' She held her torch on the serial numbers and letters. She needed evidence, real images.

'High definition. I can see the crates, but I'm going to need to see weapons if you're going to do this right,' Scott said.

'Understood,' she whispered.

'You could walk away now, Ellie. You've found enough to interest UN Weapons Inspectors,' he said, without much conviction.

She knew better. UN Weapons Inspectors would only ask questions if the US pushed them, and the US would only push them if they needed something in return. She was sitting in the Thoroughfare. She knew exactly what governments needed. A seat at this table.

She was about to open the first crate when the lights came on, flooding the room. A familiar voice called out.

'Dr Harper, please join us.'

Footsteps approached from all sides. She considered her options. Fight or flight were not possible. She raised her hands and walked slowly towards the front of the warehouse.

Kwan strode forward. His bodyguards outpaced him and met her first. They patted her down roughly and then ran a scanner over her, ripping off the goggles and shouting, motioning to her ear.

She pulled the piece out. She was now in a covered building with no drone vision, her goggles and earpiece crushed by the butt of a gun.

'Please, take a chair,' Kwan invited her cordially. 'You've done well to get this far, Dr Harper. My men will be reprimanded. You've seen the crates, I presume?'

'Yes. I've sent footage back to my people. We know what you're doing,' she lied.

'Of course, you do. You've known all along. You're just upset because we did it first. We are arming and training the Sri Lanka Army for the final stages of their war on terror.'

'Did you kill Ameena Fernando because she found out?'

'Kill Ameena Fernando? Is that what this is about?' Kwan mocked. 'We don't bother with self-righteous journalists or even mediocre bureaucrats. We don't fear international judgement the way you do. We are here to help Sri Lanka end this war and then begin a new chapter in its history.'

'You sound just like the President and his cousin. Or they sound exactly like you.'

'We are partners in the region. Is that so wrong of us? To build partnerships and treaties, to trade goods and services?'

'Goods and services?' she repeated. She hoped Arjuna wouldn't try to rescue her. The soldiers were now fully armed and on alert.

'Yes, goods and services. We live in uncertain times. Energy security, food security, water security. It is no longer just about military security. Our territorial borders are safe, but our survival is not assured.' He sat down in front of her and leaned forward. 'We don't waste time on the empty rhetoric of public good or global security, but trust that every country is entitled to do what is in its own best interests. In doing so, a stable global order will assert itself, providing security for all.'

'A global order in which you are on top.'

'Yes. Why is that so uncomfortable for everyone? America has had its time and now it's ours. People are so foolish. Better the bully they know? They'll get used to us.'

'I'm sure once we get to know you, we'll like you.' She could see soldiers taking positions at the doorways.

'Maybe, but we don't care about being liked as much as you do. We are quietly asserting our dominance in the world, and for the most part, you are too arrogant to see it. You talk too much and learn too little.'

Kwan had said, *You've known all along.* The US, Solomon and probably Redmond had known all along about the weapons and Sri Lanka's military strategy. But if they had known, why hadn't they revealed it? Why had the US kept quiet? Everything was an exchange of goods and services. What had been exchanged here in Sri Lanka? China was securing the Thoroughfare for the String of Pearls that protected its economic corridor from Africa to Asia. And the US?

'You're right,' she said. 'You should be careful doing business here, though, Mr Kwan. It's an unstable nation-state. Too many religious fundamentalists allowed into the halls of power. I wouldn't sink too much investment into it.'

'Thank you for your concern, Dr Harper. I suspect the US would like to sink more investment. There are religious fundamentalists in your White House too, but that's acceptable to you because they're the right kind of fundamentalists.'

'Perhaps.'

'Without a doubt. The US is an unstable nation-state, not the hero it thinks it is. Nor are we the villains here. We are cleaning up our air and securing our food and energy supply. We will give aid more generously and lead more courageously than you ever did.'

'All of this,' she motioned to the crates of weapons. 'This is villainy, not leadership.'

'No. As I said, we care about our country, and all of *this* is patriotism. You're an American. You understand patriotism.'

'I do, but I've never made my peace with its price.'

'There is no price too high for patriotism, Dr Harper. But I can tell you what the going rate for betrayal is. Given the falling greenback, it's surprisingly low.'

'I don't know what you're talking about,' she replied.

Kwan stood up and nodded to an approaching soldier. 'I would die for my country. I would pay any price for its safety. And I would never sell it out for sixty-eight Yuan.'

'Sixty-eight Yuan?' She didn't understand.

'Sixty-eight Yuan, at today's exchange rate, Dr Harper, is less than thirty pieces of silver.'

Thirty pieces of silver. A traitor's kiss.

'Remember that,' Kwan said. 'When you're tying up your loose ends—and ours.'

A soldier drew back a fist and hit her hard in the face. The world went black.

•

As soon as Ellie had set off for the warehouse, Arjuna called it in. He wasn't prepared to wait. Protocols existed for a reason. He asked Scott to scramble Bravo 3 and whoever else was in the area. He returned to the airport and recruited the back-up they should have had in the first place.

He led the Sri Lankan soldiers to the warehouse door, their convoy of jeeps glistening in the sun. At his request, they used their sirens, the wail sending flocks of egrets into the sky in a gale of snow-white against the cloudless blue sky.

He undid the button on his holster but didn't draw his weapon. There were seventeen soldiers behind him, carrying M16s and the jurisdiction to use them.

The Sri Lankan soldiers shouted at the Chinese soldiers who stood in formation around Kwan. Arjuna saw Ellie on the floor. His heart pounded. He kept his hands by the sides of his body.

'Mr Kwan,' he said. 'My name is Arjuna Diwela. I am US Embassy Security, although formerly of the Sri Lanka Army, joint taskforce.' Of sorts. He needed his Sri Lanka Army colleagues on side.

'Good afternoon, Mr Diwela. I believe I have something that belongs to you.' Kwan flicked his head at Ellie's still body.

'You do.' He stepped towards her. The Chinese raised their assault rifles. The soldiers behind him raised theirs.

'I've been told that Dr Harper has served her purpose. Her time is up.'

'She has a few more hours,' Arjuna said. He had to get her back to the safety of the Embassy by 1800 hours for her flight at 2100 hours. It was 1630 hours and Colombo was a four hour drive from Hambantota *if* they were lucky. They wouldn't make it.

'I have very particular instructions in relation to her,' Kwan said. 'From someone more senior than you.'

Something wasn't right.

Dr Harper has served her purpose. What purpose?

'I have instructions too,' Arjuna lied, thinking fast. 'From someone more senior than all of us.' It was a bluff; although he usually left the risky plays to Ellie, he had learned a few things during his time with her.

He had more firepower than Kwan, but if this escalated, he would still lose soldiers. Bravo 3 was twenty minutes out and would only arrive in time to pick up the bodies. Again. 'I trust we don't have a problem here?' he asked the diplomat, not breaking eye contact.

Kwan looked at him closely, then at the soldiers behind him. 'None at all.'

Arjuna tried to control his exhale, trapping his relief inside his chest. In Sinhalese, he rapidly instructed the men to stand down, then checked Ellie's pulse and breathing and whispered a quick prayer of thanks. He gathered her in his arms and held her for a moment. He stood up and stumbled. She was heavy for such a small person.

•

When Ellie awoke, her face ached, her head was throbbing, and air rushed towards her through an open window. She jolted up and tried to run, but was restrained. She looked down to see a seatbelt.

'The report?' she asked, tenderly touching her face.

'It's safe,' Arjuna said.

'What happened?' she asked.

'Kwan's soldiers roughed you up a bit. He said he had instructions from someone senior, about what to do with you.'

'Sounds ominous,' she said. Who was Kwan taking instructions from? Most likely Dilshan Perera, she thought.

'Aside from an impressive bruise on your face, you seem to be intact,' Arjuna looked at her, worried and relieved. He was driving them on a highway, but she didn't know to where.

'You got me out?' she asked.

'This time. You haven't learned a damn thing, have you, Ellie?' he said. 'When I found you, I wasn't sure you were even alive.'

'Sweet of you to worry,' she said.

He slowed the car and pulled over. His hands were shaking where they gripped tightly to the steering wheel. He turned his face away from her to the window, inhaled deeply and then exhaled. He released the steering wheel and then rearranged his fingers around it, the colour returning to the skin of his burned hand in a sunset of patches.

'I'm sorry.' She reached over and took his left hand, raised it to her face and then kissed it. 'I'm sorry, Arjuna. Thank you.'

'You may not value your life anymore, Ellie. But there are other people who do. Other people who would risk their lives for you. People who would mourn you if you're gone.' He swallowed hard, eyes straight ahead. 'You matter to me.'

'You matter to me, too. The clock on Solomon's protection has run out. Are we headed back to Colombo?' She instinctively looked around for approaching vehicles. They needed to keep moving.

'Yes, Colombo,' he replied. 'I'll stay with you until the end.'

29

THEN (2005)

Gajan returned to the clinic. The blackness in his fingers had spread. Most of the hand needed to be amputated, but he refused.

'We have to go,' he said urgently. 'A new shipment is coming this afternoon. Commander Seran says the seller is coming too, from India. He wants to talk to him about new weapons.'

'Why would he come himself?' Arjuna asked. 'It seems risky.'

'I don't know. I think he's meeting all the Tiger commanders. We are going to begin fighting again.' Gajan flinched as Arjuna gave him his antibiotics injection. 'The commander says we must end it with a big bang, in all the cities. That's why the supplier is here.' He slid off the examination table.

'Where are you going?' Ellie asked.

'To take you to the jungle,' he said. 'To show you the supplier. It's a three-hour walk.'

'Wait a minute, Gajan. We can't just go running into the jungle,' Ellie said.

'Bring your soldiers. The tall one and the nice one,' Gajan said urgently.

A frisson of warning trickled down her back. 'Where's your pendant?' she asked, holding Gajan's naked wrist. He was supposed to wear it at all times. 'Did you leave it at the camp?' Scott could lock into the camp location and get drone footage of the seller.

'I lost it in Mannar. We were swimming in the ocean. It fell off. I'm sorry.'

She held his arm a moment longer. She felt closer to Sathyan when she was with the boy.

'I'll talk to the guys,' she said. 'See if they're up for a trek through the jungle.'

•

Before they left, Ellie called Scott. He checked her sat phone and made her replace the battery with a fully charged one.

'I'll be fine,' she reassured him.

'We have Special Ops teams doing crosswords in the Embassy Rec room, Ellie. Just send them in.'

'There's no time. This is surveillance only. We'll get eyes on the seller and then we'll get out.' She inserted her earpiece and adjusted the induction loop under her shirt. 'I'll be fine,' she repeated.

'I guess BS and Arjuna are with you. I've got a drone and Bravo 9 is in position.'

'What did Solomon say?' she asked.

'Solomon doesn't debate departmental resources when our own people are in the field,' he replied. 'That's what we're here for.'

'Thank you, Scottie.'

'No problem. See you on the other side.'

•

They set off with Gajan leading the way. Sharkey, Bradfield and Arjuna were armed and wore their vests. Bradfield had kindly instructed her to stay behind them. Ellie carried a 9-mm but she hoped she wouldn't have to use it.

The walk through the jungle was slow and hard. Gajan stopped frequently to rest, the infection in his hand weighing his body down. Ellie shared her water with him until she was out. He smiled gratefully. He looked more like Sathyan today. Maybe he was growing up.

The air cooled around them and a chorus of birds echoed off the towering palmyra trees. The sun was setting, its pink and yellow hues seeping into the emerald canopy above.

Three hours later, they arrived at the outskirts of the Tiger camp. They stopped on the underside of a ridge that overlooked the small settlement. Arjuna held his canteen out to her. She refused, but when he shook it at her, she drank deeply.

'The supplier is here,' Gajan whispered. 'Let's get closer.'

'No,' Arjuna pulled him back down. 'This is far enough for now. Ellie, call Scottie to make sure he has our location. We haven't checked in for an hour.'

She unzipped her pack and reached for the sat phone. It was gone. She rifled through the bag. Her medi-kit and empty water canteen were there, but the phone was gone.

'Shit.'

'Ellie!' Arjuna hissed.

She looked up to see Gajan running down the steep side of the ridge, falling over roots and scrub, his bandaged hand held against his chest. His other hand clutched the phone. He scrambled towards the camp, sounding the alarm.

'Jesus!' Sharkey shouted. 'Fall back! Run, Ellie!' He picked her up by the scruff of her shirt and threw her down the ridge, back the way they came.

She slid down through thorny bushes, skinning her arms and scratching her face. At the sound of gunfire, she looked back at ridge. Sharkey, Bradfield and Arjuna had spread out and taken positions, using trees and fallen logs for shelter. Two provided cover, while the third emerged from behind the tree to shoot at the oncoming Tiger soldiers.

Scott could locate her phone, even if she hadn't called it in. He could still find them.

'Fall back, all of you!' she shouted. 'Fall back! We run, now.'

Too late. Sharkey cried out in pain, blood flowing from his shoulder. He clamped it with his other hand. She ran back to him and dragged him down behind a banyan tree, its aerial roots creating a fragile curtain around them.

'Fucking vest. You have to get out of here, Ellie,' he whispered through clenched teeth. 'We can hold them off.'

'I'm not leaving you.' She opened her backpack.

'No time and no options. This was planned. Not going to end well. You need to run.' He pushed her away.

'No.' She held onto him and he tightened his arm around her. 'I'll stay with you till the end.' They heard the click of a rifle being chambered above their heads.

•

They were pushed into the open circle of the camp. The Tiger cadres cheered and shook their rifles. Ellie stumbled under Sharkey's weight. He had hooked his arm around her shoulder and was leaning on her more and more, losing blood fast.

Gajan stood next to the Tiger commander. He looked flushed; with fever, regret or happiness? She couldn't tell. He was so young. How had she not realised? She had been desperate to save him. No, she had been desperate to use him and *then* get him out. She was so desperate to get him back to Sathyan, she hadn't realised that he wanted to stay right here.

Commander Seran raised his hands and the soldiers fell quiet. The jungle still squawked and sang, wildly impervious to his authority. 'We are very fortunate today. Our brother Gajan has brought us a gift: four CIA agents, hidden in a Western medical team. Who knows how many more there are out there? Pretending to help us, while spying on us for the Army. After tonight,' he walked up to Ellie. 'There will be a few less.'

He raised his gun and shot Sharkey in the forehead. A mist of blood coated her face. She shuddered, her mouth open in a silent scream. Sharkey's lanky body sagged and slipped to the ground, his blue eyes open in the dirt.

Her hands shook. Her body shook. She felt Sharkey's blood, warm on her face. Warm and full of life. She looked down at his body. Red fire ants scurried towards him, their bulbous bodies crawling on his face. They collected droplets of his blood and carried it away.

She turned to Bradfield and Arjuna. Both of them stood tall and still, bodies braced and firm. They had lost a friend. They had no weapons, but they were ready to fight and kill. People weren't born that way. The world made them like that.

Sathyan had once told her that the Tigers were the same. They weren't born ready to fight and kill. Sri Lanka's war forced them to be like that.

The commander walked over to Bradfield.

'Wait, please!' she shouted. She lunged forward and five soldiers raised their rifles to her. 'Wait, I beg you! Don't do it. We're CIA. The US government will trade for us. They will negotiate. Please don't do it.'

'*I'm* not going to do it. He is.' The commander called Gajan over and pushed the gun towards him. Gajan shook his head and took a step back. The commander retracted the weapon's bolt, sliding another bullet into place. He turned the handle towards Gajan. 'Neengal chayango, thambi,' he said, his voice reassuring. *You do it, little brother.*

The boy took the gun in his left hand. His right was clutched to his chest in pain. His eyes shone with fever, his breathing fast with infection and adrenaline.

'Please don't, Gajan,' she whispered. 'Please, think about your mother and your brother. They love you. You're not a killer.'

He turned to face her, tears streaking his face. 'How do you know what I am? I'm nothing but a spy to you. You tried to make me betray my own people, my brothers.'

'They are not your brothers. You have a brother. Sathyan. Sathyan, Sathyan.' She repeated his name like a prayer. 'He loves you. He misses you. Please.'

'This is my family now.' Gajan turned back to Bradfield but couldn't look him in the eye. His body trembled, the weapon too.

'It's okay, kid,' Bradfield said softly. 'Remember to keep that hand clean.' He looked at the gun. 'Drop it a little lower, that's the way.' He glanced at Ellie and winked.

Gajan pulled the trigger.

•

Ellie screamed and screamed and screamed. She held Bradfield in her arms as blood bubbled out of the base of his neck. Arjuna had his hands clamped on the wound but the blood wouldn't stop.

Bradfield tried to smile at her.

'Should have watched that movie, Ellie,' he whispered.

'Shh, shh.' She wiped his face gently.

'Finish it,' the commander ordered.

Ellie looked up. Gajan stood over them with his gun poised, his hand still wavering. She placed Bradfield's head gently on the ground, raised her hands and stood up, shaking her head. The soldiers around them raised their weapons as she walked slowly towards Gajan. He stumbled back.

The commander said something in Tamil. Gajan flinched and looked from him, to Ellie, to Bradfield. He stepped forward and the gun swayed from Bradfield to her. She took another step closer.

'Gajan, you don't have to do this. You have choices.'

'No. No, I don't. Stop moving. Stop moving or I'll kill you,' he cried.

She took another step and grabbed his wrist, pulling it down and twisting the gun out of his hand. She raised it in the air, holding it by the trigger guard. There was nothing she could do with it. More than twenty rifles were trained on them. All she could do was wait for help.

'Wait!' The commander ordered his men—so many of them only children. 'Wait. No one shoots her.' He moved over to Gajan and gave him another pistol. 'Finish him,' he said gently. 'The soldier has to die.' He looked at Ellie and spoke without malice. 'There are three bullets left in that gun. I'll let you use them all.'

Gajan stared at the commander, confused.

She understood. She could kill Bradfield and Arjuna. Bradfield had always told her to save a bullet for herself.

She could kill her people.

Or she could kill Gajan.

Would Scott find them? Bravo 9 should be heading towards her on a Black Hawk. Scott would find them.

She flipped the gun on her finger and held it firmly in both hands. Its black weight was cool and balanced.

Redmond called it the hierarchy of life: why we deemed some lives to be more important than others. Why we chose to kill some, in order to save others.

'Don't do it, Gajan,' she pleaded.

The boy took a deep breath in and out. He steadied his gun on Bradfield's chest, which was rising and falling in shallow gasps.

She saw Gajan's hand tighten.

She didn't hesitate. The boy reeled back from the force of the bullet and looked at her, surprised and hurt. He raised his gun once more, this time at Arjuna's head. She stepped forward and shot him again. He dropped to his knees, stunned.

He lifted the gun again, this time at her.

He was just a child.

She finished it.

•

Arjuna stood with his arms tied behind his back. His Kevlar vest had been stripped and he felt naked in the simple civilian clothes of a WHO medic. His shirt was stained with the blood from his broken nose and torn lip. Two Tiger soldiers stood at each arm, holding him upright.

Commander Seran flexed his fingers, his knuckles split where they had connected with Arjuna's bones. He took the knife from his belt and slashed it across Arjuna's chest, cutting his shirt open and leaving a thin line of blood oozing from his heart to his belly.

He could hear Ellie screaming behind him. 'Stop it, stop it! He's a high-value hostage like me! He's worth more to you alive! Imagine what you could get for him!'

The commander didn't take his eyes from Arjuna. 'He's not worth anything. A spy for the Americans, a traitor to his own country. You think I intend to trade any of you?' He shook his head. 'So many of our children are buried in this jungle. I intend to bury you with them. You and the others.'

He motioned to the pile of bodies lying in the dirt.

Arjuna heard the sound of liquid sloshing towards him. He knew it wasn't water.

He prayed for a bullet to the head.

A boy appeared at his shoulder. Arjuna recognised him from the clinic and almost smiled. The boy handed a small bucket of petrol to the commander.

'In the south, they prefer tyres,' the commander noted.

Arjuna wondered sometimes what his father's final moments were like. Did it take long? Please God, he prayed it was fast.

The commander poured the petrol onto Arjuna's chest.

Arjuna gritted his teeth as the petrol stung his open wounds. The oily smell filled his nostrils. He blinked rapidly, shaking off the sweat falling into his eyes.

'In 1983, your people hacked and burned our people to death. You tore us from our homes, our offices and our school buses. You stopped us on the streets and you asked: *What is this?*' He shook the bucket in Arjuna's face. 'What is this?' he demanded.

'Vaali,' Arjuna replied in Tamil.

When Sinhalese mobs had roamed the streets of Colombo, if their victims knew the Sinhalese word for bucket, they were allowed to live. Bhaldiya. Such a simple word. Said the wrong way, it would be their last.

Twenty years ago, that was how their war started.

The commander took a lighter out of his pocket. It sparked and flickered in the breeze. 'You burned us and the world did nothing.'

'I know,' Arjuna said. What else was there to say? He had studied his country's history. He knew more than his fellow countrymen. He cared more than his fellow countrymen. But they weren't here.

He was alone, in the jungle, with this man who had been a monster of their making. Now, a monster in his own right.

The commander turned to Ellie. 'This is your doing. You brought this on him. You interfere in our country, in our war. If you want to help us, tell the Sri Lanka Army to leave our homeland. Tell them that this red earth is ours. Tell them to stop killing our people.'

'I'll tell them,' Ellie cried. Her clothes were streaked and splattered with crimson.

Arjuna felt a familiar vibration in his chest. Too quiet, unless you were listening for it; too distant, unless you were hoping for it; too impossible, unless you were praying for it.

Ellie pulled away from the cadres and stood in front of Arjuna, trying to shield his body with hers. The wind picked up her hair, plastering thick black lines across her face. The vibration became stronger, its rhythm steady and syncopated against the erratic beat of his heart.

It was close but not close enough.

'Please wait,' she begged. 'I'll tell them exactly what you said. I remember every word. You don't need to do this. I'm sorry we're here. It was a mistake.'

'Yes, it was.' The commander flicked the cigarette lighter.

30

NOW (2009)

Ellie stood at the door and looked down the deserted street. The Embassy's HKR team would not respond to her distress call if she issued one. Scott was still watching her, but there was nothing he could do for her, now that Solomon's imprimatur had been revoked. She didn't care. She was certain she had Ameena's killer. She just wanted to look him in the eye.

It was almost midnight but she was sure he would meet her. Her message to the journalist's confidential source had been clear.

> *Narada. I know it was you. I want to know why. Meet me at the usual place. I'm alone.*

She tried the door but it was locked. She slashed away the police tape, took out her P&N set and opened the lock on the brothel door. The staff had disappeared into the labyrinth of streets after the shooting.

She followed the corridor to the atrium and looked up to where Manisha had been killed. Moonlight drifted down like a muslin canopy over a bed.

Everything was still.

She climbed the stairs to the first floor and pushed the door open. The familiar fragrance washed over her. He was waiting. She wasn't surprised but it was still painful to see him there. Betrayal hurt.

'How did you get in?' she asked.

'The back door. I never use the front. Too conspicuous.'

'Of course, you wouldn't want to be seen entering an establishment like this,' she replied.

'How did you know?' Tenby asked. He was sitting on the leather chair by the window, his body tense. He shifted the gun from one hand to the other and then back again, as though unsure of which hand he should use to pull the trigger. 'I'm sorry, Ellie, but I need to do this. Lie down on the floor. You're better trained than me.'

She complied. The wooden floor smelled of resin.

Tenby stood over her, gun in one hand as the other checked her body for weapons and surveillance.

'Get up. Slowly.' He backed away, gun still trained on her. 'Where's Arjuna?'

'In the ER, Colombo General. His nose is a mess. I didn't tell him anything. Let's keep this between us for now.'

'Why would you do that?' he asked.

'Because I'm first and foremost a US agent, even though Solomon doubts that. And I want to know for sure. I want to know why.' It was the truth.

'I want to know *how*. How did you know it was me?' His voice shook as much as his hands. He probably hadn't held a gun since his early retirement from active duty.

'I didn't at first. Not for a long time. I was looking in the direction you pointed me. I was looking at the Sri Lankans, the Chinese, even Shirani's husband. I was looking everywhere but right in front of me.'

'And then?'

'Little things, I suppose. This room has a particular smell. The incense Manisha burned here to give the room its orthodox feel. It's all over you. It's similar to something my dad's neighbour uses.' It had taken her a while to work out why it was so familiar. She lowered her hands gradually and continued. 'The hairshirt on the door. You've always been a bit of a self-flagellator and you kept scratching your neck and chest.'

'That could have been anything. I could have eczema.' He scratched nervously.

'You could. Absolutely. But then Arjuna told me Solomon's EA had sent him to pick *Solomon* up instead of *me*, and I eventually remembered that Solomon's EA is also yours now that you've been promoted to First Secretary.'

Tenby nodded. 'One of the many perks of the job.'

'No doubt. And then in the market, at Pettah, I was followed by the man on the motorcycle and the CID guys from the van, and my protection detail was nowhere to be seen. Someone had called off the team. Someone with authority—another perk of the job, you can command without question.'

'Could have been Solomon, he hates you.'

'He hates paperwork more, and it's not personal for him.' She shrugged. 'Then when we were taken to the CID building, and you didn't come for us—'

'We could have been late,' Tenby pointed out.

'I know the scramble protocols, Tenby, at least in Colombo. I worked here long enough. You delayed Special Ops because you wanted to know what I knew. You let them torture Arjuna . . .' She paused to regain control of her voice. 'Then there was this.' She pulled Ameena's ring out of her pocket. 'Manisha's final words led me to the confessional. This was in there.'

'That sicko took it. An execution trophy,' Tenby shuddered. 'He gave it to me, as if I wanted it. I left it in the confessional the day before Manisha died.'

'You thought it would incriminate her?'

'Yes, but it seems it didn't work,' he replied. 'So, protocol breaches, ecclesiastical clues and a ring were my undoing.'

'That, and at the Cricket Club, Dilshan Perera used a phrase that's more American than English or Sri Lankan. He said everyone wanted a seat at the table.'

'A culturally out-of-place idiom led you to me?'

'No, but it made me suspicious. You've been too keen to concede too much on every aid discussion. You're much better at your job than that. It made me think about who wanted a seat at the table and who had already taken the best ones. The US is on the outside here.'

'India's on the outside too,' he argued.

'Yes, but they aren't well-resourced or well-connected enough for this kind of hit. For example, tampering with the CCTV footage—not many people can do that.'

He nodded. 'Dilshan took care of that.'

She exhaled, relieved it wasn't Scott.

'Why didn't you suspect Dilshan?' he asked. 'The Sri Lankans had the most to gain by her death.'

'I didn't rule him out. Ameena was shot, and before her body was cold, a warrant was issued by an old friend of Dilshan's to confiscate all of her papers. He was looking for Ameena's final article—and I think you convinced him I could find it. That's why, when Redmond asked for forty-eight hours more in Sri Lanka, Dilshan agreed, when all he really wanted to do was put a bullet in my brain.'

'Crude but true,' Tenby nodded.

Tenby and Dilshan had used her. It didn't matter whether her diplomatic immunity was revoked or not. What mattered was that she found the article for them.

'Dilshan was looking for something, but you were *hiding* something, isn't that right, Tenner?' she said, provoking him.

'I told you to stop fucking calling me that.' The gun waved in front of her.

'I think you were Ameena's source. You were Narada, the mythological troublemaker. I think you met her here regularly and told her the secrets you'd found out about the Chinese and the Sri Lankans, from the safety of this confessional box.'

'Yes.'

'You were trying to do the right thing, trying to reveal the truth,' Ellie said. 'But then she worked out something else about you, didn't she? She worked out who you are *and* that you're a paedophile. You really did pay that kid ten dollars. It wasn't an accident. What's the going rate now, Tenner?'

'She should have stayed out of it. It was so easy. All she had to do was take the information we were giving her. It was good intel, with plenty of primary correspondence to back it up. Take it and publish it, keep the Chinese busy, that was the deal.'

'What did she threaten you with?' Ellie asked softly. 'Was she going to expose you?'

He nodded.

'Ameena used the words "palm sugar" in her notebook to describe the perks that were given to sweeten deals. The Chinese gave arms to the Sri Lankans and the Sri Lankans sweetened the deal with preferences on infrastructure contracts.'

'That's got nothing to do with me.'

'No, but I think you agreed to kill Ameena for the Sri Lankan government to sweeten a deal with them. I just don't understand the deal. Explain it to me. I'd like to know why.'

'For that proverbial seat at the table, of course. The Chinese were taking everything they wanted. We tried to undermine them by leaking intel through Ameena. It worked for a while. The Sri Lankans were getting nervous, even the Chinese. She had another big piece planned, one she'd kept secret from everyone. The story, the evidence, it was all off-site. She knew she was in trouble.'

'She just didn't know from where.'

'No, I guess not. She should have published that piece,' he said.

'But instead?'

'She started looking into me and others . . . like me. Foreign officials who were using some of Manisha's less acceptable services. Everyone does it in Sri Lanka. There's a whole tourist trade aimed at . . .'

'Paedophiles?'

'I'm not a paedophile,' Tenby said. 'I'm not, Ellie. You don't know how hard I've tried. How hard I've prayed . . .'

The sick fuck. All the praying and confessing wouldn't change that.

'How's that working out for you?'

He flinched. 'I'm not a paedophile,' he repeated.

'Diplomatic paedophiles—that's a big story, more interesting to the West than genocide. One that can't be ignored.'

'That's exactly what she should have done. She should have ignored it. You're just like her, Ellie. You never know when to stop. Too curious, too outraged by injustice, too good at your job. You need to just stop.'

'So, you stopped her?'

'Yes, I stopped her! I told Dilshan that we had intel she was planning another exposé about them. I suggested that we could assist him with the Ameena problem, in exchange for . . .'

'A seat at the table,' Ellie finished softly.

'Yes.'

'And Solomon?' she asked.

'He's the one who asked me to leak the information to Ameena in the first place. He wanted China exposed. He doesn't know about my . . . about me.'

'And the hit? Did he know about the hit, Tenby?' She tried not to raise her voice.

'No. That was between Dilshan and me. I retained someone we've used in the past. A freelancer, ex-CID. I retained him privately.'

'Without Solomon's knowledge?' she asked again.

'Don't sound so surprised, Ellie. The First Secretary of the US Embassy has his own budget and little black book of dirty contacts.' He shifted the gun again and then held it with both hands.

'And Manisha? Was that you?'

'Yes. It's a shame, I liked her. But loose ends, you know how it is.'

Ellie glared.

'Don't look at me like that. You've got your share of sins and secrets. Shirani and the kid should be on your conscience, not mine.'

'They are.' She backed towards the door, raising her arms again. 'Don't shoot me, Tenby. At least not in this room.'

'Stop moving, Ellie!' Tenby shouted. 'Stop or I will shoot you!'

She wanted him to shoot.

'Sure,' she turned and walked out the door. He ran after her, the moonlight enveloping them both in its milky shroud.

'Dammit, Ellie. Don't mess with me. I came here to kill you.'

'Then do it,' she said, looking up.

Too late, Tenby followed her gaze. Arjuna waited with a sniper rifle on the roof.

A shot rang out, but not from the direction she expected. Tenby's face exploded in a hibiscus bloom of blood splatter. His lifeless body sank to its knees. There was a second shot from the same direction. Arjuna cried out and dropped his rifle.

'No!' she shouted.

A third shot from the same direction. Tenby's torso jerked forward. It was a gratuitous bullet, sent to show that the sniper could have killed her, but didn't.

She spotted the shooter. He grabbed his rifle and folded it efficiently. He saluted her one last time and ran down to the motorcycle she knew was waiting below.

31

THEN (2005)

Ellie sat by Arjuna's hospital bed on the outside of the thick plastic dome that protected him from infection. Tubes protruded from him, as though an alien creature inhabited his burned body and was escaping through his mouth, nose and veins. A mechanical lung wheezed and breathed for him. Four small monitors showed incomprehensible lines and numbers. Every now and then, an alarm sounded and doctors and nurses rushed in, pushing her out of the way. They entered the dome and flooded his body with drugs. Twice they shocked him with electricity.

Namalie and Ellie took turns by his side for twenty days and twenty nights. When the doctors took a scalpel to his flesh and cut away the char, Namalie fled the room. Ellie stayed and watched. She owed him much more than that. She had been blind and it had cost them all.

By the end of the month, the doctors lifted the dome.

She took his left hand, which was still whole, in hers.

'I should thank you,' he whispered, squeezing her hand.
'Don't even.'
'It's okay, Ellie. You'll be okay. We both will.'
'How can you say that?'
'It's the drugs. Top shelf.' He tried to smile but couldn't. 'Bravo 9? Any casualties?'

She shook her head. 'Nothing serious.' The Special Ops team that had saved them was back at the Embassy, every one of them. No one left behind. Not even the dead. Bravo 9 had attacked the Tiger camp too late for Sharkey and Bradfield. In time for Arjuna. Unfortunately, in time for her.

Tears trailed a rebellious path down his blistered face. 'Talk to Sathyan. Tell him something that will help him sleep at night. Something that will help him move forward.'

Move forward.

'Enne manichi kolungo.' she whispered in Tamil. *Forgive me, please.*

He nodded. 'Tell him, not me.'

•

Sathyan sat opposite her in the hospital cafeteria. She wrapped her hands around a mug of scalding, bitter tea. The burning sensation helped her focus.

'I'm so sorry, Sathyan.' Ellie's voice was quiet. She couldn't get the volume and pitch right. She coughed and tried again. 'We made contact with him several times and agreed on an escape plan. He was to go with his unit on a routine reconnaissance mission on the west coast near Mannar. USAID staff were there, ready to help him break away and take him to a Red Cross ship, just like we talked about.'

She tightened her hands around the cup.

'What happened?' he said, his voice breaking. She had called him a week ago to tell him Gajan had died in a battle with the Sri Lanka Army. He'd had seven days to process the death, but now he wanted the details.

'They were ambushed, ten miles from Mannar. The Sri Lanka Army was better equipped.' She coughed again. A look flashed across Sathyan's face but was lost before she could follow it.

She sipped the tea. It burned her lips and tongue.

'The Army was waiting. The Tigers didn't stand a chance. They were outnumbered and outgunned. Our satellite imagery told us there was a fight, but we weren't allowed to intervene. A few of us got to him, but we were too late. He was already injured . . . badly. I'm so sorry.'

'Thank you, Ellie.' He pried her hands away from the mug and held them, kissed them. His tears were cool and soothing. 'I know your friend, Arjuna, was also hurt badly.'

Sathyan didn't know about the others.

'The doctors say he'll be released in about a month. His sister, Namalie, will take him home. I suspect he'd prefer to stay in the plastic bubble here, surrounded by attractive nurses.' She tried to laugh but found herself crying again.

She had to pull her shit together.

'He met Gajan too?'

'Yes. Arjuna's a good man. He was kind to Gajan. He was with him at the end, he tried to help . . .' She tried not to think about Bradfield.

'What are your plans now?' he asked.

'I'll stay for another week or so with Arjuna, just to make sure he's stable. And then I'm needed back in DC for a while. Follow-up,' she said vaguely.

'Yes, of course.' He let go of her hands, pushed the chair back and stood up.

She wanted to tell Sathyan it was her fault that his brother was dead. That because she was blinded by her feelings for him, Sharkey and Bradfield were dead. Arjuna would never be the same again. Neither would she. Neither would Sathyan.

The silence hung between them.

She touched his hair, letting it lock into the thick black curls she loved. She wanted to remember everything.

Enne manichi kolungo. She said it inside her heart.

'I'll come back,' she lied.

He held her. Kissed her. And let her go.

'I hope so,' he said. She almost believed him.

32

NOW (2009)

Ellie tugged at her suit. It felt tight around her body, suffocating her in the heat of the meeting room. Her thick hair was pulled back into an unusually neat bun, but the humidity tugged at the curls at the nape of her neck, helping them escape.

A shining photograph of the newly minted President Obama presided over them, his wide assured grin reminding her to whom she owed her allegiance. As though she would ever forget.

The door opened and Solomon entered, alone.

'Don't get up,' he said as she tried to rise.

He took a seat opposite and placed an Embassy notepad, his phone and a pen in a neat pile next to him. He threaded his fingers together and rested them on the polished surface of the conference table.

'I read your report, Ellie. Thank you for your thoroughness and candour.' His voice had its usual parched timbre, but he spoke slowly and clearly.

'You're welcome. It's standard protocol,' she replied.

'Yes. Your work in Sri Lanka has always been vital to our understanding of the country and the region. It's a complicated place.'

'Is someone listening to us right now, Solomon?' she asked.

'Excuse me?'

'Is someone listening? You're freaking me out with the formal-speak, as though a transcript of this conversation is going to be submitted to a Senate Oversight Committee.'

'It is, Ellie. The first hearing is at the end of next month, February twenty-third. The purpose of this meeting is to confirm your obligations to the United States of America and the Central Intelligence Agency, under the Espionage Act, Title Eighteen of the United States Code and the terms of your contract of employment.' His phone vibrated but he ignored it. 'Do you understand your obligations, in respect to secrecy, confidentiality and non-disclosure?' he asked.

'Yes, I understand my obligations to my country and my agency.' She swallowed hard.

'Good. It's unfortunate, the whole Tenby incident. He was a good agent.'

'He was a paedophile, sir.' Take that to the Senate Oversight Committee, Solomon.

'He was. We're looking into it.'

'He ordered the hit on Ameena Fernando,' Ellie stated, for the record.

'Yes, and now there is some justice for her. Redmond will manage the message Stateside, with her family.'

'You'll tell them she was murdered by a CIA agent because she was about to—'

'That's enough, Ellie,' Solomon interrupted. 'I said Redmond will manage the message. The ex-husband's campaign has to end. The Sri Lankan government and our Embassy wanted justice for Ameena, and now she has it. What we tell the family or the world is not relevant. It's just optics.'

'Optics?'

'Yes, *optics*. You're scheduled to take the 15.45 out of Colombo tomorrow. My driver will take you to the airport. Say your goodbyes to Sri Lanka. For real, this time. Perhaps it would be a good idea to make it once and for all. Despite your family connections here, the place doesn't seem to agree with you.' He checked his phone.

'Did you read the other report?' she asked.

'What other report?' He didn't look up from his phone.

'The one that was in the chassis of my car yesterday, but not today.' It would have been hard to find unless you knew exactly where to look. Bradfield had taught her well, but he had learned from the likes of Solomon.

'I read it.'

'And?' she asked. The report set out Ameena Fernando's entire investigation into the Chinese arms sale. It listed which weapons the Sri Lankan government had bought. There was only one purpose for those weapons. 'There are three-hundred thousand people trapped in the north-east, Solomon. Women and children. You know what will happen to them.'

He looked at her without flinching. 'No, I don't.'

'How will you manage the optics on that slaughter?'

'That's enough, Ellie. You're emotional and overwrought.'

'Bill, please.' She stood up.

'We're done here. I'll walk you to the door.' He stood up and put his phone in his pocket. 'Outside, now.'

They exited the Embassy and stood on the street, under the shade of a jacaranda tree. He lit a cigarette and offered her one, which she refused.

'The battle for historical legitimacy has always been grounded in competing mythologies, Ellie. Ancient tales of who arrived first. However, the battle has always been *won* by who has the biggest guns. Who arrived first is immaterial. Who is there last is what matters. Who stays until the end. It's the same the world over.' He exhaled a thin shaft of smoke into the air. 'What were you going to do with that report? Take it to the press? As long as the Sri Lankan government receives its foreign aid, it doesn't care about the foreign press.'

And the government would always receive foreign aid from countries like the US and China, falling over themselves to hold on to a piece of Sri Lanka. She decided to take the cigarette Solomon had offered.

'I could have sent it to the UN.' She had done that quietly before.

'Sure, so that they could issue another toothless Human Rights Council resolution. Those refugees are dead anyway. We might as well have a stake in this game.'

Ameena had left instructions with the print shop. They would post it out on the fourth of February. Ellie had failed but Ameena would not.

'Keith Tenby was a fuck-up,' Solomon continued. 'This whole thing is a fuck-up. I'm retiring after I clean this shit up.'

'Did you know about the hit on Ameena?' she asked. He was too good at his job not to know. Tenby was a spy, but Bill Solomon was a much better one.

He looked at her closely, weighing up his options, his many versions of the truth. 'I did. And I didn't stop it because I wanted what Tenby wanted.'

'Jesus, Bill. Ameena was a woman with children and people who loved her. Those people in the north—you would sacrifice all of them, for your "stake in this game"?' She felt her throat closing. She pulled off her jacket and undid her strangling top button.

Solomon looked at the tip of his cigarette, burning through the tobacco. He threw it to the ground, unfinished. 'I would do anything to protect the long-term interests of the United States.'

Solomon had cleaned up Keith Tenby. Tenby, her friend and traitor, would be given a star on the wall at Langley. His family in Boston would be told he died bravely, serving his country. Perhaps the Embassy would say it was a car accident. He didn't deserve a star next to the fallen. Next to Sharkey and Bradfield.

She said nothing.

'I am sworn to protect my country, Ellie. And so are you. Don't forget it. Have a safe trip home.'

•

Barry Sharkey. Gajan Navaratnam. Shane Bradfield. Ameena Fernando. Shirani Dennis. Renu Dennis. Manisha Gulraj. Keith Tenby.

But not Arjuna Diwela. Thank God, not Arjuna Diwela. Ellie sat on his bed and pinched him until he woke up. He smiled at her, with his broken nose and burned skin. With his almond eyes and beautiful heart.

She laughed tearfully and put her head on his chest, careful to avoid the wound in his right arm. The bullet had perforated the muscle but missed the bone. A perfect shot. They both knew it. The man on the motorcycle had been instructed to kill Tenby, to stop Arjuna and to spare her.

Arjuna put his other arm around her and held her. He had read her original report to Redmond and the heavily redacted one that Redmond would submit to State. He understood the moral compromises of war.

Rights versus security.

Someone else's rights sacrificed for their security.

'You'll be okay,' he said. 'We both will.'

'Must be the drugs talking. I can't believe they're giving you top-shelf again.' She relaxed into his body.

'I'm worth it.'

'You are. I have to go,' she whispered. '15.45 to DC.'

'You Tamils don't say goodbye. You say poite vahngo. Go and come back. Go and come back, Ellie.' He held her tightly until she stopped crying.

•

Ellie watched Sathyan enter the Hare Krishna cafe and walk towards her. She wished she was four years younger. She would tell him everything. She would leave the CIA. No, she would lie to the CIA. She would disobey them, get Gajan out and bring him back to Sathyan, alive and whole.

She would do everything differently.

She would be a different person then and a different person now.

He sat down in front of her. Hands on the table, so close to hers. 'Did you find Ameena's killer?'

She took a deep breath and allowed her training to take over. 'I'm so sorry.' She coughed to clear her throat. 'We think she was uncovering an arms deal with the Chinese government.'

'I knew that,' he replied.

'It was most likely ordered by Dilshan Perera's office, but I can't prove it.'

He exhaled. He wasn't disappointed or angry or hurt. She wished he was. She was ready for that.

'Ellie . . . you have been a daily presence in my life for four years, even though you were gone. I've hated you. I've blamed you. And still, I've loved you.'

She had felt him too. A presence in the absence. She had felt them all. 'Sathyan—'

'Please, let me speak.' He lifted his hand, then let it fall to the table. 'You owe me that.'

She nodded.

'For so long, I felt you here with me,' he continued. 'The deep joy of being with you. The deeper bitterness of your betrayal. With Ameena, it was different. It was simple and it was honest. There were no lies. No false promises. Just her. What she said and did and wrote. And it's all gone. Like Gajan.'

She realised now why he had called her and asked her to come here, to this place that used to be theirs.

He lifted his eyes. So like his brother's.

'How . . .?' She couldn't ask him how long he had known. She was too skilled to concede the truth. Too cowardly to admit it.

He shrugged. 'I'm going up north. I'm going back home. There's a group heading out next week, a local NGO. The international ones have left the war zone—government orders.'

She thought about those weapons. That geography. The refugees would be cornered in the east coast by March. They would be starving by April. They would be slaughtered by May.

She had seen it all before. 'Please don't go. Your home is lost.'

His home, still not hers. But still this hurt.

'My home is my people,' he said. 'They need me.' His eyes shone but didn't waver.

'Your people will die. We can't help you. No one will help you.' She stopped. His people would be shredded and mangled. Their remains would be pushed beneath the metal-studded hot sand of a remote strip of beach in the north-east.

'You'll maintain a "neutral distance" rather than make a "necessary intervention",' he said simply.

'Your people will die,' she repeated. She couldn't say more.

'Then I will die with them. Look around you.' He motioned to the words on the walls of the cafe. They had come here so many times that she had stopped noticing; stopped reading the scripture. 'Look,' he pointed. It was a scene from the Mahabharatha, the Hindu epic. Lord Krishna stood on his mighty chariot. Arjuna, the warrior prince, sat at his feet, his hands folded in prayer. Two sides of the same family were assembled on opposite sides of the battlefield, their armies poised. She had read the Mahabharatha. She knew how it ended. They would kill each other. They would kill each other's children.

God said to Man: *Why do you worry without cause? Whom do you fear without reason? Who can you kill? The soul is neither born, nor does it die.*

God didn't know Man the way she did.

'Goodbye, Ellie.' He picked up her hands, kissed them and left. She ran after him and called out his name. He turned and she held him one last time. She didn't want to add his name to the list of her dead. Not yet.

'I'm so sorry. Enne manichi kolungo,' she whispered. Finally. *Forgive me, please.*

He said nothing.

'Poite vahngo, Sathyan.' *Go and come back*, she said.

'Nahn poite varen.' *I'll go and come back*, he lied.

•

The man on the motorcycle watched the four white vans pull up in front of Alston Copy. He joined the drivers silently. There was nothing to say, just work to be done. The owner of the photocopying store had given him the keys and the location of the journalist's boxes. Not easily. He had shown admirable resistance.

The men loaded the boxes quickly and took them to CID. There was a kiln in the basement of the building. It was purpose-built. Wide enough to fit a body. Wide enough to fit a box of reports, and nineteen more.

•

Ellie took the newspaper from the air hostess. The headlines were not about Ameena Fernando's third article. She realised now that they never would be.

She needed to go home. She would tell Redmond that she was ready to work again. He was right to send her back. Asshole. She would buy her father some contraband KitKats. She might even accede to her brothers' requests to go to temple for Tamil New Year in a few months.

The newspaper detailed the final stages of the war in the north-east and the Sri Lanka Army's imminent victory. Somewhere further back, there was a short piece about the continuing investigation into Ameena Fernando's death. Her face stared back at Ellie. An easy smile, intelligent eyes. The pixie haircut.

Three pages later, there was an article in the international section about an aid package from the US. It was titled, 'New Road to the Deep North'. USAID had agreed to fund housing projects in the north after the war ended. They would donate German landmine detection technology and contribute to a clearing program.

US contractors had also won a lucrative reconstruction contract, building the highway that would penetrate the war-torn area and reconnect it to the rest of the country. Within the year, Colombo would be able to move goods, people and soldiers into a region defended for three decades by the Tigers and an impenetrable jungle.

The article did not specify the human rights protections that the Sri Lankan government had conceded to. They would not publicly agree to protect the rights they had never publicly admitted to violating. But the concessions were there, in the fine print of the aid package. Not nearly as many concessions as Ellie wanted, but more than she had hoped for.

The article also did not specify the military terms of the aid package. That was classified. But Redmond had told her that US naval ships and submarines would be allowed to dock at Hambantota Port when it was finally ready. And Sri Lanka would be given greater use of US eyes in the sky—satellites, monitoring the movement of soldiers, Tigers and refugees. Together, they would turn a blind eye to the slaughter.

All for the small price of a woman's life and a superpower's silence.

The price of patriotism.

Ellie tightened her seatbelt as the plane took off. She watched Colombo fall away from her grasp, the majestic palm trees and the sapphire blue of the Indian Ocean. She closed her eyes against the terrible beauty.

Sixty-eight Yuan. The price of betrayal.

In the warehouse at Hambantota, Kwan had said, 'Sixty-eight Yuan. At today's exchange rate, that's less than thirty pieces of silver.'

Thirty pieces of silver. Judas.

She opened her eyes and pulled out a pen. In the margin of the newspaper, she did some maths.

At today's exchange rate, sixty-eight Yuan was ten dollars. Tenner. Tenby. Betrayal.

She had to call Solomon.

•

Another Tardis sat quietly in the Frontal Lobe, exactly where Tenby had placed it months ago. A small black box, plugged into a computer, its activities unnoticed by everyone. It had been programmed by the Chinese to mine data from this server that was only penetrable from the inside. Fast and thorough, it reached into the US Embassy's network and explored its dark universe of secrets.

AUTHOR'S NOTE

In January 2009, the journalist Lasantha Wickrematunge was assassinated on the streets of Colombo on the way to work. He devoted his life to seeking and telling the truth. In August 2006, seventeen Sri Lankan aid workers were assassinated in Muttur (Eastern Province). They worked for Action contre la Faim, a French NGO that is committed to ending world hunger and provides food, water and sanitation. Their names were: R. Arulrajah, M. Narmathan, S. Koneswaran, T. Pratheeban, R. Sivapiragasham, G. Kavitha, M. Rishikesan, A. Jaseelan, K. Kovarthani, V. Kokilavathni, ALM. Jawffar, Y. Kodeeswaran, SP. Anantharajah, I. Muralitharan, G. Sritharan, M. Ketheeswaran and S. Ganesh. No one was ever brought to justice for these crimes. This novel was first inspired by them and it is informed by the human rights reports of civil society organisations inside and outside Sri Lanka, who courageously hold power accountable for its abuses. As Human Rights Watch says, tyranny has a witness. This book is also based on first-hand accounts from extraordinary activists, lawyers, journalists and survivors in Sri Lanka. Mikke nandri for sharing your lived experience with me. I have tried to honour you with this story.

ACKNOWLEDGEMENTS

I'm so grateful to the following people:

Robert Watkins—for everything. I adore you.

Tara Wynne—for sticking with me (it's been a long and belatedly eventful decade).

The team at Ultimo Press—and what a team: Alisa Ahmed and Rebecca Hamilton (your words, thank you); Zoë Victoria, Andrea Johnson, Brigid Mullane, Sophie Mayfield, Sandy Grant and Julie Pinkham—I feel so supported, thank you.

Uncle Chandra and Aunty Rohana—thank you for looking after me when I'm there.

Keda, Bekster, Eagle-Eye Franksy, Nat, MCC and Jay—who love Ellie and have believed her into existence.

Book Club—Sandra, Narelle, Su Lin, Carmela, Tina, Alex and Ange—Ellie and I have the best backup.

Abirami, Rachy, Shane, Havas, Namalie, Amrit and Steph G—sorry about those sub-standard drafts and thank you.

Kate Kelly—I'll meet you at the safe house.

Radhiah Chowdhury at Audible—for encouraging me to release Ellie from the white woman I thought she had to be when I first wrote her in 2016.

Caroline Overington, Dinuka McKenzie and Ashley Kalagian Blunt—for such incredibly generous endorsements.

Karen Radzyner—for valuing Ellie from the start, here's to our Ellie Harper TV series.

Create NSW—your Early Career Writer Grant sent me to Sri Lanka for research. There are some things people will only speak about face-to-face.

Writing NSW, the Australian Society of Authors and Sweatshop—for fearlessly supporting the storytellers.

Rajan Uncle (vale) and Aunty Nalaini—this novel started with an email between us in 2013 and decades of you shaping my political/personal consciousness.

Amma, Appa and Narendran—who love me and have believed my writing life into existence.

Haran/Kunji, Ellora, Kailash, Hari and Sid—the universe gave me everything with you. My heart and my life are full. Kidlets—as Krishna said to Arjuna, 'Who are you to be afraid? Rise and fight this battle, for the Self is indestructible.' Sometimes I sense what he means. Sometimes I have no idea. Love you x

Shankari Chandran was raised in Canberra, Australia. She spent a decade in London, working as a lawyer in the social justice field. She eventually returned home to Australia, where she now lives with her husband and four children. She is the author of *Song of the Sun God*, *The Barrier*, *Safe Haven* and *Chai Time at Cinnamon Gardens*, which won the 2023 Miles Franklin Literary Award.